STAY SAFE

STAY SAFE

MICHAEL LACOY

Monteverdi Press

ISBN: 978-0-9600689-6-8 (paperback)
ISBN: 978-0-9600689-7-5 (ebook)

Library of Congress Control Number: 2023915753

Monteverdi Press
Concord, New Hampshire

Scripture quotation taken from The Holy Bible, New International Version® NIV® Copyright © 1973, 1978, 1984, 2011 by Biblica, Inc.
Used with permission. All rights reserved worldwide.

Dostoevsky quotation taken from *The House of the Dead*, first published 1860–62; translated by Constance Garnett (New York: Macmillan, 1915). This work is in the public domain.

Typesetting services by BOOKOW.COM

Look at the nations and watch—and be utterly amazed. For I am going to do something in your days that you would not believe, even if you were told.

Habakkuk 1:5

There is a certain class of people, very intelligent indeed, who sometimes have utterly paradoxical ideas. But they have suffered so much for them in their lives, and have paid such a heavy price for them, that it would be too painful, almost impossible, to give them up.

Fyodor Dostoevsky, *The House of the Dead*

ONE

"Look at those idiots!" said Cole Perrot as he watched the pro-testers. "Not one of them is wearing a mask! ... It's unbelievable," he added, angrily shaking his head. Though he was outraged, Cole was not surprised. Stupidity, he felt, was everywhere these days. All across the country, from sea to shining sea, the moronic inferno was in full blaze.

He and his twelve-year-old daughter Rosa—both of whom were wearing government-recommended Pq23 respirator face masks and N16z plastic face shields—had just stopped at a red light in front of the Hancock-Beauville Medical Center. Across the street on the sidewalk stood a dozen or so sign-holding cit-izens. They were protesting the government's handling of the SPAARZ flu pandemic, and it really pissed Cole off.

"Prosecute Gerbyll!" read one of the signs.

"People Aren't Mice!" read another.

"SPAARZ Was Made in a Lab—For Profit!!" read a third.

From the passenger seat Rosa said, "What are they doing?"

"They're showing how ignorant they are," Cole said. "They want everyone to see."

"*Hey*—there's Mrs. Cutty!" Rosa said excitedly, recognizing one of their neighbors among the protesters. "Dad, beep!" the girl said, now waving at Maeve Cutty, who had not noticed them.

Maeve was holding a sign that read, "Is It a Conspiracy Theory If It's True?"

Some of the drivers waiting for the light honked their horns in support, and the sign-holders responded with jubilant waves and smiles. They all seemed to be having a good time, especially Maeve Cutty.

For Cole, it took some effort to restrain the abuse and ridicule that he wanted to unload on these right-wing imbeciles and especially on "Maeve Nutty," as he had begun to call his neighbor. More and more these days Cole was feeling the urge to explode and go off on somebody, but he did not want to do it in front of his daughter.

"Dad, beep!" Rosa repeated. She was eager to make contact with Mrs. Cutty, whom she really liked. Every Christmas Mrs. Cutty would bring over to their house gingerbread cookies with frosting and sprinkles that she made herself, and whenever they met she was always smiling and happy to see Rosa and have a little chat.

The traffic light turned green, and without a word or a beep, Cole turned into the Hancock-Beauville parking lot.

* * *

Before exiting the car, Cole took the added precaution of donning a pair of latex gloves, and he instructed Rosa to do the same. The girl wasn't too keen on this.

"Do we have to, Dad?" she said plaintively from behind her face mask and face shield. "My hands get all sweaty. It's *gross*."

"Rosa, do you really want to risk your life over a pair of sweaty hands? This place is a death trap. It's full of virus. Do as I say. You'll thank me some day."

The child pouted but silently obeyed. Now gloved-up, masked-up, and face-shielded-up, Cole confidently stepped out of the car, knowing that he and his daughter were protected. The SPAARZ virus, or any other potentially life-threatening pathogen that might happen to be lurking in the air, was of little threat to them now.

Under the blazing June sun, the two of them crossed the packed parking lot.

"It's hot," Rosa said. "My hands are already sweaty."

"Stop complaining," Cole said.

Up ahead of them, about fifty feet away, two women stood near the clinic's main entrance. One wore a white lab coat, the other was in a suit. Clinic employees, Cole presumed, taking in the scene. Just behind the women, and affixed to the building, was a large sign that read, "FOR YOUR SAFETY AND OURS: Masks are required at all times in Hancock-Beauville Medical Center. Any persons not complying with this request will be immediately ejected from the premises. Thank you." Next to this was another sign, smaller in size but no less emphatic: "Hancock-Beauville Medical Center strictly forbids smoking anywhere on the premises. Any persons caught in violation of this request will be promptly ejected. Thank you." Despite this very clear messaging, neither of the two women standing in front of these signs was wearing a mask, and the woman in the suit was smoking a cigarette.

Cole was outraged. A blast of fury erupted deep within him, from the very core of his being, and he instinctively reached for his phone. It was his go-to move whenever strangers triggered him like this. He would film the two miscreants, brazenly flouting the rules and selfishly putting other people's health at risk, and post it to his FaceFace and Chirper accounts. He might also demand to know the names of their respective bosses and file some complaints.

"Are you calling Mom?" Rosa asked.

Cole looked at his daughter. For whatever reason the girl still possessed a certain unspoiled innocence, a virginal goodness, and it made him pause. He knew that his confrontation with the two rule breakers would surely lead to an acrimonious scene. There would be threats and snide remarks and most likely some shouting and a good deal of profanity. As gratifying as it would be to

3

let off some steam, Cole grudgingly decided it wasn't something the child needed to see.

He slid the phone back into his pocket and said, "Actually, I'll call her later. When we get out."

Still, part of Cole could not let this indignity slide. The effrontery and the shameless defiance of the women were too much. Some sort of public rebuke was needed here. Some sort of public *shaming*. And then, as though the universe was responding to his will, Cole received a sort of gift. As he and Rosa neared the entrance, the maskless smoker glanced at him, and eye contact was made. Seizing the moment, Cole venomously narrowed his eyes above his face mask and waved a hand back and forth in front of his face shield, making it clear that he found the smoke to be both noxious and offensive.

Unbothered by this, the woman slightly averted her gaze and nonchalantly exhaled a billowing plume of smoke.

* * *

In the clinic lobby, a masked and gloved nurse asked Cole and Rosa if they had SPAARZ or any SPAARZ symptoms—"fever, headache, runny nose?" They said no to both questions. Their temperatures were taken and then they were tested for SPAARZ, an unpleasant and somewhat painful procedure that involved a long cotton swab inserted up their noses. The results were negative. Now cleared, now deemed clean and safe, they were permitted to proceed to the waiting room.

The space was crowded. Twenty-plus Beauvillians, all obediently masked up, sat on sofas and chairs in an attitude of bovine solemnity. Few people were talking, and those that were did so in hushed tones. In the check-in line, people stood six-feet apart on round plastic floor mats that read, in large letters, "FOR YOUR SAFETY AND OURS, STAND HERE!" This was to enforce social distancing, and to save lives. The lone receptionist sat be-hind a specially constructed wall with a plexiglass-covered win-dow. When their turn came, the new arrivals stepped up to the window and spoke to the receptionist through a touchless inter-com system.

Within seconds of joining the queue, Cole and Rosa witnessed a kerfuffle. Two men, one old, one young, started going jaw to jaw—or rather, mask to mask. The few conversations in the room suddenly stopped. Everyone stared. The problem was that the old guy refused to stand on his safety mat. Instead, he had moved into the space between his safety mat and the safety mat in front of him on which the young guy stood, and the young guy did not seem to appreciate this.

"Look, dude," the young guy was saying, "this is no time to be selfish. We all need to follow the rules, and I don't want your germs. People are *dying*, OK? People are *dying!*"

"Says who, the TV?" the old guy said with some fire. He was mid-sixties and wore paint-stained painter's pants, a plain white T-shirt, and a paint-stained baseball cap. A working man, Cole observed. As for the young guy, he was late twenties, clean cut, and wore a plaid madras shirt with chino Bermuda shorts. A former frat boy, Cole decided.

"Just stand on your mat," the frat boy said. "Nobody wants any trouble."

"*No!* I won't put up with it!" the old guy roared, irately waving an arm. "They're treating us like children! I'm paying for this shit. These damn doctors work for me! I'll stand wherever the hell I want!"

With this hostile outburst, many in the waiting room became visibly worried, even afraid. Those waiting in line appeared espe-cially concerned. The woman on the safety mat in front of Cole and Rosa looked all around in mute panic, as though searching for security guards, or help of any sort. Finding no immediate assistance, she at last gazed desperately at Cole. He pretended not to see her. And one place ahead of this woman, on the safety mat behind the angry old guy, a young mother protectively pulled her five-year-old close and backed away from the fracas, though she was careful to keep one foot on her mat.

"You want me to call the cops? I'll call the cops," the frat boy said with bravado as he pulled out his phone.

"I don't care who the hell you call," the angry old guy said. "You can call the damn president for all I care. Tell him to send in the National Guard."

This allusion to a potential armed incursion only heightened the nervous tension in the room, though one elderly woman— she was seated and had an oxygen tube attached to her nose— broke into a peal of gravelly laughter.

Then, at last, a white knight arrived. Over the intercom came an incensed voice: "*Siiirrrr!*" Everyone in the room turned to look at the receptionist behind the plexiglass window. She had risen authoritatively from her chair—she was good-sized, large and in charge—and now stood glaring menacingly at the angry old guy in the white T-shirt. Her demeanor made it clear that she was not going to tolerate any bunkum, particularly from someone who had the audacity to claim something like, "These damn doctors work for me!"

"Stand on your safety mat!" she shouted through her mask, her voice bellowing over static-crackling speakers. "Or you will be ejected from the premises! Hancock-Beauville Medical Center has a zero-tolerance policy! I repeat, STAND ON YOUR SAFETY MAT!"

The old guy looked at her, and his chest-thumping swagger slowly faded. The fire dimmed in his eyes and a look of uncertainty came over his face. He was hesitating, unsure of his next move. The room was silent. Everyone was watching, curious to see what he would do.

"*NOW!*" the receptionist hollered with searing wrath.

At this, the old guy flinched and the last mutinous flicker left his eyes. His expression grew gloomy and discouraged, and he lowered his gaze to the floor. It was just what the crowd wanted. In their face masks and face shields, the people now felt emboldened to speak up. They now felt *safe* to speak up.

"Get back to your mat," someone said quietly but with sneering contempt.

"Yeah, get back to your mat, tough guy," another person said from the back of the room, his voice a little louder, and a little bolder.

"*Yeah!*" said the woman standing in front of Cole and Rosa, now bristling with righteous fury.

"Yeah!" Cole said, adding his two cents.

Glancing around the room, the old guy took in the many scornful, half-hidden faces that were judging and condemning him. For a moment he stubbornly wavered, as though unwilling to capitulate to the herd. But once again his resolve seemed to fade, and with a sullen, dejected air, he submissively returned to his safety mat.

Delighted by this, several people laughed. One person clapped. Yet another said, "Loser!" The laughter grew louder and more profuse. Many guffawed and giggled with great glee.

And just like that, the rebellion was quashed. The dangerous man had been put in his place, publicly scolded and abased, and the people were pleased. Order had been restored to Hancock-Beauville Medical Center.

Yet this feeling of communal assurance was short lived. For there now came another ruckus.

Just behind the receptionist was a wall with a double-doorway through which you could see into the area where the SPAARZ inoculations were being given. Bodies clad in pink and blue nursing scrubs scrambled past the doorway as raised voices were heard over the intercom.

"We need help here!"

"Where's Dr. Holiday?"

"I think she's outside."

"That's not how you do CPR!"

At this last comment, a tremor of alarm passed through the waiting room. All around Cole and Rosa anxious glances were exchanged. Brows furrowed with confusion and fear.

In a near whisper Rosa said, "Dad, I know how to do CPR. Should I go help?" As part of her swimming-lessons course at the Beauville Swim and Racquet Club this past winter, Rosa had learned how to give the breath of life. If needed, she was ready to spring into action and offer her expertise.

Cole, however, was not listening to his daughter. Like all the other adults in the queue, he was craning his head to get a better look at what was happening beyond the receptionist.

Just then, a doctor in a white lab coat rushed into the waiting room. It was the doctor who had been standing in front of the building with the smoker. Now masked-up, she flew past the check-in line, went through a door near the receptionist's window, hurried past the receptionist, and disappeared through the double-doorway into the back space.

At this point, the intercom was turned off. The receptionist, who had remained at her desk, was seen to make a phone call. Her words were not audible through the plexiglass window, even though everyone in the waiting room had gone quiet and was straining to listen.

The first to break the silence was the angry old guy in the white T-shirt.

"To hell with this shit!" he said as he left his safety mat and started for the exit. "I'll take my chances. Good luck assholes!"

With extreme vexation the mother of the five-year-old scoffed as she turned to watch him go. The old guy's hostility and lack of manners, and especially his disregard for the safety of other people—in short, his complete lack of *kindness*—were clearly an affront to all she felt was right and true. But soon the man was gone, and good riddance. It meant that she, and everyone else who had been in line behind him, could move forward one place to the next safety mat.

* * *

Though the nurses had stopped calling in patients, check-in was resumed and eventually Cole and Rosa stepped onto the safety mat in front of the plexiglass window. Yet just as Cole was about to address the receptionist, there was another commotion. Into the waiting room came a pair of EMTs with a rolling gurney. The gurney had a damaged wheel that wobbled and squeaked gratingly with each rotation. Everyone in the room came to attention.

Unlike in the movies, these EMTs did not seem to be in a rush. One of them, a big guy with a prominent belly and a thick red beard that sprouted wire-like whiskers all around his blue paper face mask, sauntered up to the receptionist. Cole and Rosa stepped off to the side.

"You guys called for an ambulance?" the big guy said to the woman behind the window.

"Are you new?" she said, her voice ringing out over the intercom.

"Yeah. Both of us. First shift," the guy said as he looked back toward his partner who was manning the gurney. She was very short, maybe four foot six. From behind her mask and face shield she warily took in the room, looking from side to side with fearful eyes, as though she was leery that someone might jump out and attack her. Or maybe she was afraid that the room was filled with SPAARZ.

"What happened to Charlie?" the receptionist said.

"I don't know," the big guy said, happy to break for a little chitchat. "I heard something about someone had a nervous breakdown. Really lost it, from what they said. Too much stress, evidently. Another guy got a job selling real estate. Hell, with home prices what they are right now, I was thinking I should probably look into it myself. Why not, you know?"

"Tell me about it," the receptionist said, also happy to break for a little chitchat. "I keep getting letters in the mail from these realtors who want to sell my house. They say the market's never been hotter. But where would I move? Plus, I like my house."

"Well, you know what it is," the big guy said, as though "it" was patently obvious. "It's because of all these jerkoffs from Massachusetts. They're all moving up—"

"*Excuse me!*" said a perturbed voice.

All eyes shifted to the door beside the receptionist's window. Looming there was a nurse in pink scrubs.

"I'm sorry to interrupt," she said, "but we do have an emergency here."

"Well, I gotta go," the big guy said to the receptionist. He and his half-pint sidekick wheeled the squeaking gurney into the back room and the door closed behind them.

All through the waiting room more anxious glances were exchanged. One of the would-be patients got up from his seat and walked out.

"Sir, can I help you?" This was the receptionist, now looking over at Cole through the plexiglass window. He stepped back onto the safety mat in front of the window and explained that his daughter was here for her first SPAARZ shot. As the woman entered Rosa's name into her computer, Cole watched the scene in the back room. From this vantage he could see nearly everything. The EMTs had gotten a youngish guy—he was very skinny, with a shaved head and tattoo-covered arms—into the gurney. An oxygen mask was strapped to his face.

"... Bumble?" came over the intercom.

"I'm sorry?" Cole said, looking back at the receptionist.

"Is Rosa still with Dr. Bumble?" the receptionist repeated with irritation.

"Yes."

"Any changes with her insurance?"

"No."

Again the receptionist began typing, and Cole turned back to the action. The doctor in the white lab coat was now giving the tattooed man an injection. Cole wondered what it was. Then, realizing once more that the receptionist was speaking to him, he said, "I'm sorry—what?"

"I *said* you can take a seat and we'll call you. Or would you like me to bring you some popcorn?"

* * *

After Cole and Rosa had found a place to sit, Rosa said, "Daddy, why did the ambulance people come to the doctors?"

Cole saw his daughter was genuinely perplexed. He said, "Because someone … had an injury. And he needs to go to the hospital. This is just a clinic."

"Oh … But what happened?" Rosa said, now with concern.

"I don't know," Cole said.

Pondering things, the girl finally said, "Daddy, I'm not sure I want to get the shot."

"Rosa, not *you*," Cole said with sudden ire. Lucas, Cole's eighteen-year-old son and Rosa's older brother, was refusing to take the shot, and it was a major pain in Cole's ass. The kid was turning into some sort of reactionary crackpot. First he had been sent home from school for refusing to wear a mask. Then he had written an English paper comparing the government's SPAARZ policies—lockdowns, vaccine mandates, and supposed "censorship" of dissenting opinion—to Nazi Germany, which had gotten him suspended for three days. And finally, he had begun regurgitating all sorts of tin-foil-hat conspiracy garbage. He had claimed that the shots contained graphene oxide, a lethal toxin; that the shots were part of a "depopulation agenda" by global elites; and that the shots had more than one hundred "known" side effects, including blood clots that led to heart attacks and sterility in both men and women. All of this, of course, was utter foolishness, Cole knew. Yet because of it Lucas had resolutely declared for the past year that he would never take the jab. Among other things, this meant the boy would not be allowed to enroll at Olmsted College this fall, as the school required all students and staff to be vaccinated and boosted.

With a glum face, Rosa said nothing.

"This is about your brother, isn't it?" Cole said. "Well let me remind you, Rosa—Lucas is not a doctor or a scientist. He's just a kid who reads too much nonsense on the internet. He's just trying to be difficult. That's his new thing. He thinks he's a rebel."

The girl remained silent. She loved Lucas and didn't want him to get in trouble.

"What did he say?" Cole said firmly.

Still Rosa said nothing, though she was growing more and more distraught. There was worry on her little face.

"*Rosa,*" Cole said.

Finally the girl broke. "He said I shouldn't take it," she said with distress, feeling that she was betraying Lucas but that she had no other choice. "He said I don't need it, and that all of these soccer players are dropping dead."

Cole erupted. "*What a jackass!*" he said. People looked at him but he didn't care. "That's bullshit. *All* of it! He's just ignorant." This got more looks, people turning around in their chairs.

"*I* think he's smart," Rosa said with defiance. She didn't like it when Daddy was mean to Lucas, which was happening a lot these days. Daddy could say nasty things.

"Is he smarter than *me?*" Cole said in a curt tone.

Rosa paused to look at her father. Actually, she kind of *did* think Lucas was smarter than him. In fact, she thought Lucas was the smartest person she knew, even smarter than their mother, and *she* was a college professor. But Rosa kept this to herself.

Sensing some dissent, Cole persisted. "Is he smarter than Dr. Gerbyll? Is he smarter than the NPH? Smarter than the DCP? The FAQ? The *New York Sloth*? The *Atlantic-Establishment* monthly? CNBM? Is he smarter than Jess Murdlow?" Jess Murdlow was Cole's favorite TV pundit, one of the big stars of CNBM. Though she was a political journalist who had no medical or scientific training whatsoever, she had spent the past two years routinely mocking and "destroying" all the "anti-vax numbskulls" while vehemently promoting the safety and efficacy of the jabs, not to mention the expertise of Dr. Gerbyll and the heroic achievement of the nation's medical professionals and especially the pharmaceutical companies that sponsored her show.

"I don't know," Rosa said morosely.

"Well I do," Cole said. "What Lucas refuses to accept, Rosa, is that The Science is settled. Everybody knows this. Why else would all these people be here? And remember, you're not doing this just to protect *yourself*. You're doing it to protect everyone around you—right? We've talked about this. The vaccines work best if *everyone* takes them. And so you wouldn't want Daddy to get sick again, would you? Or your mother?" Despite both of them being double jabbed and boosted, Cole had already caught SPAARZ twice, and Rosa's mother had caught it once. "You wouldn't want us to get sick again and maybe ... *die?*"

No, Rosa didn't want anyone to get sick or maybe die. But still, she felt very confused. Part of her felt like crying, but she knew Daddy would get mad. Instead she shook her head.

"Good girl," Cole said. He wanted to give her an affectionate pat. But he remembered this might not be safe, so he held off.

The door near the receptionist's window opened and the EMTs came out with the tattooed man on the squeaking gurney. He appeared weakened but alert. With the oxygen mask strapped to his face he listlessly observed the waiting-room crowd as they all observed him back. Rosa thought he looked very sad.

As soon as the injured man was gone, Hancock-Beauville Medical Center got back to business. The door near the receptionist's window reopened and a masked nurse appeared.

"Eddie Prole?" she called out, looking around the room expectantly. "Eddie Prole? ... Do we have an Eddie Prole?"

There was no answer. The nurse consulted her clipboard. "What about, ah, Charlotte *Cupcake*? Is that right? Charlotte *Cupcake*?"

There was indeed a Charlotte Cupcake, and after another twenty minutes, during which time many people came and went, the nurse called out, "Rosa Perrot?"

Behind her face mask and face shield, Rosa smiled and shyly raised her hand, just like she did at school.

"You're next, sweetie," the nurse said with welcoming eyes. "Come on in."

* * *

Afterward, out in the parking lot under the still-blazing sun, father and daughter were in good spirits. Cole especially was in good spirits. They had done the right thing, he knew. They had affirmed their faith in Science, aligned themselves with progressive opinion, and showed themselves to be morally upright citizens who were concerned for the common good. Yes, they *had* done the right thing, and it felt very good indeed.

"That didn't hurt, right?" Cole said, smiling buoyantly behind his face mask and face shield.

"Nope," Rosa said in a cheery voice.

"You know what? Why don't we get a picture? I'll put it on FaceFace and Chirper, to show everyone how brave you are. Would you like that?"

"Mmm—OK," Rosa said tepidly, her mood now dipping. Daddy was always putting pictures of her on FaceFace and

Chirper, and Rosa wasn't so sure that she liked it. She wasn't sure why, because she usually liked taking pictures. But with Daddy and social media and people she didn't know writing things about her, it seemed … *weird*.

"Let's go over here," Cole said, motioning to a large blooming hydrangea bush. "No, hold on," he said, changing his mind, "let's do it in front of the building, by the sign."

They walked back to the clinic entrance and stood in front of the large "FOR YOUR SAFETY AND OURS" sign. Cole took out his phone.

"Are we taking off our masks?" Rosa asked.

"*No*. That would look bad," Cole said. "Now, pull up your sleeve and turn a little to the side, so people can see your bandage, OK?"

"OK."

They assumed their poses and Cole held out the phone in front of them.

"Smile!" he said. The shutter clicked and he examined the result. He wasn't pleased. His hair stuck out to one side. He neatened it with his hand and said, "Let's take a couple more, to make sure we get a good one. Try to look happier."

"Dad, I'm hungry," Rosa said after their fifth picture. She was ready to go home. "Isn't Tyce coming for supper tonight? I think that's what Mom said."

"Just a minute, honey," Cole said. He had chosen the best picture and was uploading it to Chirper. He typed out a caption —"So proud of Rosa, doing the right thing and keeping other people safe!"—and added hashtags: #bravegirl #keepingpeople-safe #vaccinessavelives. He read everything through, smiled with satisfaction, and hit send. Then he repeated the procedure on FaceFace.

Once he had finished, Cole felt a frisson of excitement. He had a very good feeling about this one. His record "likes" for a single social-media post was two hundred and seventeen for something he had written on Chirper a year earlier, in which he had eviscerated the anti-vax morons, writing: "Stop coddling these criminals. Lock them up, take their jobs, and deny them medical services. They're endangering all of us. Enough is enough!" Now *that* had been thrilling, Cole recalled—watching the "like" numbers go up, up, up, as he additionally got many positive, ego-bolstering comments from people who thought just like him. It was heady stuff—that rush, that feeling of euphoria, that feeling like he was important and universally admired. And now he had a feeling that this new post might challenge his "likes" record or maybe even smash it and go viral. Who knows? It was possible.

Cole and his daughter walked to the car, and by the time he had strapped himself into his seat, Cole saw on his phone that his Chirper account was lighting up. His "So proud of Rosa" chirp had already gotten thirteen likes, three positive comments, and two re-chirps. And boom, there it was—that chemical rush of pleasure, that full-body suffusion of ... what was it? Serotonin? Dopamine? Adrenaline? Cole wasn't sure, exactly. But whatever it was, it felt good. Actually, it felt great. It felt *wonderful*. It felt like ... life.

TWO

As she gathered the different items to take out to the patio—plates, bowls, wine glasses—Oona Pudding kept seeing *those veins*. For weeks they had been stuck in her mind, a mental image that kept repeating over and over like some song she could not shake. Not that she especially *wanted* to shake the image. Still, it was kind of driving her crazy. She had just had a session with Brad, thinking it would help, as it usually did. But this time, it had not helped at all. In fact, it may have made things worse, because with more and more urgency the veins were flashing in her mind, enticingly, insistently, maddeningly. *Those veins, those veins—*

"Hi Mom."

The voice came from behind, unexpectedly. But Oona did not flinch. She wasn't startled. She wasn't the excitable type. Temperamentally she was very cool, very rational. She was someone who liked to be in control, someone who was *used* to being in control. Which was why the vein thing was so disturbing. She turned around to see her daughter entering the kitchen, followed by her husband.

"How did it go?" she said.

Rosa, in face mask and face shield, held a reusable cloth shopping bag stuffed with groceries in her right hand, and had a flesh-colored bandage on her left arm. "OK," the child said. "Except some man maybe died."

"Nobody '*maybe*' died," Cole said brusquely from behind his face mask and face shield as he put two bags of groceries on the table.

"Did you get everything?" Oona said, giving him an unfriendly look.

"Yes."

As Rosa took off her face shield, face mask, and latex gloves, she said, "Mom, two ambulance people came right into the waiting room at the doctors, with their stretcher thing. They came to get this man who got injured. And also, some old man started yelling because he didn't want to stand on his safety mat. It was kind of funny." The girl giggled.

"*Hey*," Cole snapped, watching as Rosa stepped up to the refrigerator and opened the door. "Have you washed your hands?" It was a rhetorical question. The child had *not* washed her hands.

"Oops—sorry," Rosa said, abashed. She went over to the sink and ran the hot water.

"You got the steaks, right?" Oona said to Cole.

"*Yes*," he said with an edge. It was really pissing him off about these steaks, not least because Cole was a vegetarian. As far as he was concerned, if guests to his house wanted to eat animal flesh, they could bring it themselves. Was he running a damn restaurant here? A free steakhouse for cow killers? But he only said, "I got everything you asked."

"They'll be here in fifteen minutes," Oona said as she began to unpack the groceries. "Why don't you two go set the table."

"We don't have to wear masks tonight, do we?" Rosa asked, still scrubbing the germs off her hands at the sink. "Because of the company?"

"No," Oona said. "Not tonight. No masks."

Rosa smiled. Cole did not.

* * *

Out on the back patio Rosa asked, "What side do the napkins go on again? I always forget."

Cole had set out six plates on the table and now picked up the two steak knives for his "guests," wondering where to seat them. Though he had already removed his latex gloves, he was still wearing his face mask and face shield, partly for protection, but mainly as a protest. As an *act of defiance*. "The left," he grumbled.

"I wonder what happened to that man from the doctors," Rosa said as she placed folded cloth napkins next to the plates. "Do you think he's paralyzed?"

"Would you just drop it, Rosa!" Cole said. "You're very macabre. It's not healthy for a girl your age. I'm sure he's fine. He's probably out getting another tattoo. A big syringe on his back."

Rosa pondered this with a lugubrious air. She was convinced that the tattoo man's condition was dire. She was sure of it. Something ominous had happened at the clinic, something bad, she felt, and she was weighed down by a sense of doom. But then, all at once, her face brightened and she exclaimed, "Hi Tyce!"

With the two steak knives still in his hand, Cole turned around. A man in a tight black T-shirt, with inflated muscles and a cocksure grin, was approaching. He had come across the backyard and was holding a bottle of wine.

"Oh, look at you!" the guy said. "A Rosa is a Rosa is a Rosa. How are you, beautiful?"

Rosa giggled and glowed, beaming with delight. Cole frowned, his face twisting with bitter enmity beneath his mask and shield. He was not happy. He was not happy at all. This was going to be, he knew, a very long and challenging night.

* * *

The dinner party had been Oona's idea. Tyce Creamer, Cole's neighbor, was currently dating Linni Mudge, a secretary in Oona's department at Wendover College. Oona and Linni had been friendly over the past few years. They occasionally had lunch or went for a drink, and more recently Oona had joined a local gym that Tyce and Linni belonged to. Evidently a certain chumminess was developing between the three of them, and Cole was not pleased.

One year earlier, Tyce had moved into the house next door. The place was larger and fancier and considerably more expensive than Cole's house, with luxuries that Cole could only dream of. Among other things, it had a custom-designed pool with pool house and bar, an in-ground ten-person hot tub, and a professionally landscaped yard with a Japanese koi pond and stone waterfall.

On the day of his arrival, as the guys from the moving company were unloading his things, Tyce had moseyed onto Cole's property while Cole was spraying his front lawn with a garden hose. Seeing this stranger—he was taller and younger than Cole, mid-thirties to Cole's mid-forties—Cole had been both concerned and perplexed. Not only was the guy not wearing a mask, but he had on a red trucker hat with an American flag and a T-shirt that read "BORN TO PUMP." What the hell is this, Cole had wondered—some kind of joke? A prank by the new neighbor? Throughout his teens and twenties and even to a certain degree up to today, Cole himself had been a satirical ironist, and so he could recognize the type. In his school days and after, among him and his friends, wearing a trucker hat with an American flag would have been a hysterical gag, an inside joke on all the clueless squares. Same with that "BORN TO PUMP" T-shirt. Yet Cole sensed something *off* about this character coming across his lawn. Specifically, the guy had a football player's physique, an unnaturally muscular body that could only have resulted from countless hours spent at a gym, huffing and grunting while downing protein shakes and injecting steroids into his ass. No, this was no comedic postmodernist. *This*, Cole suspected, was a genuine New Hampshire redneck.

Cole let up on the trigger of the hose gun and the water stopped spraying.

"How ya doin'?" said Stars-and-Stripes Guy.

Through his Pq23 respirator face mask and his N16z plastic face shield, Cole cautiously said, "Hi."

"I'm your new neighbor," the guy said, stepping closer and offering his hand for a shake. "Tyce Creamer."

Cole flinched back as though a nude leper were trying to embrace him—or rather, a nude leper infected with SPAARZ. Not only did he make no movement to shake his new neighbor's hand, but he kept his finger on the trigger of the hose gun, should he need to defend himself. "*Tyce Creamer?*" he said.

"Yeah," the guy said, still extending his hand.

Cole vacillated. He did not want to touch this person. He did not think it safe. "Uh, sorry," he finally said. "My hands are dirty. I've been working in the yard."

"Oh … that's cool," Tyce Creamer said, looking a touch embarrassed. He withdrew his hand.

There was silence, then Tyce said, "What's your name?"

"Cole."

"Well, it's good to meet you, Cole," Tyce said with an amiable smile.

Cole did not return the sentiment. "Where are you moving from?" he asked.

"Here. I've been in Beauville most of my life. I grew up on the Heights."

"Ah—a *local*," Cole said, smirking to himself. He had been correct: Stars-and-Stripes Guy *was* a redneck. Beauville Heights was strictly low-rent—fast food restaurants, dollar stores, methadone clinics. White Trash, USA. Cole now suspected the guy was some sort of drug kingpin, for how else could he have afforded the house next door?

An awkward conversation ensued. Tyce asked Cole if he had a family; if he worked locally; if he liked the neighborhood. To each question Cole gave a terse, unenthused answer. He asked nothing in return about Tyce Creamer.

"Well, I should have you over for a beer sometime," Tyce then said, as though to wind up their chat. "You could bring the family. Use the pool."

Cole shrugged. "Uh … sure. Maybe. I'm actually not a drinker." This, of course, was not true. Not even close. But Tyce Creamer would never know, Cole felt. "We're pretty private here," he added.

There was another silence, and at last Tyce Creamer seemed to get it. His formerly polite, affable, and very earnest expression now darkened. With a false, mirthless smile he slowly nodded his head. "OK. I understand," he said. Then, with a meaningful glint in his eye, he winked and said, once again, "It was good to meet you, Cole."

A day or two after this, Cole noticed that his new neighbor had hung a good-sized American flag near his front door, and that settled everything. Cole now had no doubts—this Tyce Creamer clown was a fascist and most likely a racist to boot. There goes the neighborhood, Cole had thought. Their idyllic upper-middle-class enclave on quiet Lilac Lane had been invaded by a nativist brownshirt. In response, Cole purchased a large rainbow flag and hung it near *his* front door. He also put up a "This Home Hates Hate" sign in his front yard, right next to Creamer's property. If nothing else, he felt, the two of them now knew where the other one stood. Which was A-OK with Cole. After that their only contact had been the occasional stiff wave and fake smile when they happened to see each other in their front yards.

This neighborly détente, alas, was about to come to an end …

* * *

"How ya been, Cole?" Tyce said in a booming manly voice, as he came onto the patio with an unmasked face and an outstretched hand.

With spirit-sinking resignation, Cole realized there was no getting out of this one. Still holding the steak knives in his left hand, he shook Tyce Creamer's hand with his right, and promptly winced at the vicelike force of the man's grip.

From behind a pair of smoke-tinted sunglasses, Tyce said, "I've been waiting a year for that handshake. It feels good to press the flesh, you know? It's how men connect." He grinned slyly, flashing a set of titanium-white teeth, and gave Cole a friendly yet stinging slap to the side of his shoulder, which jostled Cole and caused him to wince yet again.

"*Tyce*," Rosa said excitedly, eager to draw his attention back to herself, "Lucas showed me some of your videos. They're *really* cool."

"You think so? Which ones did you like?"

"The workout ones. Last night I did some pushups. Four. You want to feel my muscle?"

"I don't know—will it hurt my hand?"

Rosa giggled merrily. "See? Feel," she said, now raising her right arm and energetically flexing her bicep.

"Oh wow!" Tyce said. "Look at that." He bent over, extended his hand, and did as requested, squeezing the tiny straining muscle between his thumb and forefinger. "Ouch!" he cried and comically jumped back. "I knew it would hurt!"

Rosa was delighted, pealing with more giggles.

Amid this nauseating banter, Cole took a moment to discreetly size up his neighbor. For whatever reason, this Creamer made him feel … *uneasy*. There was something disquieting about him, something beyond the surface vulgarity and buffoonery, something that Cole simply did not trust.

Tyce had a shaved head, though given the discernible stubble pattern on his scalp it was clear he hadn't done it because he was balding. He had a precisely shaped beard and a square, virile jaw. He wasn't good looking in a Hollywood sense but he had presence, Cole had to admit. He was abundantly confident and self-assured in a way that was vaguely aggressive, or perhaps *intentionally* aggressive. He was also in fantastic shape, which no doubt partly explained the confidence. Under his too-tight black T-shirt his gladiator muscles noticeably flexed and rippled with each movement. There was an outsized vitality about him, a dynamic masculine vibe, and it unsettled Cole. It put him on the defensive. Cole was especially aware of something else: Creamer's arms were riddled with popping veins, and not just his forearms. Down each of his bulging biceps there coursed a single prominent vein, as thick and long as a number two pencil.

* * *

Hearing laughter and voices outside, Oona went straight for the kitchen window. The guests had arrived. *He* had arrived. A tingly thrill passed through her body, electrifying her flesh. For the third time in the past hour Oona stepped into the bathroom off the kitchen and looked in the mirror. She inspected her hair and made sure no gray strands were visible; then, with the subtlest of smiles, she admired the discreet bit of cleavage that showed in her scoop-necked top; and last, she stared worriedly at her face. The tiny lines around her eyes and mouth, the first hints of the wrinkles to come, filled her with anxiety and a pang of dread. She was becoming obsessed with those tiny lines, staring at them more and more each day. She was getting old, passing her prime, and it was happening fast. But then she scowled at her reflection and scolded herself, irritated that she would think in such a retrograde manner. She was a career woman, not a housewife! An *intellectual*, not a cookie baker—and so why should she care?

Why should she fall prey to patriarchal norms of social worth? Why should she give two shits about capitalistic criteria of female value? She was above all of that, and she should know better. Oona left the bathroom and went out to the patio.

* * *

"Hey, there she is!" Tyce said, finding a new target for his manly charm attack. In one smooth motion he removed his sunglasses, hung them from the collar of his T-shirt, stepped toward Oona, gripped one of her arms, and gave her a kiss on the cheek.

Cole's mouth fell open. Rosa was dumbstruck. Even Oona was taken aback, though she did not seem particularly upset. Her face and her eyes had lit up, shining with stunned delight. It was their first-ever kiss.

"Thanks for doing this," Tyce went on with vivacious good cheer, unaffected by the surprised looks of his three hosts. "I can't believe it's taken so long for us to get together. I mean, we're next-door neighbors, right?"

Now flushed and frankly aroused, Oona found her gaze drifting unthinkingly to Tyce's right bicep, where that thick vein now seemed to be visibly throbbing. "Oh, you know," she heard herself mumbling, "the pandemic and ... uh ... everything else. But *here we are!*" she added with sudden girlish glee, her voice rising steeply in pitch. Now beaming, she shined her radiant eyes directly into his.

Cole was baffled. Rosa was baffled. Neither of them had ever known Oona to be either gleeful or girlish, or even beaming for that matter.

Then, as the red flush slowly ebbed from her cheeks, Oona realized something was amiss. Looking all around she said, "Where's Linni?"

Tyce shrugged and gave her a cryptic half-smile.

"What—is she running late? ... Is she doing her *hair?*" Oona joked and abruptly broke into a peal of maniacal laughter. Her

25

eyes flashed riotously and most of her teeth shone in her gaping mouth.

Cole was horrified. Rosa was horrified. They stared perplexedly at Oona, wondering who this person was.

"No," Tyce said with a cocky grin.

"Is she ill?" Oona said, now concerned. "Did she come down with something? *SPAARZ?*"

"Actually ..." Tyce said, both reluctant and amused, as though he was somehow pleased with himself but did not want to boast, "we just broke up."

"You just *broke up?* Come on!" Oona said.

"I'm serious. About an hour ago."

Oona went silent, staring at him questioningly.

He shrugged again and said, "Anyway, I brought this." He handed her the wine bottle.

Oona mechanically received it and said, as if to confirm that she had heard him correctly, "You just broke up with Linni ...? An *hour ago?*"

"Yeah. Though it had been coming. For weeks. Maybe longer."

"But didn't you guys just get together?"

"Not really. It started in April. So, four months."

"It's June," Rosa interjected. "That's three months."

Tyce laughed. "You got me, Rosa!"

The child giggled, her face glowing.

So many things were going through Oona's addled mind. She looked at the bottle in her hand and wondered how it had gotten there. She held it out to Cole. "Would you open this?"

From behind his mask and face shield Cole sneered resentfully, annoyed at his wife's presumption. But he took the bottle and went into the house.

"OK, you need to tell me what happened," Oona said to Tyce. "I'm ... *concerned* about Linni. Rosa, go help your father."

"Why?" the girl said, instantly displeased. Something weird was happening here, she felt. Something *very* weird. And plus, she wanted to talk to Tyce.

"Because I *said*," Oona replied, giving the girl a dark look.

Rosa didn't budge. "It only takes one person to open wine, and that's Daddy's job."

"*Rosa*, I need you to bring out the food. Daddy's going to be grilling. Get the meat and the potato salad. Everything's in the fridge."

An obstinate look came over the girl's face. She stayed put.

"Rosa—*now!*" Oona said.

The girl pouted and scoffed and finally went into the house.

Oona turned to Tyce. "Let's sit down," she said with an alluring smile. "I want to hear all about it."

* * *

"What an asshole," Cole muttered to himself.

"Who?" Rosa said, turning to look at him from the refrigerator.

"Nobody," Cole said. He had removed his mask and face shield, and was now opening the bottle his neighbor had brought. It was a Burgundy Pinot Noir, a *grand cru* no less, which still had its price sticker: $260. Cole had been planning to serve a $12 Oregon Chardonnay.

"Showoff bastard," he mumbled acrimoniously.

"*Dad*, you keep talking to yourself—it's creeping me out!" Rosa said, as she took the steaks out of the refrigerator. "Oh gross! This meat's bleeding!" she shrieked, looking at the cow flesh and the red juices that had seeped onto the plate.

Cole removed the cork with a slight pop, sniffed the open mouth of the bottle, and was immediately intrigued: the wine smelled lovely, a tantalizing aroma. He poured out an inch or so, swirled it around in his glass, inhaled its complex scents, then soaked his mouth with liquid pleasure. It was ... blissful. Astoundingly good. Maybe the best wine he had ever tasted. "Oh man," he moaned, shutting his eyes with coital-like rapture.

"Is it good?" Rosa said.

"*No*," Cole said, opening his eyes and resuming his resentful temper. "It tastes crappy."

"It didn't sound like it," Rosa said doubtfully. She took the steaks outside to the grill and Cole quickly refilled his glass, making it a double, and took another mouthful. The taste, the *experience*, was truly blissful, and somehow this moment of high-end pleasure—$260 worth of liquid luxury—reminded him of his own relative poverty, and his mood plunged. Though he lived better than most people on planet Earth, Cole himself earned a fairly modest income. It was Oona, the "celebrated professor," who was primarily responsible for their nice house and pretty much everything else they had.

Hoping to get his buzz back, Cole reached for his phone. He wanted to check his social media and see how his "So proud of Rosa" post was doing. He had done this as soon as he and Rosa had arrived at the Beauville Co-op, following their trip to the clinic, and he had done it again while they had been waiting in the check-out line to pay for their groceries, and then again just after they had gotten home. And now, with bleak disappointment, he saw it was just more of the same. The deluge of likes, comments, and re-posts and re-chirps that he had been hoping for had yet to materialize. And at this point, it was looking more and more likely that they would *not* materialize. The FaceFace tally was thirty-six likes, nine comments, three re-posts. The Chirper tally was forty-two likes, thirteen comments, seven re-chirps.

"How many likes did my picture get?" Rosa said, coming in from the patio.

This irked Cole, and even embarrassed him a touch. Was he really that transparent? That *desperate*? "I don't know," he said. "I haven't checked. I was just reading a text. From a friend."

"Will you help me bring out the rest of the food?" the girl said.

A cell phone left on the counter started ringing. Rosa picked it up, read the caller ID, then went to the sliding glass door to the patio.

"*Mom*, it says 'Linni.' Should I answer?"

"*No.* Don't touch it."

* * *

"I feel like you're holding back on me," Oona said with a charmed smile and a flirty sparkle in her eye. She and Tyce were seated at the patio table, side by side. "You're being evasive."

"No. Just self-respecting," he said. "I never talk about a woman behind her back. It's very beta."

"Oh, so *that's* it—you're a *gentleman*. An *alpha* gentleman," Oona teased. "Is that what you're saying?"

"I guess it depends on how you define 'gentleman,'" Tyce said, giving her a bit of the flirty eye sparkle right back.

"See, what I don't understand," Oona went on, her expression shifting from alluring to analytical, "is that there was obvious chemistry between the two of you. I could see it at the gym. You and Linni seemed very happy together. And this was just days ago ... *Days*," Oona added emphatically.

"Sure. There was definitely chemistry there. Both ways," Tyce admitted.

"So then what happened? ... Did you meet someone else?"

Tyce quietly laughed, watching her with cool amusement—a spider watching a fly.

For her part, Oona was watching Tyce's teeth. They were well-formed teeth, strong and unusually white. Fake white, of course. Cosmetically enhanced. Something that normally would have struck Oona as tacky and superficial. But on him it was somehow ... wildly attractive. "Well," she said, "it's pretty obvious you're the one who ended it. Otherwise she'd be here and not you. Hopefully you weren't an ass."

"She knew where things stood," Tyce said. "I made it clear from the beginning. Actually, I made it clear *before* the beginning."

"Come on, *tell me*," Oona said confidentially. "What happened? You cheated?"

He grinned and shook his head. "No."

"*Linni* cheated?"

He laughed. "No."

"Then *what?*" Oona said, squirming with curiosity. "She wanted something?"

"Yes."

"Ah," Oona said. "What—*marriage?*"

He laughed again. "No."

"*What?*"

"She wanted us to be exclusive."

"Exclusive?"

"Monogamous."

"Oh," Oona said, now understanding. "So you're *not* a gentleman. I had a feeling you weren't."

* * *

When Cole returned to the patio he had the wine bottle in one hand and a wine glass in the other. The glass was half filled and the bottle was half empty.

"I thought you didn't drink?" Tyce said to him.

"Me?" Cole said with surprise as he set the bottle on the table between Tyce and Oona. "Who told you that?"

Tyce made another cryptic smile. "I guess I'm thinking of someone else."

"Why don't we start cooking," Oona said, meaning that Cole should start cooking.

"Hey Tyce." This was Lucas, coming from the backdoor of the garage. He had been out playing pickup soccer and was dressed in shorts and sneakers.

"Hey there, big man," Tyce said. "How've you been?"

Lucas stepped up to the table and gave Tyce a fist bump.

"I watched the live stream on Monday," the boy said. "It was really good."

"Oh, yeah? Cool. What did you like?"

"I liked the diet questions, because I'm really getting into that. But I also liked that story about the guy who caught his wife cheating. It was pretty funny."

From the grill, Cole watched this exchange in amazement. '*Big man*'? A fist bump? Since when, he wondered, had his son and his redneck neighbor become buddies? When had it happened, and *how*? It was incredible. First Rosa, then Oona, and now Lucas—all fawning over Creamer. What the hell was happening to this family?

Rosa came outside with a large wooden bowl filled with salad.

"What's that bandage on your arm?" Lucas said.

Rosa made a guilty face. "Dad made me do it."

Lucas glared at his father.

"I didn't make you do anything," Cole said sharply to the girl. "You did it for your own safety. And for the safety of everyone in this house."

"You didn't make Lucas do it, only me," she said with a sullen look.

"Well, when you're eighteen we'll let you make your own stupid decisions just like your brother. Till then, your mother and I know what's best. And I don't want to hear any more about this for the rest of the night, from either of you."

"What about the tattoo man?" Rosa said. "Can I tell Lucas about that?"

"No."

She told him anyway.

* * *

The whole party—the four Perrot-Puddings plus Tyce Creamer—was now seated at the patio table. Dinner was served.

"Tyce, don't you want some salad?" Rosa said.

"No. I'm all set, Rosa. Thank you."

"Are you sure? It's *really* good," the girl said, trying to tempt him with her voice.

"He's a carnivore," Lucas said matter-of-factly. "He doesn't eat vegetables."

"What's a carnivore?" Rosa said.

"He just eats meat. Meat, butter, and dairy," Lucas said.

"Just *meat*? No vegetables?" Cole said, looking at Tyce.

"No. No vegetables," he said.

"*What?* That's crazy!" Cole said indignantly, as though personally offended. "How can you not eat vegetables?"

"I don't care for them. They're not healthy."

"Oh, come on!" Cole said. He was becoming enraged. "They're not healthy?"

"No."

Cole scoffed with derision. "Did you hear that?" he said to Oona. "Vegetables aren't healthy ... And what about fruit?" he said, turning back to Tyce. "Do you eat that? Or is that not healthy too?"

"No, I don't eat fruit. Too much sugar. I just eat animal products," Tyce said patiently.

"Of course," Cole said. " 'Too much sugar.' What about grains? Rice, quinoa?"

"No."

"*Nuts?*"

"No. Just animal products."

"I don't understand," Cole said, now flabbergasted. "How are you even alive?"

"He looks healthy to me," Oona said, taking a bite of her vegan veggie burger.

"I *am* healthy," Tyce said, cutting off a piece of steak. "This is the healthiest I've ever been. I've got the energy of a teenager."

This got Oona's attention. Her eyebrows rose, and she contemplated him with an intrigued expression.

"I like steaks," Rosa piped up, though she too was eating a vegan veggie burger.

"Good for you, healthy girl," Tyce said, winking at her.

Rosa beamed.

"I'm thinking of going carnivore too. I've been doing a lot of research," Lucas said, as he chewed a bite of the steak that Cole had originally bought for Linni.

"Not while you're living here, you're not," Cole said, as he cut off a piece of his vegan veggie burger. "We're not cow killers in this house. This isn't the Stone Age. You want to eat murdered animals, you can go live in a cave."

"What's the Stone Age?" Rosa said.

"People are curing themselves of all sorts of problems on carnivore," Lucas said. "Autoimmune diseases, emotional problems, acne, fatigue, leaky gut. Just by eating animal protein and fat."

"Where did you get this nonsense?" Cole said.

"From his video. And his live stream," Lucas said.

"Whose live stream?" Cole said.

"Tyce's."

Cole looked questioningly at Tyce.

"He's on MyToobs," Rosa explained. "He's famous."

"That's not true," Tyce said, grinning with false modesty and making it clear that it probably was true.

"He has a channel," Lucas said.

"A *channel*?" Cole said with sneering disbelief, as though Tyce himself was not present.

"Yeah," Lucas said. " 'Bro2Bro with Tyce Creamer.' He has two-hundred-thousand subscribers."

"Two hundred and twenty," Tyce added helpfully.

"Two hundred and twenty thousand," Lucas said.

"That's a lot," Rosa said. "I can't even count that high."

"It *is* a lot," Oona said, taking a moment to once again glance longingly at the vein on Tyce's well-developed bicep.

Tyce was relishing the attention.

Cole could not believe this. Any of it. "*You* have a MyToobs channel?" he repeated, staring heatedly at his guest. "With two-hundred-and-twenty-*thousand* subscribers?"

"Yep."

"You're kidding me."

"No."

"He's not," Rosa said earnestly. "I saw it."

"Are you on Chirper?" Cole said.

"I am. I just broke a hundred-and-fifty-thousand followers, even though they're shadow banning me. Otherwise it would be way more. Probably double. Maybe half a million."

"*Come on*," Cole said, now growing visibly upset. He himself had seventy-eight Chirper followers. "Are they real?"

"Sure," Tyce said.

"Are you on FaceFace?"

"No. Nobody's on FaceFace."

"My dad is," Rosa said. "He's always on FaceFace."

"Now wait," Cole said testily, trying to process all of this. "You said your channel is ... what was it called?"

" 'Bro2Bro with Tyce Creamer.' "

"What the hell *is* it? What's your angle?"

"It's a men's lifestyle channel. I started off with health and fitness videos, about ten years ago. I was running a personal-training service and I uploaded a couple videos for my clients, and without even expecting it, they kind of took off. So I made more and the channel started to grow. Then I added nutrition advice, and that was popular too. Funny enough, I was a vegetarian at the time, so I ended up taking all of those down after I went carnivore and started making carnivore videos. The thing with MyToobs is, your channel can be short-lived if you don't evolve. If you have just one message, people learn it and move on. So you have to keep growing, adding new content. About three, four years ago I started with more social-psychological topics. You know, dating advice, relationship advice, societal analysis—"

Cole was incredulous. "*You* give relationship advice?"

"Yeah."

"And you make money off this?"

"*Cole*, stop being so nosy!" Oona shrieked, glaring at him with extreme exasperation. "God, it's embarrassing!"

"It's OK," Tyce said calmly. "Yeah, the channel makes money, but not as much as the books. That's where—"

"Hold on, hold on, hold on," Cole said, cutting him off and looking as though he was starting to feel ill. "You've published ... *books*?"

"Yeah. Three of them. I'm doing a series. They're really taking off."

"I don't believe it!" Cole snapped, now with outrage. His feeling was that books and writing were properly reserved for people of a different sort than this Tyce Creamer. They were for people who were *serious*. People who were progressive and intellectual. People like himself, for instance. That this vulgar cretin could be called an "author" was too much for Cole. It was indecent. It was obscene. It was an insult to everything he held dear. "I don't believe it!" he said again, nearly shouting.

"Dad, that's rude!" Rosa said, her little eyes burning with reproach.

"I just read the first one," Lucas said. "It's really good. I'm definitely reading the next one."

Tyce gave Lucas a fist bump.

Cole was dumbfounded. All this past year he had assumed that Stars-and-Stripes Guy was peddling opioids or weed. Or that maybe he was a pimp or some sort of con-man grifter. But instead Creamer was ... a popular author and an online celebrity?

It was incredible! With astonished eyes Cole turned to his wife, to see if she was thinking the same thing. But Oona, with a rapt, dreamy expression, was gazing fixedly at Tyce.

* * *

Cole was seated up in bed, with his reading light on, when Oona came out of their en suite bathroom. She had brushed her teeth, removed her clothes, and now wore just her bra and cotton mom panties.

"What a jackass that guy is," Cole grumbled. "A complete phony. Could you believe him?"

"Who?" Oona said distractedly. Her thoughts were focused entirely on Tyce Creamer: his veiny arms, his shining white teeth, and especially his flirtatious behavior. Oona was fairly convinced that he had been coming on to her.

"What do you mean, '*who*'? Who do you think?" Cole fumed, observing his wife's nearly nude body. He loved Oona's curves, and always had. They were one of her best features. And now, in his tipsy state—they had gone through two and a half bottles that night, most of which was drunk by Cole himself—he felt a distinct twinge of tumescence.

"You mean Tyce?" Oona said irritably as she went over to her bureau. She opened a drawer, withdrew an old T-shirt, turned her back to Cole—because she knew he was leering at her—and put it on.

Now checking out his wife's ass, Cole had to admit it wasn't quite what it had once been. Same with her legs. "Yes—*Tyce*," he said biliously. "*Tyce Creamer*. What kind of a name is that anyway? It sounds pornographic."

Oona bristled with annoyance as she got into bed. "Who knows?" she snarled, hoping to make it clear she was in no mood to listen to him bitch for the next half hour.

But Cole seemed to miss the hint. "He's so in love with himself," he went on. "Those bleached teeth and that too-small T-shirt—I bet he shops in the kids section."

Oona rolled her eyes.

"And did you see the price tag? On the wine?" Cole said. "He did that on purpose. *Guaranteed.* It was a crass move!"

Despite herself, Oona smiled. She too had noticed the price tag, and had thought it … flattering. She felt it had been done to impress *her*. "Maybe it was a mistake," she said.

"Yeah, right. And why the hell did he even come over in the first place? You're friends with Linni, not him."

"We're not *that* close," Oona corrected him.

"But you're closer to her than to him. And so if she wasn't coming, then that should have been the end of it. He should have stayed home."

"He said he didn't want to be rude, canceling at the last minute."

"Well that makes sense. They did make us buy them steaks. It would have been rude of him not to come over and eat them."

"I don't know," Oona said pensively. "I think it showed a certain amount of …" She paused, searching for the right word.

"Social ineptitude?" Cole offered. "Narcissistic psychopathy?"

"*Boldness*," she decided. "It showed boldness."

"I'll tell you what shows boldness," Cole said, "naming your MyToobs channel 'Bro2Bro with Tyce Creamer.' That shows boldness."

Oona, lying beside Cole in their marriage bed, laughed. Cole had made her laugh often in their early days, but less so more recently. Much less so. "Well, yes. It is a bit tacky," she admitted. "But so what? He seems to be doing pretty well."

"Did you know about all this? His MyToobs channel and his twenty-million Chirper followers?"

Over the past few months Oona had watched a number of Tyce's videos, after first learning about them from Linni. "Not really," she fibbed.

"And what about the books? Did you know that Lucas was reading him?"

"No," she said, now telling the truth.

Cole said, "I'm telling you, this really bothers me. The next thing you know, the kid will be wearing a trucker hat with an American flag on it—and not as a joke."

Again Oona laughed, picturing her son in a trucker hat and thinking it was possible. Lucas had been very rebellious over the last year, standing up to his father and his school and just about everyone else around the issue of SPAARZ. Oona admired it. She herself had never rebelled, not in any significant sense. In almost every way possible she had done exactly what was expected of her.

Cole, noting the improvement in Oona's mood, felt his own mood improve as well. It had been many months since they had gotten along like this, chatting easily and sharing private laughs. Thinking he might take advantage of the situation, he turned toward her and put his hand on her lower abdomen.

"Cole, no," she immediately said. "You're drunk."

"So what, you're drunk too."

He caressed one of her breasts, moaning, "*Mmmmmm.*"

"Cole, *stop!*" she shouted with fury.

Startled, he pulled away from her as if a snake had just bitten him. Even worse than her angry voice had been the flash of hatred in her eyes. It was a look of pure loathing, and it wounded him.

"I don't feel like it!" she said.

"When do you *ever* feel like it?" he said, now becoming angry himself. "It's been a year, Oona! *Or more!* I can't even remember who was president the last time we screwed!"

She did not back down. In fact, it was just the opposite. Glaring fiercely at him, she bellowed, "Are you *kidding me*?" She was happy to see his anger, and raise it. "Are you *fricking* kidding me?"

Cole paused, taken aback by the strength of her feeling.

"Did you *really* just say that?" she went on, her scornful eyes baring down on him from just inches away.

He paused again, now wondering what verbal line he had crossed. Nothing he had said was factually incorrect: they *hadn't* had sex in more than a year and it was because Oona herself never felt like it.

Seeing her husband hesitate, as he often did when they argued, Oona redoubled her attack. "I just can't *believe you*. I really can't!"

Cole seemed to wilt. "I'm ... I'm sorry," he said uncertainly, since he didn't quite know what he was apologizing for. "It was ... insensitive," he offered, feeling this might placate her.

"I'll say!" she said.

Still, Cole was puzzled, and he briefly considered asking how, exactly, he had offended her. But he knew this would lead to a fiery lecture about something that he should have already known. Something to do with patriarchy and oppression and white-male privilege, and so Cole kept quiet.

"I just need some time," Oona finally said, softening her tone.

"OK. Well ..." he said cautiously, afraid of stepping on another mine, "you *have* said that before. A few times. Maybe we could, you know, see a therapist. A couple's therapist."

Oona shut her eyes hard, as though from extreme vexation, and raised a hand for him to stop. "Cole, I just can't take this right now. I'm done with this conversation."

She turned her back to him, switched off her reading lamp, and assumed a sleeping posture.

Minutes passed in silence, and Cole suffered. He hated it when they fought like this, when he didn't even know *why* they were fighting. It made him feel guilty. It made him feel lonesome. It made him feel confused and lost. Presently he said, "Oona?"

She was still on her side with her back to him. She said nothing.

"Oona, I'm sorry. I'm sorry for what I said."

There was no reply.

"And I want you to know," he went on, "that I'm here for you … When you're ready."

At last, Oona made a response—or rather, she made a sound. It was an ambiguous sound. It could have been a muffled sob, or possibly a mocking scoff. Cole wasn't sure.

"Oona? *What?*" he said quietly and with sensitive concern, looking at the back of her head by the dim light of his reading lamp. "What was that? Oona, are you OK?"

"I'm trying to *sleep!*" she growled. "Go to bed!"

For Cole, it was yet another humiliation. Another pie in the face. It burned him, *she* burned him, and he felt the impulse to lash out. He was teeming with animosity and resentment, years and years of it. He was choking on it. But rather than venting his rage at his wife, he did what he always did in these situations —he stifled it, he tamped it down.

* * *

Too upset to sleep, Cole reached for his phone on the bedside table. He wanted to see what was happening on Chirper and FaceFace. Though it was not something he would have cared to admit, Cole was addicted to social media. It was central to his life and his emotional well-being, like breathing and regular bowel movements. It was his connection to the world, to the zeitgeist, to all the *real action* taking place beyond his boring paltry life in Beauville, New Hampshire. And more importantly, it was the one place where he could genuinely express himself, the one place where Cole Perrot could truly be Cole Perrot. As such, he had put a lot of effort into the crafting of his public persona. On Chirper, his handle was @zarathooostra, a nod to his grad-school days and a tipoff to the digital masses of his sophistication and ironic wit. His banner photo was of him marching amid a dense crowd, with a raised fist and a snarling face, at a social justice rally in Boston, pre-pandemic. His profile photo was a headshot of him in his Pq23 face mask and N16z face shield with the caption, "I Stand With Gerbyll." For his bio he had written, "Seeker of justice, despiser of lies. Antiracist feminist radical. Speaking truth to power since 1976. Just be kind. He/Him." It was all there, Cole felt—all the things that made him *him*. On FaceFace and Chirper he regularly posted urgent political messages and attacked all the morons and fascists who thought differently than he did. But he also posted more personal things, such as quotes from revered philosophers—Nietzsche, Schopenhauer, Foucault —as well as videos of his favorite bands and pictures of meals he had eaten.

Now, he first looked to see where things stood with his "So proud of Rosa" post. As he had feared, the likes and comments, on both Chirper and FaceFace, had mostly dried up. It was dispiriting, and his mood dipped even lower. A number of people had even written negative comments. On FaceFace, one of his so-called "friends" had written, "There's no evidence that kids actually need these shots. They may even be harmful." This was from a guy named Pedro Leboeuf. Cole had barely known Leboeuf at college twenty-five years earlier and had never seen or talked to him since, outside of FaceFace. Normally Cole would have responded to such a preening display of ignorance and negativity with a clever yet devastating put-down. Cole put a lot of thought into his online put-downs. They were, he felt, a sort of public art form, social displays of intelligence and wit reminiscent of the verbal swordplay made famous at the court of Louis XIV. Glory and praise could be had with a sparkling bon mot or a cutting riposte. Yet tonight Cole did not have the energy to compose a clever insult for Pedro Leboeuf. There was no fire in his veins, no desire to engage in digital combat. Instead, he just deleted the comment and "unfriended" Leboeuf who wasn't a friend in the first place.

Typically Cole would have spent the next hour or more scrolling through his feeds, reading about and commenting on the day's various outrages. But a nagging curiosity led him in a different direction. He clicked over to Amazin! and, with a vague sense of foreboding, typed "Tyce Creamer" into the search window. The results were worse—or *better*, depending on how he looked at it—than even he could have imagined. Tyce Creamer, Cole's Stars-and-Stripes muscle-bound price-tag-flaunting titanium-teethed loser neighbor, was indeed a published author. However, the title of his book series—it was called, unbelievably, "Don't Be a Bitch"—was so gloriously vulgar and offensive that Cole would have shouted and hooted but for fear that he would wake Oona. Regardless, he derived much satisfaction at this confirmation of his longstanding suspicion of his neighbor's moral turpitude. "Don't Be a Bitch"? Ha! The man—the *buffoon!*—was an out-of-the-closet, unashamed, in-your-face misogynist. For Cole it was too comical, and too perfect. The fool had dug his own grave. Surely his cancelation was imminent.

But then Cole looked a little closer and his spirits plunged—plunged to great, dark depths. Book one in the series was entitled, *Don't Be a Bitch: Transform Your Body and Transform Your Life in Thirty Days!* It had 9,486 ratings, nearly all five stars. How was this possible, Cole wondered? Nine-thousand-plus ratings, nearly all five stars? Those were best-seller numbers. Presidential memoir numbers. Charles Dickens and Leo Tolstoy numbers.

He scrolled down to the first reader review. It was headlined "Life Altering," and began, "Bros, I didn't think it was possible, but Tyce is just as good on the page as he is on the screen. I was afraid this might be some sellout bullshit rehash of his videos, but there's a lot of new info here that really busted my balls, in a good way. His writing is both entertaining and engaging, with humor and insights that really raise the bar for other influencers in the dudiverse. Mad props to my boy—"

Cole could not read any more. It was sickening, and depressing. What was wrong with the world? What was wrong with this country? It was a conspiracy of cretins, a confederacy of clowns. One idiot writes a book, and nine thousand idiots on Amazin! give it a five-star rating. Cole clicked back to the series page to see if maybe this was an anomaly, to see if book one's success was just a fluke. It wasn't. Book two was entitled, *Don't Be a Bitch: From Simp to Pimp—How to Become a Dominant, High-Value Male*. It had 8,872 ratings, nearly all five stars. Book three was, *Don't Be a Bitch: The Sissyfication of America and How to Resist*. 12,944 ratings. Nearly all five stars.

A bleak melancholy came over Cole. Not only was Creamer younger and fitter and richer than him, but he was also a successful author. A well-known author. How could life be this unfair? This unjust?

As if this weren't enough punishment for one evening—and Cole was, it must be said, just a *tad bit* masochistic—he clicked over from Amazin! to MyToobs and did another search. And there it was: "Bro2Bro with Tyce Creamer." The man did indeed have a MyToobs channel, and he did indeed have two-hundred-and-twenty-thousand subscribers—220,683 to be exact. Going back ten years, Creamer had made a whopping one hundred and fifty-six videos. Some of the titles were, "Six Steps to Increased Testosterone—Your Lady Will Thank You!"; "Charisma: I Wasn't Born This Way—You Can Learn Too!"; "Success Is a Mindset, Failure Is a Choice"; and "Playa Don't Get Played: 10 Signs That She's Cheating On You." This last title alone had gotten more than 1.6 million views.

It was more than Cole's battered heart could take. Melancholy gave way to despair. Crushing, soul-killing, full-body-paralyzing despair. Cole had always felt a certain kinship with Sisy-phus—a man who valiantly struggled on despite the opposition of the gods. But now Cole felt more like Sisyphus's unknown kid brother—the one who had stumbled, fallen, and been pinned helplessly and for all eternity under an immovable rock. Cole was down, and he could not get up. No, life is not fair, he thought. It is not fair at all.

He turned off his phone, switched off the light, and tried to sleep.

THREE

The next morning, Lucas marched into the kitchen and made his grand announcement. He was wearing his "Your Ignorance Isn't My Problem" T-shirt. With brassy aplomb he said, "I decided I'm going full carnivore. Starting today. I'm done eating crap food."

Cole, the lone recipient of this important news, was standing at the stove. With a spatula in his hand and three kale breakfast burgers sizzling in a skillet, he gazed incuriously at his son. He was hungover, depressed, and catatonically exhausted. It had taken him forever to fall asleep last night, and after he finally did, he woke at four a.m. with an anxious mind and a racing heart. For the next few hours he lay wide awake, worrying about his problems and also about how he could not fall back asleep. By the time he started to feel drowsy his alarm clock went off.

To his son he merely replied, "Congratulations." He turned back to the stove, flipped over the kale patties, and said, "Get a plate. They're almost ready."

"I'm serious, Dad. From now on I'm just eating meat and dairy. Preferably grass-fed, though it does cost more. Hopefully Mom won't mind—"

"Lucas, I'm in no mood for your shit right now, OK?"

"Why, are you hungover?"

Cole did not respond to this. He didn't have the energy. Instead he flipped over the kale patties again and said, "They're done. Get a plate."

"Dad, I mean it. I'm finished with that stuff. Processed foods are poison. And so are vegetables. Have you ever heard of oxalates or goitrogens? Or lectins? Or saponins or phytates? I'm telling you, I'm done. I'm only eating clean animal products."

"Fine," Cole said, removing the skillet from the burner. "Have fun with the colon cancer. You can be the one kid at college with a colostomy bag."

The boy was unfazed. "Meat doesn't cause cancer," he said. "Not if it's unprocessed, and especially not if it's grass-fed. That's just corporate propaganda. Did you ever see a lion with cancer? Or for that matter, a lion that was fat or had bad teeth?"

Cole frowned, tiredly. "You know Lucas, this might surprise you, but I don't know any lions." With the spatula he transferred the patties to a plate and said, "Where's your sister? If you're not going to eat this, I'll give it to her."

"I think she's still sleeping ... And did you know," Lucas went on, happy to share more of his newfound wisdom, "that Plato says in *The Republic* that the masses shouldn't be allowed to eat meat? Did you know that? It's to keep the people weak, so the elites can control them better. It's true. I read about it last night."

"That's because Plato was a fascist," Cole said. "Did you read about that too? Go get your sister."

Right on cue, Rosa belted out a terrified scream from her bedroom on the second floor. She had never been one to shy away from a good scream, be it over a spider or a scary movie, but this sounded serious. And immediately after the scream came her terrified voice, shrieking, "*Mom!*"

Lucas ran for the stairs and Cole followed. When they entered Rosa's room they saw the girl lying in bed with Oona hovering at her side.

"What is it?" Rosa was saying. All up and down her left arm were strawberry-colored splotches of varying sizes and shapes. They were on the same arm as the bandage.

46

Oona tentatively reached out a hand to touch the splotches but then seemed to think better of it. "I don't know, honey. It looks … like a rash. Or something."

"I told you!" Lucas said, glaring accusingly at Cole.

"What is it?" Cole said to Oona.

"I don't know," she shrugged. "Sun rash?"

"Were you in the sun yesterday?" Cole said to Rosa.

"Yes," she sniveled. "But why isn't it on my other arm? Or anywhere else?"

"It's the vaccine," Lucas said.

"Would you shut up, you jackass!" Cole said, turning on his son.

Rosa started crying.

"Good job, Lucas," Oona said crossly.

"Rosa, this has nothing to do with the vaccine," Cole said.

"Then why is it on the same arm?"

"I don't know. It's just a coincidence. Your mother and I had three shots each and nothing ever happened."

"That's not true," Lucas said. "You felt like shit for a week after your first shot, and you got bad headaches after your second."

"That only meant it was working!" Cole hollered. "Boy are you thick!"

"I'm scared," Rosa said with tears spilling down her cheeks.

"It's because your brother is an idiot!" Cole said. "Stop listening to his nonsense." To Oona he added, "It's probably psychosomatic."

"I don't know, it's pretty … unusual," she said, reexamining the splotches. "It wouldn't hurt to take her in," she added, glancing at Cole.

"I have to be at work in half an hour," he said.

"*Cole*, my day is *completely* booked," Oona said. "I need you to help out here."

* * *

47

"Hmmm," said Dr. Bumble as he examined Rosa's arm. He wore a face mask and latex gloves. "Could be a food allergy. Or maybe some sort of poison ivy. Were you out in the woods yesterday? Out, uh, *walking* with your boyfriend?" He chuckled jovially and gave her a knowing look.

The comment, and particularly the look, unsettled Rosa. It creeped her out. She turned her worried eyes to her father, who was also in the examining room.

"No, she wasn't," Cole said from behind his mask and face shield.

"What about soaps or lotions?" the doctor said to the girl. "Have you started with a new brand? Something you weren't using before?"

"No."

"And what's this bandage for?"

She told him.

"Oh, good. That's good," he said.

"Do you think that's what caused it?" Rosa asked.

"What, the vaccine? Oooh, no. No no," Dr. Bumble said in a breezy voice. "No no."

"But it's all on the same arm," she said.

"Nope. No no," the doctor repeated. "That's just a coincidence. In some cases, people report fatigue, or sort throat, or other flu-like symptoms, post-shot. But that just means it's working. But I've not heard anything about a rash like this. No, Sharon, it's just a coincidence."

"My name's not Sharon. It's Rosa."

"Oh, that's right," Dr. Bumble chuckled again. "Busy morning," he explained.

"See?" Cole said to Rosa. "It's just a rash. Now stop listening to your brother, and show a little more faith in The Science. Dr. Bumble is a professional. He knows what he's talking about."

* * *

"*Cole?*" said a surprised voice. "Are you just getting in?"

Hoping to have entered the work space unnoticed, Cole stiffened with irritation. To get to his desk he had to pass by his boss's office. It could be, and often was, a real pain in Cole's ass. In the upbeat, easygoing, *team-player* voice he had perfected for moments such as this, he said, "Oh, hi Dig—how are you? Yes, just getting in. I sent you an email."

"Yes, I got it," Digby Cotton-Espinoza said from behind not one but two blue paper face masks. Along with shots and boosters, masks were still required of all Wendover College faculty and staff, and a number of folks were regularly double masked for extra protection. Digby was seated at his executive-style cherrywood desk and, as always, his office door was wide open. As Head of the Office of Student Affairs, a post he had held for more than thirty years, he liked to keep a close eye on all the comings and goings of his six-person staff.

"But I thought you said you'd be in by ten?" he went on. "It's nearly eleven-thirty."

"Yeah, I know. I'm sorry," Cole said with genuine-sounding contrition, gazing humbly at his boss through his plastic face shield. "Things ran late at the doctor's. Typical, right? But the important thing is, Rosa's OK. It was just a rash. We were *very* concerned."

"And you left early yesterday—three o'clock, I believe," Digby added with dour disapproval.

Cole felt a twitch of hostility. He had, on more than one occasion, imagined pummeling Digby's doughy humorless face. The man was in his early seventies and had pouchy jowls that jiggled when he spoke. For some reason those jiggly jowls really annoyed Cole. Thankfully the old fool would be retiring at the end of the month, as Cole was expecting to take his job. He had already sat through two interviews—one with Digby himself and the other with Human Resources—and all seemed set. Still, the thing hadn't been made official, so Cole felt it best to remain respectful, at least for the time being. He thus assumed a submissive attitude and said, "Yes, that was to take Rosa for her SPAARZ vaccination. It's important to us that she's protected."

"I see," Digby said, watching Cole with enigmatic eyes. Then he said, "And how is Dr. Pudding? Is she well?"

Cole felt another twitch. Digby, like everyone else at Wendover College, showed marked deference to Oona—or "Dr. Pudding," as they all called her. It bothered Cole. In fact, it bothered him very much. "Yes. She's fine. But she's ... she's busy at the moment. Writing another book. So I had to take Rosa. Both times."

"Hmm ... yes. I understand," Digby said, now with a glimmer of amusement in his red-rimmed eyes. He had gone to Harvard in the late Sixties, something he frequently liked to remind his staff about. *"Days of hope and rage,"* he liked to say, becoming mistily nostalgic. He also liked to go on and on about his interests in Edmund Wilson, Shaker furniture, and the musical instruments of Renaissance Italy—Digby himself played the sackbut in the Wendover Monteverdi Society. He had met his wife, Salma Cotton-Espinoza, née Espinoza, at a Northern California commune where he had lived for two years following his undergraduate days in Cambridge.

"And how is the Multisex Bathrooms report coming?" Digby went on, now gazing gravely at Cole. "You're nearly finished?"

Digby had "tasked" Cole with researching the cost and feasibility of converting all current men's and women's dormitory bathrooms into non-gender-specific spaces in which all students would shit, piss, and shower together regardless of preferred pronouns. Unthrilled by this assignment, Cole had in turn "tasked" it to a junior member of the staff.

"It's coming. LaKeesha is helping out," Cole said. "We're almost there."

"It'll be ready by next Thursday?" Digby said, lowering his chin so as to peer over his horn-rimmed spectacles and give Cole an extra-meaningful look. "Dean Munchausen is expecting it. He's leaving for Maine that weekend, and he wants all of this to be settled before then."

"Yes," Cole assured him. "It'll be ready."

"Very good," Digby Cotton-Espinoza said, and he turned his attention to his computer, signaling to Cole that their little tête-à-tête was finished.

* * *

LaKeesha Lovette sensed a presence at her side and quickly turned her head. It was Phony-Ass Cole. He was gazing down at her with his phony-ass smiling eyes. Seated at her cubicle with earphones on, LaKeesha had been watching an old SugaGirlz video on her computer. She paused the video but did not remove the earphones.

"Yeah?" she said bluntly, her tone just a hair's-breadth shy of being disrespectful. She wore a blue paper face mask—just one —and no face shield.

"Hey LaKeesha—sorry to bother you," Cole said.

She just looked at him, knowing damn well that behind his face mask he was making his phony-ass smile to go along with his phony-ass smiling eyes. It had taken her some time, maybe two or three months, but she had finally figured out that Cole's extra-polite manner was a sham. And not just a sham, but even a way to put people down, the way his smiling eyes seemed to laugh at you. When she had first gotten this job—it would be one year this September—she had wondered why all these college white folks were so extra polite to her, Cole especially. She thought maybe it was because they were rich and educated and that that was how rich and educated white people acted. But then she noticed that these whites who were extra polite to her weren't that way to each other. In fact, some of them were kind of nasty to each other. And once she realized their politeness was fake, a put-on for the black girl, she also realized something else. These rich educated whites were kind of afraid of her. Which was to say, she could tell they were cautious and hesitant whenever they interacted with her, like they didn't want to say the wrong thing, or be uncool, or be thought a racist or something. Whatever it was, she didn't like it. It bothered her. It made her suspicious. She would much rather work with working-class whites as she did before this job. Half of her best girlfriends were working-class whites. But working with them meant working retail or fast food, and there was no way in shit she was going to give up this cushy-ass 55k-a-year job just to hang with her girls. She could do that on weekends.

"What can I do for you Cole?" she said, giving him a bored look.

"Oh, *hey*—that's the SugaGirlz," he said, looking at the paused video on her computer screen. "*Yo do me, do me now, boy!*" he sang, bobbing his head as he repeated the lyrics to the group's big hit from the mid-Nineties. "That's old school, girl!" he added, trying to "talk black." "I don't think you were even born when that came out."

"Mm-hmm," she said, unimpressed.

"So, yeah," he said, now in a lowered, confidential voice, "I was wondering if we could do a little *catch-up* on the Multisex Bathrooms report."

"What do you want to know?"

Cole raised his eyebrows and nodded meaningfully in the direction of Digby's open office door—from this angle the old guy could not see them but he was no doubt listening. In a hushed voice Cole said, "Why don't we go to the conference room?"

* * *

As they took their seats on opposite sides of the table, Cole looked at LaKeesha with his extra-friendly, wholly-non-threatening, "I'm-one-of-the-good-whites" smiling eyes. He wanted her to know that he was on *her* side—the side of history, the side of progress, the side of *justice*. And why not? It had been Cole himself, in fact, who had pushed for the hiring of LaKeesha Lovette.

After a staff-assistant position had opened up in the Office of Student Affairs in June 2021, word had come down that, under no circumstances, would any white or "white adjacent" people be considered for the job. Basically, anyone "not black" was strictly verboten. Following the shooting death that May of Davonte Boothe by police outside of Philadelphia, and the mass nation-wide protests that had followed, the Wendover College Office of the President had sent out a series of outraged press releases condemning racism in general and systemic American racism in particular, noting as well that the college would redouble its ef-forts to hire more black staff and more black faculty and enroll more black students. Through such efforts, the college was com-mitted, as President Blanche Hogg declared, to "leading the way in making the world a safer, more diverse, and more equitable place for all people, and especially for People of Color."

Yet despite an aggressive marketing campaign for the open staff-assistant position—in which none of the whites, Asians, Latinos, and other non-blacks knew that their applications had gone straight into the trash—only three acceptable candidates were contacted for an interview. One of them promptly with-drew his application, stating that he had "decided to go into real estate." The second candidate, a recent graduate of a respectable private college with a degree in classics, had become the clear favorite after he had dazzled Digby at his interview. Digby had mentioned his interest in Italian Renaissance instruments and his membership in the Wendover Monteverdi Society, and was then astounded to learn that the candidate, Clifford Blue, not only loved Palestrina and Gabrieli but that he also "revered" the sack-but. "A beautiful instrument," Clifford Blue had said. "A rich, complex, majestic sound. I'd love to hear you perform sometime."

Digby had wanted to hire Clifford Blue right there. Cole, made uncomfortable by the instant rapport between his boss and this potential colleague, sensed an alliance in the making that at some point might prove problematic to himself.

Cole therefore put all his support behind candidate number three. LaKeesha Lovette had graduated from Beauville High School and, after working a series of menial jobs for a number of years, had begun taking night courses at the Wendover Extension School. She had wanted, as she explained in her interview with Digby and Cole, "to better herself." Six years later, just after Davonte Boothe's murder, she graduated with a BA in Business Administration.

For Cole, LaKeesha Lovette was the perfect candidate: a diversity hire that posed absolutely no threat to himself. Given her education and work history—she had been a night manager at Pepe's Burritos on Main Street in Beauville and a merchandise stocker at Giganta-Mart on the Beauville Heights—LaKeesha would likely remain a staff assistant for the entirety of her Wendover career. That meant one less person who might challenge Cole's position and ambition in the Office of Student Affairs.

"But Dig," Cole had said as he and his boss deliberated the merits of the two candidates, "LaKeesha checks all the boxes: black, female, underprivileged, Wendover Extension School. She's an HR wet dream! She's a *Wendover* wet dream!"

Digby solemnly shook his head, woefully conflicted. "I know, I know. But Clifford is *such* an interesting young man. My God, he's even read *To the Finland Station*—for fun! And who cares if he's not a woman? He *is* black, and that's primarily what the administration wants ... No, this is *my* department! We're going with Clifford, and that's *that*."

But that wasn't *that*. For just as Digby had begun to type an email to inform Clifford Blue that he should be expecting some very good news in the next couple of days from Wendover Human Resources, Clifford Blue sent an email to Digby: he had decided to join the Peace Corps and would soon be leaving for Azania. "I'm sorry I won't get to hear your sackbut or further discuss Wilson. Thank you again for your kind consideration ..."

Shortly after this, a press release and a university-wide email was sent out announcing that, "LaKeesha Lovette '21, has become the first Black woman Wendover Extension School graduate to join the administrative staff of Wendover College." For Cole, it was a moment of great triumph and deep personal gratification. A moment to savor. Once again, he felt, he had done his part in fighting injustice, helping the downtrodden, and making a better world.

"So where do we stand with the Multisex Bathrooms report?" he now said to LaKeesha. "Have we made any progress?" He was assuming the answer was no, and that he would have to work his ass off for the next eight days to get the report ready for the Dean. Quite frankly, today wasn't the first time he had caught LaKeesha at her desk watching old-school rap videos.

But she surprised him. "It's basically finished."

"*Finished?*" Cole said.

"Yeah. I just need to punch in the figures from the architect. The meeting's on Monday."

"The *meeting*? What meeting?" Cole said. "And what architect?"

"I sent you an email."

"I don't remember ..."

"The college's architect—Parkman Associates. You told me when you gave me this thing that they'd be tasked with coming up with preliminary plans and estimated costs."

"Right," Cole said, now remembering.

"So I took care of it."

"You took care of it," Cole muttered, staring at her.

"Yes."

Nodding meditatively, Cole wondered if he had maybe underestimated LaKeesha Lovette. "And what about the actual report," he went on, now in a more probing tone. "You know, the actual *writing*. The analysis part."

"I already told you. It's basically finished."

"But how?" Cole said.

"It was easy," LaKeesha said. "At the beginning you told me we were copying Thaxter College on this. You said they had gone multisex bathrooms ten years ago and that we looked—how did you put it, 'prehistoric'?—for still having men's and women's bathrooms. So I called their Student Affairs Office and asked if I could see a copy of the feasibility report they did. The lady said, 'I don't see why not,' and they emailed it to me that afternoon."

For Cole, up was now down, six was now nine. The world had gone topsy-turvy. What LaKeesha had done was ... *pure genius*. Pure *bureaucratic* genius. She had saved herself two or three weeks' worth of soul-destroying drudgery by doing something no one in this office would have ever thought to do. He was, Cole realized, dealing with a special mind here. But the plan was not without potential problems.

"You *plagiarized* Thaxter's Multisex Bathrooms report?" he said.

"*No*," LaKeesha said in an openly rebukeful tone. "I used it as a *model*. A 'template,' as it's called in the business world. I took a course on this. Is some of the language similar? *Yes*. But this isn't a PhD dissertation on subbuts, is it?"

"Sackbuts," Cole gently corrected her.

"*Whatever*. The point is, everyone here knows 'feasibility' in this case is bullshit. The college wants to go multisex and our report gives them exactly what they want, how 'multisex bathrooms will benefit both students and society and blah blah blah.' Like I said, all that's left for us is to get the drawings and figures from the architect and plug them into the report. Which I can also do since you don't know how to use ProWerksX."

ProWerksX was the new software the college had implemented across all administrative offices to produce reports and other important documents with graphs, spreadsheets, and images. Cole found it tediously perplexing, and refused to use anything but Word and Excel.

"Well ... OK," he said uneasily. "It sounds like we're on schedule. But send me a copy as soon as it's ready. So I can review it and, uh, make any necessary corrections."

A look of mistrust came into LaKeesha's eyes. "Are we finished?"

Cole nodded and she left the room. Watching her go, Cole felt faintly apprehensive. Yes, he had definitely underestimated LaKeesha Lovette. He would have to give this situation a little more thought.

* * *

"It was the best ... sex ... I ever had," said Linni Mudge, choking up between her words. "The best ... sex ... *of my life*. So ... *incredible* ... so ... *otherworldly*. And his body ... *oh God!*" With affecting, silver-screen pathos, Linni's eyelids fluttered, and a single glistening tear broke forth and slowly rolled down her sculpted cheek.

She and Oona were seated at an outdoor table at the Uriah Heep Bookseller Café, just off the Wendover College campus. All around them on the crowded terrace people had paused their chewing and their conversations and were straining to listen. Oona, who had agreed to meet Linni for lunch so they could "talk" about her breakup with Tyce Creamer, was at full attention too.

"In one of his videos," Linni went on, wiping her eyes, "he says that when a guy first has sex with a woman, he should make sure to give her 'the best lay of her life.' That way, she'll always remember him and keep coming back for more. But with Tyce, *every time* we had sex was the best sex of my life. Every ... single ... time ... He always brought it, Oona. It was magical. *He* is magical."

As yet another tear rolled down Linni's cheek, a dreamy and even reverential look shone from her perfectly symmetrical face. It was as though she was remembering some cherished moment of Tyce-given bliss. Among the women who had been raptly listening from nearby tables, Linni's last comments had elicited an array of responses. Some of the ladies appeared amazed that such exalted heights of pleasure were even humanly possible; some appeared skeptical of Linni's tale and dismissive of her operatic presentation; still others appeared to be wondering how they too might get some of this action. The nearby men, by contrast, appeared nervous and fidgety, particularly those who were with women.

"I'm telling you Oona, Tyce has secret knowledge," Linni said with reddened eyes. Then, leaning forward, she added in a near whisper, "Secret *sex knowledge*. Things that aren't in his videos." Of course Linni was aware of her audience, and she was more than happy to perform for the crowd, but she did not want to give *too* much away.

For her part, Oona found herself becoming more aroused with each additional revelation. Linni's ecstatic ravings about Tyce's body and his pleasure-giving prowess were stoking both her curiosity and her desire. Trying to control herself, trying to maintain a semblance of *dignified restraint*, she said, in a manner that was almost professorial, "Now when you say '*secret sex knowledge*,' what do you mean, exactly? Do you—"

"And he's such a *brute*! *Such* a brute!" Linni burst out, cutting Oona off. The girl was too absorbed in her feelings, too engrossed in her *drama*, to field questions just yet. She needed to tell her story, she needed to get it out.

In this instance, Oona did not mind. "A *brute*?" she said, now doubly, *trebly* intrigued. Images of wild, ape-like sex scenes flashed in her mind. Scenes of violence and wanton abandon.

"Yes!" Linni eagerly affirmed. "He said, '*There's the door!*' "

Bewildered at this, Oona said, " 'There's the door'?" She was trying to envision a sex act that involved a door, but her mind remained blank.

Just behind Linni and directly in Oona's line of sight sat two young women who had been listening right along. They too seemed perplexed by the suggestion of "door sex."

Linni nodded sadly and replied, "It's what he said when we broke up."

"Oh," Oona said, understanding with some regret that the topic had shifted and that there would be no "door sex" story. With her interest momentarily flagging, she took a bite of her neglected turkey wrap sandwich. Now chewing she said, "What happened?"

"I don't know if I can talk about it," Linni said. "It's too intimate."

Oona found that hard to believe. She took another bite of her turkey wrap, and waited.

Linni said, "All I wanted was ..." A shade of embarrassment passed over her face, and she briefly lowered her eyes. "All I wanted was ... for us to be ... *exclusive*. That's all I asked."

Oona, of course, already knew this; Tyce had told her the previous evening. With her mouth filled with turkey breast, guacamole, lettuce, and spinach-flavored pita bread, she responded with a nod and a perfunctory, "Mm-hmm."

Linni's brow creased with mistrust. "Did he tell you?" she said hotly.

"What? *No*," Oona said with her mouth full. "No."

"Did you talk about me last night? Did you talk about ... *us*?" Linni said with a wounded look.

"*No*. Not at all," Oona said, adding a touch of affronted outrage to her voice. She could perform just as well as Linni. "I would *never* have gone there. I would never have allowed it.

What happened between the two of you is private. As far as I'm concerned, it's none of my business."

"Thank you, Oona," Linni said, grateful and reassured. "Thank you." She sipped her peach kombucha, then continued. "I just wanted us to be exclusive. That's all … It feels weird to say that, because I know in a way that we *were* exclusive. I mean, we were together almost all the time, so when could he have been seeing other girls? When I was *asleep*? When I was at work? When I was at the grocery store? I don't know. Maybe I shouldn't have said anything. Maybe it was too soon. But we were *always* together anyway, almost every night, so what was the big deal? But then he said, 'I told you when we first started that I'm not looking for anything serious. I want my freedom.' And I said, 'That's what I want too! We can be free *together*!' But he just laughed. He *laughed*, Oona."

At this, one of the two young women seated behind Linni— they were still following every word—shook her head with disgust, as though revolted by the baseness of men. Her friend, clearly feeling the same, repeated the gesture.

"And I admit, I got mad," Linni went on. "I was pissed. I said, 'Are you seeing somebody else?' But he wouldn't answer. He wouldn't answer! And then I got even more pissed and I said, 'If you can't make a commitment to me, to *us*, then I'm leaving!' I said that, Oona. I did."

"Good for you," Oona said. "And what did he say?"

"He said …" Linni paused, her voice quavering. "He said … 'There's the door, *baby*.' "

"Oh. Right," Oona said.

"That's when he said it."

"Gotcha."

"Can you believe that, 'There's the door, *baby*'? I'm *not* his baby!" Linni said, now with pique.

"Mm-hmm," Oona said, chewing another bite of her turkey wrap.

"Was that too much to ask, Oona? For us to be exclusive? I mean, we *love* each other. We always have. For three months now."

"Did *he* say he loved you?" Oona asked.

"Well ..." Linni said. "Not *specifically*. But I could *tell* that he did. It was obvious. He didn't need to say anything."

"Hmm," Oona said.

"The problem, Oona, is other women. *That's* the problem," Linni said, now with seething disdain. "These, these *hussies*, they think, just because Tyce is hot, and rich, and famous, that they can just walk up to him and offer him a blowjob. Really, they just throw themselves at him—*even when I'm right there!* You've seen it, haven't you? At the gym? But it happens everywhere. At bars, at restaurants. At the pet store one time. But the thing is, Oona, Tyce needs me. He *needs* me. We're perfect together. We were made for each other. People can see that. And he knows it. He *knows* he needs me, and he knows we were meant to be. I think he's just scared. He's scared of love. *True* love."

Oona saw the two young women behind Linni shake their heads and roll their eyes with exasperated disappointment. All along they had been listening with sisterly solidarity to Linni's tale of romantic woe, but just like that they had withdrawn their support. Linni had lost the girls' allegiance and also their respect. Oona felt the same. She marveled at Linni's self-delusion and wondered at how passion could make an otherwise intelligent woman—for Linni *was* an intelligent woman, as among other things she had read and favorably commented on two of Oona's books—so downright stupid. How did such things happen? How could people lose control like this? It seemed absurd. Yet truth be told, Oona herself had little experience of romantic angst. When, indeed, had she last been upset over a man? Twenty years ago? Thirty? *Ever?* In the past there had been crushes and infatuations, and even tender feelings she had thought were love. But never anything like this. Never anything agonizing or life-convulsing, and certainly never anything that would make her act like such a fool as Linni was acting now.

"But he'll come back," Linni was saying. "I know he will. He just needs some time."

"Have you spoken to him? Since the, um, breakup?"

"No. He's not returning my calls. Or my texts. Or my emails."

Watching Linni, with her sad eyes and vulnerable expression, Oona got an idea. She tilted her head slightly to the side in what she thought was a gesture of sympathy, and gazed into Linni's eyes with what she thought was a look of compassion. "Linni," she said, "do you think it would help if ... if *I* talked to Tyce?"

Behind Linni the reaction was swift. Like the chorus of an ancient Greek drama, the two eavesdropping young women turned their suspicious eyes directly on Oona. They sensed mischief afoot. Vile, treacherous, loathsome mischief. It was creeping at Linni's door, hiding in the shadows and preparing to pounce.

"Would you do that for me, Oona?" Linni said, her face shining with hope and appreciation. "Would you do that?"

"If you want," Oona said graciously, as though she was prepared to do anything to help a friend.

"Oh, thank you, Oona. Thank you!"

"I just want you to be happy," Oona said.

For the two young Furies behind Linni, this was enough. Convinced of Oona's back-stabbing intentions, her evil-bitch villainy, they bitterly shook their heads and glared at her with smoldering feminine wrath. Then one of them put on her blue paper face mask and stood, and the other one did the same. Then together the incensed duo marched off, though not before giving Oona a pair of nasty, curseful looks.

Oona ignored them. She could not have cared less.

"But what will you say?" Linni asked.

"I'll say ... I'll say what *you* say," Oona said thoughtfully. "That you and Tyce are perfect together, and that he's making a big mistake. And I'll also tell him that, if he waits too long, he'll lose you to another man, and that he'll always regret it."

"Oh, Oona, that's *good*!" Linni said. "That's really good. Yes, say that. And also tell him … tell him that—I'm here for him, when he's ready."

* * *

"Mom, I don't feel good."

"What's wrong?"

"I feel sick."

"How do you mean?"

"I just feel sick."

"Is this about your arm?"

Rosa's arm was still covered in ugly red splotches.

"No."

"Then what? Do you have a stomach ache? A headache? I'm not a mind reader, Rosa."

Oona was in a rush. After her lunch with Linni she had been too agitated, too worked up, too inflamed with desire, to go back to her office and write. Her editor was expecting the first three chapters of her contracted new book—they were already a month overdue—but Oona had no interest in writing. She only wanted to go to the gym. Tyce was usually there late afternoon and she wanted to get there before him. It would look more natural that way.

"I don't know. I just feel sick," Rosa said.

"Rosa, that's not an answer."

"I feel really tired. I just want to sleep."

The two of them were in the kitchen. Oona had already changed into her workout clothes and was filling her water bottle. "Then take a nap," she said.

"I already did. Mom, those tights are too tight. Everyone can see your bum."

"Rosa, I thought you were sick?"

"I am."

"Then go back to bed. Take another nap."

"I don't want to. It's boring."

"Well I have to go. I'm late."

"Your boobs are popping out too," the girl said. "You look half naked!"

"Rosa, I don't want to hear it. This is normal workout attire for grownups. I'll see you for supper."

"Also, Mom?"

Oona had already started for the door. She stopped and looked back. "What?"

"Lucas is in the backyard. Naked."

Rosa wasn't laughing. "You mean he has his shirt off?" Oona said.

"No. Everything."

Oona reversed direction and went out to the backyard.

Lucas was reclined in a chaise longue. Naked.

"Mom!" he said indignantly. "You could have warned me!" He reached for the T-shirt by his side and covered himself.

"Lucas, what the hell are you doing? Are you trying to get arrested?"

"*No.*"

"Lucas, we're surrounded by houses here. People can see you."

"They're all at work."

Oona shook her head. "What are you doing?" she repeated.

"I'm getting sun."

"OK, great. But why are you not wearing shorts?"

"Because I'm sunning my balls."

"You're sunning your balls," Oona said, mystified.

"Yes," Lucas said. "It doubles your testosterone."

"Sunning your balls doubles your testosterone?" Oona said doubtfully.

"Yes."

"Who told you that?"

"Tyce."

"*Tyce* told you?"

"Well, not *personally*. It was in one of his videos."

Oona sighed. "Lucas, you're eighteen—don't you have enough testosterone as it is? At your age it should be coming out of your ears."

"I want more … It feels good."

"The sun on your balls?"

"*No*. The testosterone. You get it when you exercise, and also when you eat meat, and when you get sun. It helps you gain muscle and feel more aggressive."

"Wonderful. Just what the world needs. Another aggressive man."

"That's not true. Men are becoming weaker. Testosterone levels worldwide are dropping. They're about fifty percent what they were in the 1950s. Sperm counts are way down too. I've seen the data."

"Fine, Lucas. Sun your balls," Oona said, now turning for the garage. "But if the police come, call your father to bail you out, not me."

* * *

Oona's workouts at the gym—it was called "BuffBodz Pro Fitness" and was the swankiest gym in Beauville—typically ran from thirty minutes to an hour depending on whether she did cardio or weights. Today, however, she had already been at the club for nearly two hours, waiting and waiting for Tyce Creamer to arrive. With each passing minute she lost a little more self-respect. So as not to look conspicuous—like a desperate middle-aged woman hoping to "bump into" someone, for example—she had run on the treadmill, ridden the stationary bike, lifted dumbbells, and done reps on every weight machine in the place. Now her arms ached and her knees hurt. Yet just as she decided that she had had enough humiliation for one day and was preparing to leave, Tyce came through the door.

All at once the energy in the club changed. A palpable electric charge infused the place. People stopped what they were doing and became attentive. The women especially seemed affected, as girls in their sports bras and form-fitting booty bottoms became extra alert. Some observed Tyce discreetly, as though wanting to conceal their interest. Others ogled him unabashedly, as though wanting to make their intentions clear. Still others had an air of dreamy forgetfulness, as if they had gone mentally to another, better place.

The male response was less complex. "Yo Tyce!" a guy said and gave him a soul-brother handshake. Another said, "What's up, dude?," as he and Tyce slapped each other's hands, back and front, then concluded it with a fist bump.

As it turned out, Tyce was moving through the club straight in Oona's direction. She, inexplicably, froze. Her body froze. Her *brain* froze. She could not move, she could not think.

Then, out of nowhere, a young blonde in tiny shorts with long athletic legs swooped down on Tyce like some ravenous hawk. The girl was half Oona's age but clearly twice as bold. She looked like a cross between a runway model and an Olympic track star. With supreme self-assurance she gave Tyce a coy smile that seemed to say, "This *might* be your lucky day, playa."

Just as he had done the previous evening at Oona's house, Tyce flashed his sugar-white teeth, removed his smoke-tinted sunglasses and hung them from the collar of his too-tight T-shirt, and gave the blonde beauty a kiss on the cheek. Everyone in the gym was watching, women and men. It seemed a sort of Darwinian moment. A Darwinian *performance*. The two hottest people in the place had found each other and asserted their dominance over the rest of the less-fortunate herd.

Oona's mood dropped to the floor. She wanted to slip out of BuffBodz unnoticed, get her forty-two-year-old non-model, non-Olympian body back to her car and onto the road. Yet before she could slink away and head for the rear exit, she froze yet again. Tyce and the blonde were coming her way.

"Oona, how are you?" he said as he closed down on her, his bleached teeth shining and his animated eyes sparkling with film-star charm. Of course he was maskless, as was nearly everyone else in the gym, including Oona herself. Unlike the day before, however, Tyce did not greet her with a kiss. Instead he touched her upper arm in a friendly, chummy way, and said, "Last night was great." He explained to the blonde that he and Oona were neighbors and that he had had dinner with her and her family the previous evening. Then to Oona he said, "This is Ingrid."

Of course it is, Oona thought, as she craned her neck to look up into Ingrid's very pretty, very blue, and very self-satisfied eyes. Ingrid did not extend her hand or say hello or even give Oona a nod. She did not acknowledge her in any way. Instead she smiled coolly and turned her attention back to Tyce with an appreciative, proprietorial air, as though she was admiring a champion stallion. *Her* champion stallion.

Blatantly snubbed—by a young trollop barely old enough to drink—Oona's impulse was to take ahold of Ingrid's foot-long ponytail, yank her to the floor, and stomp on her delicately shaped Nordic nose. Stomp, stomp, stomp … Then Oona realized that Tyce was looking at *her*, and that he was waiting. And then Oona further realized that she had not yet spoken. She had not yet said a single word. She became flustered and frantic. Something witty was called for, something to prove she was more than just a pair of tits and long legs like Miss Hitler Youth here. Quickly, and with a forced laugh, she said, "You know, my son is home sunning his balls." Yet as soon as the words had been said, Oona cringed, instantly regretting them. She tried to laugh again, but couldn't. Her cheeks turned red.

A look of leery disgust wrinkled Ingrid's formerly flawless face. She gazed at Oona as though she was some sort of sicko, a monstrous pervert.

Tyce also appeared taken aback, but minus the grade-school theatrics. "Oh …" he said with mild confusion. "That's good," he added politely, as if to help her out. "Good for him."

"He said it boosts testosterone," Oona said, trying to recover. "He said he saw it in one of your videos."

"*Ah* … Right. I remember that one," Tyce smiled.

"You said you were going to show me those new squats," Ingrid said to Tyce. She smiled coaxingly and placed a hand on his veiny bicep.

Oona's face darkened. The bitch was touching his vein! *Her* vein!

"It was great to see you," Tyce said to Oona, amiably patting her on the shoulder and giving her a cheery wink.

As the alpha couple walked away, Oona found her eye focusing squarely on Ingrid's shapely young ass. Tragically—for Oona, that is—the ass was heartbreakingly glorious. A gluteus maximus for the ages. And with each step the girl took, a slight half-moon of that glorious gluteus peeped out nakedly from beneath her extra-short booty bottoms.

Oona felt thoroughly beaten, crushed and deflated, as though all the life had gone out of her.

* * *

She was in her bathroom, stripping off her smelly gym clothes and filling the tub with hot water, when her phone rang from the bedroom. She went to check it. The caller ID said "Linni." Oona sighed, feeling annoyed. She decided not to answer it. Then she changed her mind. "Hi Linni."

"*Oh, Oona!*—can you talk? Something awful happened."

"Yes, but I've only got a few minutes. I'm going to put you on speaker phone—"

"Oh don't! Can people hear us?"

"No, I'm alone. I'm about to take a bath. I overdid it at the gym," Oona said as she went back into the bathroom.

"You were at the gym? When? Did you talk to him?"

"I went this afternoon."

"Was Tyce there?"

"He came in just as I was leaving," Oona said, watching the water cascade into the tub.

"Was he with that slut Ingrid?"

"Uh—"

"We just had a fight. Oh, it was awful. And now I'm banned from the club!"

"No."

"Yes."

"Who did you fight?"

"Ingrid. She's such a bitch! It was all her fault!"

"What happened?"

"I went after work, and when I got there Ingrid was all over him. She was wearing her short-shorts, the ones where half her ass hangs out. It's because she doesn't have any tits."

"What caused the fight?" Oona said. The tub was nearly filled. She turned off the water and set the phone on the flat edge of the bath, next to Brad.

"I told Tyce we needed to talk," Linni said, "since he wasn't returning my calls, or my texts, or my emails. He said it wasn't cool that I came there, and I said, 'What do you mean it's not cool, I'm a member here!' And then Ingrid stuck her pointy little nose in it, saying I should leave, and I said, 'Maybe *you* should leave you skinny bitch, and stay the hell away from my boyfriend!' That's exactly what I said, Oona."

"Good for you," Oona said with mild interest. She had removed the last of her clothes and now stepped into the tub, lowering her achy body into the warm water. The pleasurable sensation was instant, like a soothing, all-over caress. It almost felt like being hugged.

"Thanks," Linni said. "But then she *laughed*, Oona. She laughed at me! She's like twenty years old! Who the hell does she think she is?"

"She does have some attitude."

"I know. I was so mad I could hardly speak … That's when I did it."

"What?"

"Oh, it's too embarrassing."

"Tell me."

"I squirted her."

"You squirted her?"

"Yes, with my water bottle. The white plastic one I have, from the 'Walk for Timmy' walkathon? The little boy who had cancer? You've seen it."

"OK," Oona said, though she had no recollection of the object.

"I just pointed it at her and squeezed. It shot a long stream right into her face. It was dumb but I was so mad. Of course she screamed and made a scene. Everyone was watching. Then one of the managers, Rick, the one with the hair plugs, he said I had to leave and not come back. I hope he doesn't mean it. It would be a disaster. I mean, how will Tyce and I work out together?"

"Mmm, yeah—that's a good question," Oona said, thinking this maybe wasn't such bad news. Linni's banishment from Buff-Bodz meant that she, Oona, would have more access to Tyce. Of course there was still Ingrid to consider.

"It's horrible, Oona. A complete nightmare. And Ingrid said she's going to press charges. It's outrageous! Just for squirting her with water? She really is a bitch. Do you think I should call a lawyer?"

"Uh, I don't know," Oona said, becoming bored with the conversation and now eyeing Brad with a deep pang of longing.

"My father's best friend is a lawyer. I'm thinking—"

"Sorry, Linni, hold on … *What is it honey?*" Oona called out to the wall as she held up the phone for Linni to hear. "*OK!*" she added. "Sorry Linni but I have to go. Rosa needs me."

"Oh," Linni said with disappointment. "OK … But Oona, do you think I should call Tyce? You know, to discuss this?"

"Linni, I think you should do … whatever feels right."

Oona turned off her phone and reclined deeper into the comforting bath. The water was up to her chin. For some time she lay motionless with her eyes closed. She was finally relaxing, finally decompressing from her many stresses and worries and frustrations. Gradually the desire came over her for a more intense experience of pleasure. Oh yes, she was ready. She reached for Brad, her sixteen-inch heavy-rubber sex toy. It looked like a flesh-colored billy club, a weapon of lethal intent. But for Oona it was a weapon of bliss. Brad vibrated, Brad penetrated, Brad lighted up her life. She had bought the thing six months earlier, online, and had it shipped discreetly to her office at the college. Since then Brad had been her one source of joy, her one unfailing escape from her oppressive, unsatisfying life.

She clicked the thing on and it began to hum and throb. She gripped it with both hands at the base, closed her eyes, and gently pressed the tip along her cheeks and neck. The vibrations roused her flesh and also her mind. Slowly she lowered Brad down her body and into the bath. The water stirred energetically, making bubbles and wavelets. A smile blossomed on Oona's face. She was picturing Tyce Creamer—his veins, his muscles, and his fake-white teeth—and soon she was imagining many other things as well.

* * *

Afterward as she was drying off with a towel, Oona paused to examine herself in the mirror. Her face, she knew, was not her strong point. She was no beauty, no head-turner like either Ingrid or Linni, both of whom had been genetically gifted. Oona's nose was too big and her eyes were too close together. She had always told herself that she was a six out of ten on the looks scale, though deep down she thought it was more like a five. Things improved, however, with her body. Though she was short and had unattractive feet, she indisputably had fantastic legs and a most magnificent bust. In high school and college, on days when she felt depressed because she was unpopular and lonely and completely ignored by the good-looking boys, she would go into the bathroom, remove her shirt and bra, and—like now—admire herself in the mirror. Her breasts were still mostly magnificent, Oona felt, despite three decades of gravity. When she had ballooned out at fourteen her similarly well-endowed grandmother had advised her to always wear a bra, including to bed, otherwise by forty "your knockers will be down at your waist." Whether this prediction actually might have come true Oona would never know, for she had always followed the advice.

"Oona?" came a voice from the other side of the bathroom door.

It was Cole. Oona recoiled and raised her arms to cover herself. The door was unlocked. All he had to do was turn the knob and he could come in. "*What?*" she said gruffly to the door.

"What are you doing?"

"I'm just getting out of the bath."

There was a pause, then, "Can I come in?"

In his voice Oona heard boyish insecurity and even a touch of childish pleading. It repelled her and she winced. Watching the door, she made no reply, still worried he might turn the knob and enter.

"Oona? … Can I come in?" he repeated, now with whiny desperation. The door remained shut. He was too timid to open it. Too respectful, too afraid.

This was her husband, and Oona could not bear it. She could not bear his whimpering neediness, his cowering self-doubt. It was viscerally repulsive to her, and, unable to control herself, she shouted, "*No!* Go away!"

FOUR

"I don't feel good," Rosa said as she came into the kitchen.

"Still?" Cole said, holding a spatula at the stove.

The girl nodded drearily. "I feel weird."

"Well your arm looks better," Cole said. The strawberry-colored splotches had started to fade. "Are you coming to the Farmers Market?" he added brightly.

"I think so."

It was Saturday morning, and Cole was in good spirits. *Very* good spirits. But he was always in good spirits on Saturday mornings. It was his weekly mood high-point. He was free from the office and would not have to go back for two whole days. On Sundays his mood sank, mainly because he knew that he would have to return to work the next day. And on Saturday evening his mood also dipped because he knew Sunday was just hours away and Saturday was almost gone. But *Saturday morning*—well, *that* was the best, and for Cole Saturday mornings in summer also meant the Beauville Farmers Market, which he loved.

Now Oona entered the kitchen. She looked, Cole noted, just as dissatisfied as she usually did—vaguely bothered, vaguely resentful, vaguely pissed off. For her, Saturday morning seemed no better than any other morning. Cole said nothing to her, and she said nothing to him.

"Mom, I don't feel good," Rosa said.

"What's wrong?"

"I feel weird."

"Weird?" Oona said, stepping over to the coffeemaker.

Rosa nodded.

"Did you take an aspirin?" Oona said, pouring herself a cup.

"No."

"Do you want a kale burger?" Cole said to his wife.

"Sure."

Lucas entered the room.

"Here he is—Beefsteak Bob," Cole said with an acerbic grin.

"Yep, the only healthy person in this house," Lucas said, giving it right back. "I've already noticed a change. I have more energy and my mood has improved. It's what happens when you take out the carbs."

"It's been three days, Lucas," Cole said smugly. "We'll talk in a week, after you've become good friends with Mr. Constipation. Trust me, you'll be begging for a salad and a banana."

"No I won't. Fiber is actually bad for you. It's indigestible," the boy said.

Cole chuckled darkly. "Whatever you say, Lucas. Whatever you say."

After Cole had finished cooking and distributing the kale burgers, home fries, and toast he joined Rosa and Oona at the table. Lucas then sat down with a one-pound square block of raw ground beef on a plate, taken straight from the plastic package. His mother, his father, and his sister looked at him.

"Are you forgetting something, Lucas?" Oona said. "You know—the *cooking part?*"

"No. I'm eating it like this," the boy said as he stuck a fork into the meat and brought a hunk of it to his mouth.

"Eeeewwww—that's *gross!*" Rosa said. "It has blood in it!"

"No it doesn't," Lucas said, chewing the raw cow flesh. "It's just juices. They drain the blood after they slaughter the cow."

"I feel bad for the cow," Rosa said sadly.

"You like cheeseburgers," Lucas said.

"I know but ..." She didn't finish the sentence.

For Cole, a militant vegetarian of twenty years, this was too much. It felt personal. "Are you doing this just to *piss* me off?" he burst out. "Is that what this is, Lucas? Are you trying to *piss me off*?"

"Cole," Oona said.

"No, he's trying to be provocative!" he said. "That's your thing now, isn't it?" he went on, glaring at the boy. "You want to piss people off! First it was the vaccines and the masks, now it's the caveman diet. What's next, Lucas, are you joining the Flat Earth Society? Well let me tell you something, kid—the Earth is round! It's *round*!"

"I'm doing this," Lucas said, coolly yet firmly, as he forked off another chunk of ground beef, "because I want to be healthy, and I want to gain muscle. I'm done being a pussy."

"That's a swear," Rosa said, looking from Lucas to her mother and expecting her to step in. But Oona ignored this.

"No it's not," Lucas said. "I'm talking about wimpy guys. Not the other thing."

" '*Wimpy guys.*' Listen to him," Cole grumbled, munching on his kale burger and shaking his head. "This is unbelievable."

"But why raw, Lucas?" Oona said. "Is cooked meat for pussies?"

"Mom!" Rosa said.

"No," the boy said. "Raw meat is healthier. When you cook it you degrade the enzymes and the vitamins, especially if you overcook it. And cooking itself creates carcinogens."

"What nonsense! Where do you get this stuff?" Cole said.

"Tyce. He has a video—"

"Tyce? *Tyce?*" Cole exploded, looking at Oona. "Can you believe this? You let a redneck brownshirt move into your neighborhood and the next thing you know your kid's eating raw hamburger and using the word 'pussy'! I'm telling you, I looked into this guy, this *Tyce Creamer*. Do you know what his books are called? His books that your son is reading?"

Oona did in fact know what Tyce's books were called, as she had already looked them up on Amazin!—several months ago. But she said nothing.

" 'Don't Be a Bitch'!" Cole said, answering his question. "That's what they're called—'Don't Be a Bitch'! The guy is a misogynist racist fascist. He's everything that's wrong with this country!"

"*I* think he's nice," Rosa said, sticking up for Tyce.

"Have you actually *read* his books, Dad? Or watched his videos?" Lucas said. "Because you might want to do that before you, you know, *slander* him. I *have* read one of his books and I've watched a bunch of his videos, and I've never heard him mention anything to do with race or mainstream politics or either of the parties. Not even once! It's so stupid what you're saying. You don't even know him."

"I don't have to know him, Lucas, to know he's an asshole!" Cole roared. " 'Don't Be a Bitch'? 'Bro2Bro with Tyce Creamer'? The bleached teeth and the steroid muscles? What more evidence do you need? Anyone with a thimbleful of brains can see the guy is a complete clown!"

"He doesn't take steroids, Dad. He made a video saying how bad they are."

"Well he's still a clown!"

"A 'clown,' " Lucas repeated, smirking with amusement.

"That's right, he's a *clown*!" Cole said aggressively. "A redneck fascist clown!"

Lucas shook his head, still smirking. "You're just jealous," he said quietly, looking at his raw hamburger.

"*Excuse me?*" Cole said. "What did you say?"

"I said you're just jealous. Of Tyce. He's popular and successful and he publishes books and makes videos that get millions of views. What have you ever done?"

"*Lucas*—that's enough!" Oona shrieked, pointing at her son as if he had insulted *her*. "You are really pushing it, young man!"

"He started it," Lucas said.

"You know what? It's fine. It's *fine!*" Cole said to Oona, and then, turning his furious eyes on his son, he said, "If you want to eat your raw cavemen burger and read your 'Don't Be a Pussy' books, I could care less. It's Saturday morning, it's sunny out, and I'm going to the Farmers Market, and you, Lucas, can go screw yourself!"

* * *

For the Perrot-Puddings, the Beauville Farmers Market was the closest thing they had to a shared family ritual. The market was held Saturday mornings, May through October, and since their arrival in Beauville a decade earlier, the family had regularly attended the market with religious devotion. Part of the ritual involved the family walking the eight blocks to get there, rather than taking a car. This way, they got exercise and fresh air and did not pollute the planet. Despite the breakfast table animosities, today would be no different.

Cole was already waiting in the living room, the place where the family assembled before heading out. In addition to his Pq23 respirator face mask and his N16z plastic face shield, Cole was attired in his typical Saturday-morning summer outfit: knee-length cargo shorts (the same style he had worn as a teenager), slip-on surfer sneakers (which he had also worn as a teenager, even though he had never gone surfing even once), and one of his alt-rock band T-shirts. Cole sort of collected the T-shirts, unofficially, just as he collected the bands' vinyl records. Some of the shirts were twenty years old and had been purchased at concerts and indie record shops while he was in college and graduate school. He liked obscure hipster bands, brainy noncorporate groups that the mainstream conformos had never heard of. Bands with edge, bands that gave the middle finger to the Man. Bands like Porcupyne, the Jizcums, Vile Bodies, the Smack Grannies. Today he was wearing his Idiot Gurus concert T-shirt from their 2003 "Tuna Fish Tango" tour, which he had seen in Chicago.

Rosa came into the room. She too had on her face mask and face shield.

"You all set?" Cole said.

"Yep," the girl said, smiling happily behind her mask. Like her father, she too loved the Farmers Market.

Now came Oona, followed by Lucas.

"All right, are we ready?" Cole said in a chipper voice, eager to depart. "You got your mask, Lucas?"

"Cole, stop it," Oona snapped.

Unlike the rest of his family, Lucas had refused to wear a mask for more than a year now. He had taken a lot of grief for it, too. Mainly insults, lectures, and dirty looks, at school, in grocery stores, and especially at home from his father. But the boy had held firm, citing various studies and the opinions of numerous doctors and scientists that masks were essentially useless against SPAARZ. The boy had even showed his father a video dating from the start of the pandemic in which Dr. Gerbyll himself, the government's leading health authority and the primary driver of mask and vaccine mandates, claimed that masks provided no meaningful protection against SPAARZ. "Fake news," Cole had claimed. Now, instead of responding to his father's latest gibe, the boy shook his head with pity.

Pleased with his put-down, Cole grinned at Oona. "All set?" he said.

She nodded, and then Cole noticed something.

"Where's your mask?" he said to her. "And your face shield?"

Oona made a look of tired resignation. "I don't think it's necessary. Not at this point," she said. "Plus, we'll be outside. They say the sun prevents transmission ..."

Lucas laughed triumphantly.

Cole was aghast. Over the past two years he had obediently followed government and news-media messaging on the pandemic, including the wearing of masks both indoors and out. Like all other critical thinkers, Cole compliantly followed The Science. Thus he wore his face mask and face shield while mowing the lawn and driving alone in his car and even when taking the trash to the curb. He did it for his safety and also for the safety of others. It was a health issue but also an ethical one. He was saving lives and alerting everyone around him that he cared, that he was both enlightened and kind, and that he especially wasn't one of *them*—one of those dangerous anti-Science redneck nitwits.

"Oona, what are you doing?" he said, looking stunned and even betrayed. "The DCP still advises—"

"Cole, just stop. Let it go," she said, becoming irritated.

"I can't believe this!" he said hotly. "I really can't!"

"I think the worst of the pandemic has passed," she said.

Rosa then stepped forward and declared, "If Mom's not wearing her mask, then I'm not either!" The girl took off her face shield and her face mask and threw them on the sofa.

Gloating victoriously, Lucas headed for the front door. Oona followed, and Rosa, with a joyous grin, did too.

* * *

Fuming at Oona's apostasy from The Science, and feeling quite frankly as though she had plunged a dagger in his back, Cole remained peevishly silent as he trailed behind his family on their eight-block walk. They could all go to hell, he thought. Yet when they finally arrived at the market—a closed-off section of Union Street in front of Beauville City Hall, jam-packed with vendors' tents and tables and shoppers—Cole's mood instantly rebounded. For here, he felt, were his people. The Farmers

Market was a homey mix of progressive "save-the-planet" politics and 1960s-hippie "Do-your-own-thing-man" sensibilities. There were organic farm stands, artisan cheesemakers, artisan jam-makers, artisan winemakers, artisan soap- and candle-makers, fair-trade coffee bean sellers, and gourmet gluten-free bakers, along with information booths dedicated to pressing social issues such as climate change and transgender rights. There were pockets of entertainment too. One week you might see a blue grass band and, a little farther off, a street poet; the next week, an accordionist and a barbershop quartet. Today, at the near-end of the market, were two gray-haired Boomers with acoustic guitars. They both wore cutoff dungaree shorts and leather sandals, and one had on a T-shirt that read, "Why Be Normal?" They were now playing a sentimental Woodstock-era ballad about parents teaching their kids well ...

Cole stopped to listen. A small crowd had gathered and he noticed that some were masked, but most were not. Something was changing, he thought, and it bothered him. When the song ended he clapped halfheartedly.

Rosa came up to him. "Can we get a muffin?"

Every Saturday the family got a muffin. Today they got a muffin. Though Lucas did not, since he now only ate meat. After that, the shopping began. The Perrot-Puddings ambled down the bustling street, checking out the vendors' many tempting offerings. Cole bought a dozen heirloom tomatoes, a half dozen organic cucumbers, a pound of Indonesian dark-roast coffee beans, some goat's-milk yogurt, and a bottle of elderberry rosé wine. Oona bought a bottle of hand-crafted vinegar, a loaf of chocolate-cherry bread, and a jar of blueberry black-garlic jam. Rosa bought some peanut butter cookies, her favorite flavor for the past two summers.

"I want to buy some grass-fed steaks," Lucas said.

"Did you bring any money?" Cole said.

"Mom, can I have some money?" Lucas said.

"Hey, there's Mrs. Cutty!" Rosa said.

"Oh, great," Cole muttered, as he watched his daughter skip over to one of the information tables. Lucas followed.

"We should say hello," Oona said to Cole, making it clear by her look that she wasn't crazy about it either, but that it was the polite neighborly thing to do.

Cole scowled but grudgingly obeyed his wife.

Maeve Cutty, or "Maeve Nutty" as Cole called her, had been publicly advocating against the experimental SPAARZ vaccines for nearly two years. She had been a nurse at Beauville-Hancock Medical Center but had gotten fired for refusing the clinic's mandate that all doctors, nurses, and staff take the jab. In response, she organized regular protests outside the clinic. She wrote letters to the *Beauville Patriot* and started a FaceFace group for people opposed to vaccine mandates. And when the *Beauville Patriot* refused to publish her letters and FaceFace banned her group for "spreading disinformation," she doubled down. She made her own website, originally entitled "Nurses for Freedom" but which had recently been renamed "Nurses for Freedom Against the Global Coup d'État." The site aggregated pertinent articles by likeminded "truthers" and also included videos of Maeve herself interviewing luminaries in the so-called "anti-vax" and "conspiracy theory" worlds. Her initial thinking on the issue had been that the vaccines were not advisable for the simple reason that they had not been sufficiently tested. To her mind it was patent lunacy to force billions of people to take an experimental drug with unknown side effects for a flu that was only slightly more dangerous than a typical strain. That, at least, had been her initial thinking. Since then, as new data and studies and testimonies had begun to emerge, her theory was that the vaccines were killing and harming millions of people across the globe, and that they were part of a concerted effort to destabilize countries and their economies as the means to usher in a central bank digital currency, followed soon after by a one-world government controlled by oligarchs and their hired technocratic elites. And how did Cole know all of this? Because every now and then he would peruse Maeve Nutty's website, seeking to keep abreast of current "thinking" on the lunatic fringe. Depending on his mood, the site would either infuriate him or provide extreme hilarity, proving yet again just how colossally stupid some people could be.

"Hi Mrs. Cutty!" Rosa said, stepping up to Maeve's table.

Maeve had been standing alone, unvisited by the crowd of shoppers. There did not seem to be much interest in what she was offering. Her table was covered with an assortment of leaflets and brochures and was fronted by a large-lettered banner that read, "Freedom Isn't Free! The Predator Class Wants to Enslave You and Your Family. Educate Yourself and Resist!"

"Hello Rosa, how are you sweetie?" Maeve said, giving the child the warm smile of a favorite aunt, before greeting the rest of the Perrot-Puddings.

Cole tried his best to be civil. It was Saturday morning, after all.

"Look what happened to my arm," Rosa said, as she exhibited what remained of the red splotches.

Maeve, who was in her early sixties, squinted to take a look. "Oh my," she said with restrained alarm.

"It was *way* worse before," Rosa said, excited to tell a dramatic story. "It was bright red and gross. I had to go to the doctor."

Maeve Cutty's expression grew more concerned. She was a slender, gentle, kind-hearted woman who was nonetheless unafraid to state her beliefs. Around her neck she wore a small silver crucifix and on her button-down shirt she wore an array of pins. One read, "Last Year's Conspiracy Theories Are This Year's Facts." Another read, "Nuremberg 2.0." A third read, "Gerbyll Lied and People Died," and a fourth read, "Psalm 106:38."

She looked tentatively from Cole to Oona and said, "Did she …" But Maeve did not complete her thought, as she felt her question might be considered indelicate. The vaccines, as she had well learned, could be a touchy subject.

Cole and Oona remained silent, both of them looking uncomfortable.

Lucas, who did not look at all uncomfortable, answered the unfinished question, "Yep. She got the vaccine. My dad made her."

"*Lucas,*" Oona said sternly. Then to Maeve Cutty she explained, "It was a family decision."

"Yes. Of course," Maeve said politely, clearly disquieted but trying to maintain an affable, neighborly air.

"Rosa's protected now. And so are we," Cole said with a shade of aggression. "We believe in Science."

Lucas said, "What about the science that says the countries with the highest vax rates have the highest rates of death, and the countries with the lowest vax rates have the lowest rates of death? What about that science, Dad?"

Oona shot her son a warning look and Cole said, "Lucas, I'm *not* going to do this with you. *Not now.*"

"Yeah, because you know I'm right," the boy said.

"*Lucas!*" Oona snapped.

The boy made a fretful face, looked off to the side, and shook his head.

Maeve Cutty thought it best to change the subject. "And how was your graduation, Lucas?" she said. "That's so exciting." The boy had graduated from Millfield Academy, a private day school in Beauville, the previous Saturday.

"It was OK. I'm just glad to be out of there," he said. "And thank you for the card, and the money. That was really nice. I was going to come over."

"Oh, you're welcome," Maeve said. "I feel like I've watched you grow up. And soon you'll be heading off to Olmsted College."

"Actually, I decided I'm not going," the boy said.

"Yes he is," Cole said.

"No I'm not," Lucas said. To Mrs. Cutty he said, "Olmsted makes all students take the vaccine—the shots and the boosters —and I refuse."

Maeve looked again at Cole and Oona. She seemed both saddened and conflicted, as though she wanted to speak up but was afraid of offending them.

"He's just going through a rebellious streak," Oona said reasonably. "Come August, when all his friends are getting ready to go off to their schools, he'll change his mind."

"No I won't," he said. "And it's not even just about the quote-unquote vaccines anymore. Why would I want to spend four years with a bunch of brainwashed morons? Most of those kids are cowards and fools. Colleges today are just woke indoctrination camps. Screw that. I can take free classes online, and I won't have any debt."

Cole exploded. "You know what, Lucas? Here's an idea. Instead of Olmsted College, why don't you apply to clown college? I'm sure you'll fit right in."

"What's this? Can I read it?" Rosa said. While her parents and brother had been bickering, yet again, the girl had been looking over Mrs. Cutty's leaflets. She now reached for one that was entitled, "20 Reasons Not to Give Your Child the SPAARZ Vaccine."

Seeing the title, Oona and Cole both cried, "*No!*"

Rosa flinched back, startled by the force of their voices.

"Maeve, it was great to see you, but we have to run," Oona said. Maeve opened her mouth to speak but Oona wasn't interested. She quickly ushered her kids away, back in the direction they had come.

"I wanted to read that thing," Rosa whined.

"I think I'm going to get a donut before we go," Oona said with maternal cunning.

Rosa's eyes lit up. "Can I get one too?"

"Hey, there's Tyce!" Lucas said.

"Oh for frick sake!" Cole muttered as he spotted their buff neighbor twenty feet away, in line at one of the vendors' tables.

Oona became keenly aroused. Her flesh tingled with pleasure and her head felt light, even a little dizzy. It was *him*. And then she also noticed *her*—Ingrid. The Blonde Bitch. She was standing at Tyce's side.

"*Oh!* It's the Perrot-Puddings!" Tyce said with exaggerated ebullience as he saw the family coming his way. He gave Lucas a fist bump, then shined his winning smile on Rosa, saying, "Look at you, Rosa. That skirt is *very* pretty on you."

The girl blushed crimson. The skirt, which modestly reached below her knees, was old and starting to be too small but it was one of her favorite things. It was pink and covered with cartoon drawings of smiling puppies. "Thanks," she said, beaming shyly.

Ingrid promptly stepped closer to Tyce, as if to make it clear he was taken.

"*Oona*—how are you?" Tyce said in a playful, mock-dramatic voice, as if they were old pals and seeing her now was the highlight of his day. He stepped toward her, took hold of both her upper arms, and kissed her on the cheek.

Everyone present was visibly affected. Ingrid's brow creased with testy surprise. She considered Oona old, frumpy, and totally unattractive—especially that big nose. Rosa too looked on with testy surprise, feeling something like jealousy toward her mother. Why did Tyce keep kissing *her*, the child thought? She's *married*! Even Lucas was unsettled by the kiss. He questioned the appropriateness of the gesture and decided that, in fact, it kind of bothered him. What was Tyce thinking? As for Cole, although most of his face was covered by his mask and face shield —he was, in fact, the only person present who was properly protected—his splenetic eyes made his feelings clear. He did *not* approve of the kiss. It was shockingly offensive, a blatant and perhaps intentional act of disrespect toward himself! The racist redneck was purposely goading him. Cole felt compelled to say something. He felt compelled to *do* something. But he ... he did not want to make a scene. Not in front of all these people. So he did nothing.

But no one in this circle was half as affected as Oona herself. Not only had she not expected the kiss, but as Tyce had released her upper arms and pulled away, one of his hands had grazed the side of her breast. It sent an erotic charge all through her body, setting off a second wave of tingly feelings. Flummoxed at this, flummoxed at everything, Oona struggled to make sense of the situation. The firm strong feel of his hands gripping her arms, the kiss itself, and then his fingers sliding across her unsuspecting boob, had all turned her on. But what the hell, she wondered? He had kissed her cheek at the dinner party the other night and had even flirted with her, or so she had thought; then he pretty much ignored her at BuffBodz when he was with this blonde tart Ingrid; and now, in front of Ingrid and also in front of her family, he kisses her again? And what about the hand-to-boob thing? What was *that*? Was it intentional, or accidental?

"How ya been, Cole?" Tyce was now saying, as he offered his hand for a shake.

Shrugging stoically, Cole accepted the hand and promptly winced under Tyce's vice-like grip. He emitted a slight groan, smarting from the pain.

"The 'Idiot Gurus'?" Tyce said with some puzzlement, looking at Cole's T-shirt.

This gratified Cole. Very much. Tyce was obviously a hip-culture philistine, a clueless white-bread square, and it was now evident for all to see. The buffoon had been publicly unmasked, so to speak. "It's a band," Cole said smugly. "They're not main-stream."

"Cool," Tyce said with complete indifference, and then added, "This is Ingrid."

Cole redirected his attention. Taking in the girl, he seemed to instantaneously lose his capacity for verbal speech. And even though he knew it was not socially acceptable, certainly not for a highly educated and politically sensitive man such as himself, he found he could not prevent his eyes from greedily exploring this female masterpiece. Slowly, lingeringly, his gaze went from her blue-eyed, plump-lipped, lingerie-catalogue face, to the two *very visible* nipples that were poking through her form-fitting top, down to the teeny-weeny white shorts that barely covered what at one time would have been called her "privates," and at last to her long, eye-magnet legs, which noticeably stirred his blood. At some point, Cole regained his sense of propriety, and also his ability to speak, and said, "Oh, uh … hi."

"And you remember Oona?" Tyce said to Ingrid, continuing the introductions.

"Not really," Ingrid said, giving Oona a snooty glance. "Are you a waitress? I kind of think I've seen you before."

"She goes to BuffBodz. And she's not a waitress," Tyce gallantly interjected. "She's a prominent academic. She's a bigshot at Wendover. She's written famous books."

This delighted Oona. Immensely. "Well …" she said, glowing modestly. "I wouldn't say *famous*."

Cole rolled his eyes, feeling the rage bubble up. This was unbearable.

"Books?" Ingrid said, as if she was faintly familiar with the concept. "Like what? Sherlock Holmes?"

"No, political science," Oona said, happy to take the Blonde Bitch down a few pegs. "I focus on the intersection of politics, global capitalism, and technology. In particular I'm looking at the displacement of the sovereign nation-state by the rise of the NGO and the international decision-making class. Have you read Jacques Attali? Alvin Toffler? Samuel Huntington? Or maybe the Fabians or the Frankfurt School?"

Ingrid's face had gone blank at "political science." She became suddenly very unsure of herself and turned her panicked eyes to Tyce, as though hoping he might intervene.

87

With a wry grin, Tyce took his cue and continued the introductions. "And this is pretty Rosa … and Lucas, my main man."

Rosa waved with little enthusiasm. She had not missed the fact that Ingrid was not wearing a bra, nor that nearly every inch of her bare legs were exposed due to the teeny-weeny shorts. The poor child was now reassessing whether she liked her favorite skirt anymore. All of a sudden it seemed stupid.

"Say hello, Lucas," Tyce said. His tone was both supportive and commanding, like a firm parent trying to encourage a timid child.

"Hey, uuh, how's it going?" Lucas mumbled, not quite knowing what to do with his gaze. He felt too bashful to meet Ingrid's eye and was too embarrassed to stare at the rest of her, which was what he very much wanted to do.

"I'm ready to leave," Ingrid said to Tyce with a bored look, as if to say this whole scene was very much beneath her.

Tyce's expression hardened and he gave Ingrid a blunt stare. "OK. But I'm *not* ready to leave," he said. "I'd like to talk to my neighbors. If you want, you can wait in the car."

Ingrid gaped at him with stunned eyes. Her queenly, self-assured demeanor fell flat. "Uh … no. It's OK," she stammered, now shaken with insecurity. "I'm fine."

Turning back to the Perrot-Puddings, Tyce resumed his cheerful air and asked what they had bought. Oona and Rosa spoke simultaneously, explaining and displaying their various purchases. Rosa even offered Tyce one of her cookies, though he politely declined.

"I want to buy some steaks," Lucas said.

"Hey, this is the place," Tyce said, motioning to the vendor beside them. "I was about to buy some myself. I get all my beef from this guy. It's top-notch."

The sign at the booth read, "Honeycutt Hill Farm: Grass-Fed Meats and Pasture-Raised Eggs."

"Mom, can I get some steaks?" Lucas said.

Smiling charmingly not at Lucas but at Tyce, Oona said, "Sure, we can get some steaks … What do you recommend? I'd love to hear your thoughts."

* * *

I'd love to hear your thoughts. The words, and the schoolgirlish manner in which they had been said—Oona's face beaming un-selfconsciously, radiating a nauseating mix of adoration and delight as she gazed up at Tyce Creamer—had played continuously in Cole's mind all the rest of the day. Still in his Idiot Gurus T-shirt, he was now grilling beef steaks and veggie burgers out on the patio, and wondering if he should be concerned. Wondering if he should be concerned about Oona and Tyce Creamer. Given Oona's lack of interest in sex, however, he felt there was likely nothing to worry about. But still, he kind of had a bad feeling. He simply did not trust this Creamer clown, this redneck himbo. Cole finished off his second glass of elderberry rosé and poured himself another.

"How are the steaks doing?" Oona said, coming from the kitchen with a large salad bowl.

"They're almost done. They smell *disgusting*," Cole lied, for in fact he found the aroma of the charring cow flesh rather … appetizing. The juices in his mouth were definitely flowing.

"*Hey*—what happened to the wine?" Oona said. The bottle was more than half empty.

"It's good," Cole said unapologetically. "I should have bought two bottles."

Oona poured herself a glass and glanced discreetly over at Tyce's place. She had been thinking about him all day. Or rather, she had been *obsessing* about him all day, pondering and analyzing and enjoying again and again his unexpected compliments about her work, the kiss in front of the Blonde Bitch, and the sly boob caress in front of Cole, which she now was convinced had been intentional. To her, it could mean only one thing. Tyce Creamer was attracted to her, physically *and* mentally. It was obvious.

Lucas came outside. "Mmm—smells good!" he said with enthusiasm and maybe a little teasing. "Finally, some man food."

Cole snorted derisively. "Yeah, the *murdered cow* smells great —the greasy smell of death!"

"Call your sister," Oona said.

Lucas went back into the kitchen, yelled "Rosa, come and eat!," and returned to the patio. He joined his mother at the table. "I'm psyched for this steak," he said.

"Me too," Oona said giddily, giving him a conspiratorial grin.

The boy stared curiously at his mother. She had been acting strange all day—bubbly and happy and even a little bit silly. On the walk home from the Farmers Market, Rosa had told a series of very unfunny Knock-Knock jokes, to which Oona had laughed and laughed. Lucas had found it perplexing, and very weird.

"Here you go," Cole said, setting down before his son a plate with a medium-rare grass-fed ribeye. "And I hope you enjoy it. With each bite you're increasing your carbon footprint and destroying the planet."

"That's bullshit," Lucas said mildly. "Cows represent less than two percent of US greenhouse gas emissions, which is more than fifty percent less than agricultural crops. And far more land is deforested globally to grow vegetables and other crops than to raise cattle. The whole 'meat is destroying the planet' line is just more corporate propaganda. Follow the money, Dad. You really need to wake up."

To this, Cole had no ready retort. He was not up on the latest greenhouse gas statistics. But more than this, Cole was wondering how Lucas could possibly be the product of his own sperm. The two of them had absolutely nothing in common. Not one thing. Had there maybe not been a mix-up at the hospital?

"Where's Rosa?" Oona said.

"I called her," Lucas said.

Rosa came out of the house and everyone gaped. The child had taken a pair of scissors to her favorite skirt and was now wearing a teeny-weeny pink mini with smiling puppy faces that barely covered her bum cheeks.

"Rosa—what the hell did you do?" Oona said sharply.

"*What?*" the girl said with feigned innocence.

"Don't 'what' me. Where's the rest of your skirt?"

"I like it better this way," she said. "It's more comfortable."

Oona scoffed. "It's more '*comfortable*,'" she grumbled, shaking her head. "Sure it is."

Offended by the sarcasm, Rosa made a look of injured dignity and sat at the table in stony silence.

Cole offered her a plate with a cooked veggie burger.

"I want steak," the girl said, looking up at him.

Cole was aghast. "*What?*" he cried.

Lucas laughed.

"I want steak," Rosa repeated. "I like it."

"You see what's happening?" Cole said angrily, addressing Oona. "*You see?*" He did not mention Creamer's name, but his irascible meaningful look made his thoughts very clear.

Oona only said, "She can have some of mine."

Just then, from Tyce Creamer's pool, there came the sound of merry human beings. The pool was concealed behind a tall privacy fence, no more than forty feet away, that ran along the property line between the two houses. There was a joyful female laugh, followed by a joyful female scream, followed by a joyful manly laugh. Then came two mirthful bantering voices, one male, one female: "Come here!" "Nooooo!" "Ah, gotcha! Hahahaha!" "Nooo! Nooo!" "Hahahaha!" Next came a splash and another splash, after which was more laughter and more splashing.

All four Perrot-Puddings had gone quiet, listening to the wild revelry on the opposite side of the fence. Oona's mood sank faster than a cannonball. She was sure the female elations had come from the Blonde Bitch, who was likely gallivanting about in some string bikini. Cole and Lucas were also thinking of Ingrid —Cole mentally picturing the girl's eye-popping legs from earlier that morning, and Lucas picturing her perky nipples. Rosa, meanwhile, was thinking it would be fun to go swimming.

"*We* should get a pool," the girl said sullenly, breaking the silence.

"It's too expensive," Cole said, ticked off that Tyce Creamer was once again intruding into his life—and riotously enjoying himself in the process.

"Actually, it would add value to the house," Lucas confidently asserted. "And if home prices keep rising, which is likely, then you'd make a nice profit from it if you ever sell. Quite frankly, it would be a great investment."

Cole, who by now was more than a little tipsy, had heard enough. With sneering disdain he said, "Lucas, is there any subject that you're not an expert in? Any field of human knowledge that you haven't mastered? Why don't you give us a lecture on, oh, I don't know, Gödel's theorems, or Schrödinger's cat, or maybe the latest theories on Bigfoot. Or how about you just get right to it and tell us the meaning of life. With your towering intellect, I'm sure that's an easy one. Please, we're all ears."

Lucas looked wounded at this. He said nothing.

Cole bitterly finished off his wine, then refilled his glass with the last of the bottle.

"Hey, I was going to drink that!" Oona complained, glaring at him.

"Do you think Tyce would let us come swimming too?" Rosa said.

Oona, imagining what she would look like in a bathing suit next to the Blonde Bitch, said, "No. He has company right now."

"Can I ask him tomorrow?" Rosa said.

There were more splashes, followed by more joyful female screams and more joyful manly laughs. Oona was becoming irate. She downed the last of her wine, then turned to Cole. "Do we have another bottle? Of anything?"

Pleased that Oona had made the suggestion rather than him, Cole gladly went into the house.

"This steak is awesome," Lucas said. "Mom, I'll eat yours if you don't want it."

"No, I want it," Rosa said. "I hate veggie burgers!"

Oona did not respond to either of her children, for just then she saw an astonishing sight. Into the grassy space between her house and Tyce's, there now appeared Linni Mudge. She was coming from the direction of the street and was marching with steely determination straight for Tyce's pool. Glancing to her left, Linni briefly raised a hand and said "Hi Oona" without slowing her purposeful stride. She continued onward, went up to a gate-door in Tyce's fence, opened it, and vanished into the pool area.

All of the Perrot-Puddings had witnessed this, including Cole who had just come out of the house with an uncorked bottle of Malbec. Immediately, Oona dropped her fork, shot up from her chair, and silently rushed to the fence.

"What the ...?" Cole said, staring in wonder. "*Oona!*" he added, now in a hushed voice, as he did not want Creamer and company to hear.

Oona ignored him.

Now Lucas rose from the table. He followed after his mother, and Rosa followed after him.

"*Hey!*" Cole said, again in a hushed voice. "You two—*get back here!*"

They ignored him as well.

Hunched low at the foot of the fence, eager to hear every word that was said on the opposite side, Oona now saw Lucas as he crept up from behind. "Get back to the table!" she hissed.

"No, I have to see this," he said in an excited whisper.

The fence, however, presented a problem. It was six feet high and Lucas was five foot nine. He looked all around for something to stand on but there was nothing except a soccer ball lying on the grass. He decided to give it a try.

"What are you doing?" Oona whispered as Lucas placed the ball against the base of the fence and carefully stood on it.

"I have to see this," he said again.

"Lucas, *no*. Get down!" Oona whispered. "You're going to crack your skull."

"What's happening?" Rosa whispered, hovering behind her mother.

"Rosa, get back to the table!" Oona whispered, now noticing her daughter.

"Lucas isn't," the girl said.

Wobbling slightly as he stood atop the ball, Lucas steadied himself with his hands and gingerly peeked over the fence. Already there were heated words coming loudly from the pool. "Holy cow!" Lucas said quietly, staring in amazement.

"What?" Oona whispered.

"What happened?" Rosa whispered.

"Ingrid is topless!" Lucas whispered.

"Then get down, Lucas. Go *back* to the table!" Oona said.

"Screw that," the boy said.

"What are they doing?" Rosa said to her mother.

"Rosa, I'm telling you, go back to the table. This is ridiculous."

"No. I want to listen too."

On the other side of the fence the argument was escalating. All of the Perrot-Puddings could hear it, including Cole who had returned to his seat at the patio table:

Linni: "We need to talk, Tyce. I'm done playing around! Why haven't you returned my calls? Or my emails? Or my texts? This is *not* the way you treat the woman you love!"

Tyce: "Linni, this is wrong. What you're doing right now is wrong. This is trespass. This is breaking and entering."

Linni: "Oh yeah? And what is *she* doing? *She's* trespassing!"

Tyce: "No, she's not. She's my guest."

Ingrid, offended: "Your *'guest'*?"

Tyce: "You know what I mean."

Linni: "Tyce, we need to talk. Just you and me."

Tyce: "Linni, I'm sorry, but it's over."

Ingrid, heatedly: "Yeah you … you *psychopath*! It's over—can't you see that, you idiot?"

Linni: " 'Psychopath'? *You're* calling *me* a psychopath? Ha! That's rich! Ooooh yeah—that is *really* rich!"

Tyce: "Linni, come on. I think you've been drinking, and I think you should just go home and sleep."

Linni, sarcastically: "You know something, *Ingrid*, I had bigger tits than you when I was in the sixth grade."

Ingrid, also sarcastically: "I know Linni, it hurts. You're what, thirty? Thirty-five? You can always get a cat."

Linni, screaming: "I already have a cat, you *skinny bitch!*"

Lucas, riveted by this as he balanced himself atop the soccer ball, muffled a laugh. To his mother he whispered, "I think Linni is really plastered. She's swaying and kind of stumbling." Then, renewing his surveillance, Lucas said, "Oh, *damn!*"

There had just been the sound of a hand smacking a face, followed by a female shriek of pain and shock.

"What happened?" Rosa said.

"Linni just hit Ingrid!" Lucas whispered.

Rosa's mouth opened into a big O and she covered it with one hand, staring wide-eyed at her mother. Then she said, "Mom, can you hold me up so I can see?"

"Rosa, go back to the table," Oona said. "I'm not telling you again."

"I don't want to," the girl said.

The shouting and the shrieking became louder.

"Ingrid is bleeding!" Lucas reported. "I think she has a broken nose. It's really coming out."

Ingrid, now sobbing: "You *bitch*!"

Tyce: "Linni, *leave!*"

Linni: "Not till we talk."

Ingrid: "I'm calling the police."

Tyce: "Ingrid, don't. This doesn't have to go any further. She's leaving—"

Ingrid: "To hell with that! I'm bleeding all over. If my nose is broken, I'll sue both of you assholes!"

Tyce: "*Hey*—come here!"

Lucas whispered, "Ingrid just went into the house ... Now Tyce went into the house ... And now Linni went in." Lucas laughed. "This is insane." He watched for another half minute, saw nothing, then stepped off the soccer ball and assumed a crouching position like both Rosa and Oona, though this wasn't exactly necessary since they all were well concealed behind the fence.

"That was pretty wild," Lucas said, still in a hushed voice. "Linni really smacked Ingrid, and Ingrid had blood all on her face and down her chest. I'm going to finish my steak." He went back to the table.

"Mom, why did Linni hit Ingrid?" Rosa said.

"She's just upset. And I think she had too much to drink. Some people can't control themselves."

But the show wasn't over just yet. Not long after the Perrot-Puddings had resumed their supper at the patio table, they heard an approaching police siren.

"Ingrid called the cops," Lucas speculated, looking greatly amused. "I have to see this."

Lucas, and then Oona, and then Rosa, rose up and headed into the house.

"You guys are pathetic," Cole said contemptuously, shaking his head and knocking back more wine.

The trio passed through the kitchen and into the living room, which provided a wide-screen view of Tyce's front yard. Two Beauville Police cruisers were now parked on the street. A lone cop stood in Tyce's front yard while the others were let into the house.

"The Cuttys are watching too!" Rosa announced.

Across the street, Maeve Cutty and her husband Andy stood at their bay window, observing the scene.

"Is Linni going to jail?" Rosa said.

"I think she is," Lucas said. "In fact, I think she's pretty screwed. She trespassed, she hit somebody, and she's shitfaced. What a dumb-ass."

Fifteen minutes later, Linni was taken out in handcuffs and put into the backseat of one of the cruisers, which promptly took off. Soon afterward, two other cops escorted Ingrid—who was now fully dressed and holding a clump of tissues to her nose— to the second cruiser, and it also took off. Tyce himself, Oona noted, was nowhere to be seen.

* * *

That night, Oona couldn't sleep. It was past twelve and Cole was loudly snoring. Typically she would have elbowed him in the ribs and demanded that he stop. Now, however, she got up and checked on Lucas and Rosa. They too were asleep. She went into the kids' bathroom but did not turn on the light. From the window she could see the side of Tyce's house and much of his backyard. The pool area was dark except for a section that was illuminated by light from the back of the house. No people were seen. All was still.

Returning to her bedroom, Oona crept past Cole snoring in the marriage bed and entered their bathroom. She quietly shut the door, flicked on the lights, and sat on the toilet to think. For some time she pondered the situation, questioning, calculating, weighing this possibility and that. And finally she thought, yes. Yes.

She sniffed one armpit through her T-shirt, wrinkled her nose at the pungent smell, and rolled on some deodorant. She brushed her teeth, brushed her hair, put on the jeans she had worn that day, and slipped downstairs, barefoot.

Quiet as a thief she crossed the patio toward the house next door. The moon was nearly full, bright enough to light her way. The air was warm and fragrant and the grass was damp on her feet. As she opened the gate-door and entered the pool area she felt a heady rush of emotion. She was scared. She was nervous. She was thrilled and excited. She felt very much alive. Exuberantly alive.

She walked around to the back of the house and stood before a two-story plate-glass wall that stretched across the entire width of the home. Facing the pool, the plate-glass wall enclosed a large open-plan space that was both a kitchen-dining area and a living room. Tyce was there now, on the living room side. He was seated at a work station, with his back to her. There were multiple computers with large monitors, video equipment including cameras on tripods, and video lights atop metal stands. At the moment he appeared to be watching a video. Oona stepped closer to the glass wall for a better look.

The video, it turned out, was of Tyce himself. He was speaking to the viewer, saying words that Oona could not hear. The video then paused, and Tyce the person (as opposed to Tyce the screen image) began working the keyboard. Without hesitating Oona knocked a single knuckle against the glass.

Tyce coolly turned around, unflustered by this late-night interruption. From the light of the room spilling through the glass wall he saw Oona. There was a glass door in the glass wall and Tyce came over and slid it open.

"Hello," he said with the faintest of smiles, looking wholly unsurprised to see her.

"Hi."

He waited, his eyes studying her. When he noticed her bare feet, his faint smile turned into a faint smirk.

"I came to talk," Oona said, her heart thumping wildly. "About Linni."

"Sure you did," Tyce said, his smirk becoming a tad more pronounced.

Oona said nothing. He was looking fully into her eyes and she could tell he saw everything: her desire, her fear, her awkwardness, her giddy excitement.

He stepped back from the door and she went inside. She tried to play it casual. She tried to play it like this was no big thing. She gave the kitchen a mindful gander. Everything was stylish and sleek, very contemporary—the large restaurant-style stove, the large marble-topped island. Apart from an empty wine bottle and two empty wine glasses atop the island, there was no clutter or even a dirty dish anywhere in sight. Sauntering on, Oona went into the living area, which also was stylish and sleek. There was a black leather sectional couch, lush green palm plants taller than herself, a fireplace made of black steel, and all of his video and computer equipment.

"This is where you make your videos?" Oona said over her shoulder in her best nonchalant voice.

"Yeah. I was just doing some editing. I like to work at night."

She turned and looked him in the eye. Her pulse was pounding hard. She felt she could barely breathe.

He said, "Take off your shirt."

Oona nearly shuddered right there. "You first," she said.

He did as she asked.

"Oh my," she gasped. "Oh my."

* * *

Around four a.m., Oona was quietly sobbing. She lay naked in Tyce's king-size bed. The man himself was asleep beside her, deeply and serenely at rest, like Samson before his haircut. By the dim glow of the hallway light, Oona was watching him, and remembering. Without question she had never experienced anything like *that* before. His energy, his power, his uninhibited brutish dominance—for her, it was entirely unprecedented, something she had thought was solely the stuff of daydreams and romance novels (not that she had ever actually *read* a romance novel, but she knew the basic gist of them). Regardless, Linni had neither lied nor exaggerated about Tyce Creamer—in any way. Everything she had said about him had proved true.

And so why the tears? Oona wasn't exactly sure. She couldn't pinpoint a predominant emotion. She wasn't weeping precisely from joy, or sorrow, or relief, or exhilaration, or guilt. Rather, she was weeping from a combination of *all* of these, every single one, to greater and lesser degrees. And it worried her. It scared her. She was not the type—like Linni, for example—to become emotionally unhinged. She was a scholar, an intellectual. A woman that other women looked up to. A woman that *men* looked up to. These strong convulsive feelings were thus both strange and unwanted. But at the same time—oh, how wonderful it felt! How wonderful it felt to have been, for the first time in her life, so thoroughly and so gloriously sexed!

Without waking him, she gathered her clothes, dressed, and padded barefoot down the stairs, out of the house, and across the cool dewy grass to her home. It was nearly four-thirty when she got into bed. Cole was not snoring at the moment, and she was grateful. It was still possible, she felt, to get a few hours' sleep.

FIVE

"Oh, *damn*," Lucas said. He was standing at the stove, cooking bacon, and was looking at his phone.

"What?" Rosa said. She and Cole were seated at the table, eating the pancakes Cole had just made.

"Zach LaFontane died."

"When?" Cole said.

"Who's that?" Rosa said.

"Last night. He's the drummer for Zeitgeist Monkeys," Lucas said, still looking at his phone.

"What happened?" Cole said with grim interest. After the Idiot Gurus broke up, due to the heroin overdose of their singer, the lead guitar player, Dave Gnabry, formed Zeitgeist Monkeys. Cole had two of their albums on vinyl, though he thought the band pretty much sucked.

"They're not sure. They say it was a 'sudden death,' " Lucas said. He then read aloud from his phone, " 'Paramedics tried to revive him but he was pronounced dead at the hospital.' Damn! Another one. It's the vaccine!"

"Oh shut up!" Cole snapped. "Would you just shut up!"

"What?" Lucas shot back. "Dave Gnabry made everyone in the band get the vaccine, and Zach LaFontane didn't want to. Gnabry said either he gets the shot or he had to leave the band."

"You're such a crank, Lucas," Cole said. "According to you, anyone who dies nowadays it's because of the vaccine. It's idiotic beyond belief!"

A week earlier the actress and standup comic Loni Summerville had been performing a live routine, which included a number of jokes about "anti-vax shit-tards," when she suddenly collapsed on stage. Thinking this was part of the act, the audience had laughed uproariously. It turned out that Summerville, who was triple jabbed, had had a fatal heart attack. Though the press had so far remained mum on the cause of the heart attack, Lucas had attributed it to the vaccine.

"It was probably a drug OD," Cole said.

"That's bullshit," Lucas said. "Zach LaFontane didn't drink or smoke and he was always saying how drugs are bad. He was also a vegan and he meditated every day. It says he collapsed in a hotel room while he was playing a video game."

"He died of the vaccine?" Rosa said, looking worried.

"*No*," Cole said. "Your brother is just being an asshole. *Again*."

"Yeah, right," Lucas said. "People are dropping dead all over the place and I'm the asshole. Do you know what an ad hominem attack is?"

Cole erupted. "Yes I do know what an ad hominem attack is you smarmy little shit! And people are *not* dropping dead all over the place! That's just conspiracy theory garbage!"

"No it's not. It's happening everywhere and people know it but they're trying to hide it. I saw an article about 'Sudden Adult Death Syndrome' the other day. Supposedly all of these 'sudden' and 'unexpected' deaths of healthy people have to do with 'climate change' and eating red meat. It's such a joke. This country is so corrupt. The whole thing!"

Oona came into the kitchen looking physically pained. Her entire body was achy and sore, every inch of it. "Would you two please *stop*?"

Rosa said, "Mom, Zach La … something, died. Of the vaccine." The girl looked like she was about to cry.

"Way to go, kid!" Cole said to Lucas. "Scaring your little sister. It's *pathetic*!"

"You just don't want to admit you were wrong," the boy said. "That's why you're mad. You're projecting."

"*Stop it!*" Oona screeched. "Both of you!"

"You guys know I'm right," Lucas said. "But Dad will keep making Rosa get shots just so he can post it on Chirper."

Cole's eyes filled with murderous rage and he grabbed his half-finished glass of orange juice and threw it against the wall. The glass broke and the orange juice splattered in all directions.

"*Cole!* Are you crazy?" Oona shrieked at him with stunned eyes.

Rosa started crying and ran from the room.

"That's on you, buddy!" Cole shouted, pointing a finger at Lucas. "That's on *you!*"

"*Lucas*, you go and apologize to her," Oona said. "Right now!"

The boy was appalled. "*What?* That's not *my* fault! *He's* the one who—"

"Right now!" Oona repeated.

"Mom, I was just trying to explain—"

"*Now!*" she yelled.

Lucas turned off the stove, removed the pan with his half-finished bacon from the burner, and started off to find his sister. "Don't eat my bacon," he said as he went.

After the boy left the room, Oona said, "What the hell is your problem? I can't believe you just did that! You can't control yourself in front of your children? It's unbelievable! That's how they learn bad behavior!"

"He pisses me off!" Cole said. "More and more every day. It's becoming personal!"

"He's just going through a phase," Oona said. "It's normal."

"And he shows me no respect! None at all!" Cole added.

Oona made no comment, though she did slightly roll her eyes.

After a silence Cole said, "I saved you some pancake mix. You slept a long time."

"I was tired."

"What happened to your arm?" Cole said, now noticing a bluish, hand-sized bruise just beneath the sleeve of her T-shirt.

Oona looked where he was looking. "Oh ... that's ... I slipped in the shower."

"You 'slipped in the shower'?"

"Yes."

"When?"

"The other day. It's nothing," she said, thinking it was likely not the only bruise on her body.

"Well you should probably cover it up," Cole said. "People might think I've been beating you."

"I doubt it," Oona said. "Is there any coffee left?"

Cole said there was and Oona poured herself a cup.

"I hope you plan on cleaning that up," she said, glancing at the juice-stained wall and the broken glass on the floor below it.

"I will."

Oona sipped her coffee and ate a slice of Lucas's bacon, taking it from the pan. "Mmm," she said, munching. "It's good." She ate another slice and soon found herself musing about last night, mentally revisiting various images, and words, and acts.

When the doorbell rang, Cole was sweeping up the broken glass and Rosa and Lucas were upstairs. Oona's first thought was that the visitor might be Tyce. She shot up from her chair, said "I'll get it," and scurried into the living room with a thumping, hopeful heart.

* * *

It was Maeve Cutty.

"Oh," Oona said, frowning glumly. "Hi Maeve."

"Hi, Oona. I hope I'm not bothering you," Maeve said with a sheepish look.

"Uh, no. I was just about to eat breakfast but ... that's OK. What can I do for you?"

"Well, this may be a little awkward. But I've been thinking about Rosa. And the marks on her arm ..."

Oona's lips tightened, and she readied herself to be offended.

"You see," Maeve went on, "I've been studying the SPAARZ vaccines for some time now, reading scientific papers and talking to various researchers, and I'm worried about what the S3-k enzyme may do, or may be doing, to Rosa. And so I—"

"The 'S3-k enzyme'?" Oona said. She had not heard of this.

"Yes, it's part of the ... Oh, hello Cole."

Cole had just come to the door and now stood beside Oona. He was not too happy to see Maeve Cutty.

"I was just telling Oona that I have some concerns about Rosa," she said. "About the, uh, vaccine."

For the second time that morning Cole felt the desire to commit a violent act. He did his damnedest to remain calm, though not necessarily civil. He gave Maeve a cold, spiteful stare.

Maeve turned her attention back to Oona and said, "So we now know that the S3-k enzyme is very toxic. Originally we were told that it stayed in the shoulder, after inoculation, and that it was degraded there and was then harmlessly excreted from the body. But this has proven to be untrue. Autopsies are showing that the S3-k enzyme spreads to all the organs in the body, which is why we are seeing dramatic increases in sudden—"

For Cole, this was enough. Having just gotten an earful of ignorance from Lucas, he sure as hell wasn't going to get another one from Maeve Nutty. With barely restrained fury he said, "Maeve, let me tell you something. We are *not* anti-vaxxers in this house. We are not Luddites. We are not Flat Earthers. We believe in Science, OK? *Science!* Which means we believe that the Earth is round and that the moon isn't made of cheese!"

"But I'm not anti-vax either," she said.

"Then I guess that wasn't you I saw at the Farmers Market yesterday with the 'Gerbyll Lied and People Died' pin? And the

'20 Reasons Not to Give Your Kids the SPAARZ Vaccine' fliers? That was what, an alien body double?"

"*Cole*," Oona said.

"I'm not anti-vaccine," Maeve earnestly repeated. "I support vaccines that have been properly tested and proven safe. But these haven't been. And we now know that these current SPAARZ vaccines neither provide immunity nor prevent transmission."

"Maeve, I'm sorry," Cole said in a very unsorry voice, "but are you a scientist? Or a researcher? Do you have a PhD or any significant lab experience in virology or immunology?"

"No. But I *am* an experienced nurse."

"OK. You're a *nurse*," Cole said snidely and with a belittling smirk. "And so you want me to believe that you—a *nurse*—know more about the safety and efficacy of the SPAARZ vaccines than the entire US medical establishment? The NPH, the DCP, the FAQ, the medical schools, and the pharmaceutical companies? You know more than all of those people *combined*? A fired nurse from Hancock-Hicksville Medical Center in Beauville-Hicksville New Hampshire?"

"*Cole*," Oona said.

"But excess deaths are up," Maeve said humbly, overlooking the insults and patronizing attitude. "Long-term disability claims are up. Miscarriages and stillbirths are up. Infertility rates are up. Heart disease. Cancers—"

"*Maeve*," Cole interrupted in a near shout, "if all of this were really true, even one little bit of it, don't you think it would be in the news? Because essentially what you're talking about is the biggest crime in the history of medicine. Maybe the biggest crime in the history of the United States, period. *That's* what you're implying. And you're also implying that literally thousands and thousands of medical and scientific professionals are in on this crime, and that nobody in the media and in the government—not *one single person*—knows anything about it. The only people who know about it are you and a handful of whack-jobs with access to a keyboard and the internet."

"Cole, that's enough," Oona said, and she turned to her neighbor. "Maeve, it's nice that you're concerned about Rosa, and we appreciate it. But quite frankly, this is none of your business."

"OK. I'm sorry. But would you just take a look at this? For Rosa's sake?" Maeve held out a flier. "It's an S3-k-enzyme detox protocol. It's important for Rosa's long-term health that she—"

Cole snatched the flier out of Maeve's hand and crumpled it into a ball. "You know something Maeve," he said with seething animosity and a maniacal grin, "it's because of people like you that my son may not be going to college. Why my son is scaring his sister half to death with lies and misinformation. And basically why the kid is turning into a *complete asshole*! So here, take your damn flier and get the hell off my property." He held out the crumpled paper and Maeve Cutty meekly accepted it. She then looked at Oona, as though hoping she might change her mind, but Oona did not.

"Well, I am sorry," Maeve said. "I just wanted to help."

"*Goodbye Maeve*," Cole said.

Maeve lowered her eyes, turned, and went down the walkway to the street.

* * *

That afternoon, Oona stepped out onto the patio in a fifteen-year-old bikini. It seemed to fit a bit tighter than it once did—both the top and the bottom, though particularly the bottom.

"What are you *doing*?" Lucas said with surprise.

"What are *you* doing?" Oona said with surprise.

The boy was out on the grass beyond the patio, shirtless and in shorts and sneakers, and had just been caught flexing his right bicep muscle while admiring it.

"I'm working out," he said.

"Since when do you work out?" Oona said.

"Since last month. I'm already getting results," Lucas said and proceeded to demonstrate. He jutted his elbows out, clenched both fists in front of his belly, and flexed mightily. A look of strain showed on his face as the modest muscles on his skinny frame—chest, abs, arms—became a tiny bit more defined.

"Impressive," Oona said drily.

"I do pushups, air squats, planks, pull-ups, sprints. You don't need to go to a gym to get fit. You're just wasting your money."

"Mm-hmm," Oona said with waning attention. She was repositioning one of the chaise longues so that it looked away from Tyce's house. She didn't want him to think she was spying on him.

"And what are *you* doing?" Lucas said, repeating his original question. "And what are you *wearing*? You're kind of creeping me out, Mom."

"I'm getting some sun, Lucas. Just like you."

"Since when do you get sun? And since when do you own a *bikini*?"

"You know Lucas, my life didn't start when you were born."

"I didn't say it did," he said. And deciding the conversation was going nowhere, he got back to more important matters. He dropped down to hands and toes and started pumping out a set of pushups. "One, two, three …" he counted off in precise military cadence.

As Oona was settling into the chaise longue, her phone rang. It was on the ground beside her chair, and her first thought—which sent a thrill through her nearly naked and extremely pale body—was that it was Tyce. He had been watching her through the window, *spying on her*, and he wanted her *now*. He wanted her and her naked body this *very minute*! But then it occurred to her that Tyce did not have her number. The phone's caller ID read, "Linni." Oona groaned. For some moments she hesitated, then she picked up. "Hi Linni."

"*Oona*, thank God. Can you talk?"

"Yes, but only for a few minutes. I'm working."

"OK. Are we on speaker phone?"

"No. Go ahead."

"Well ... did you see what happened last night?"

"You mean, apart from when you walked across my lawn and went into Tyce's pool? No, I didn't see anything. Though I did hear sirens at some point ... That wasn't you, was it?"

"Oh, Oona, it was awful. Though I think your son was watching. I saw him looking over the fence."

"Lucas?" Oona said naively, watching as the boy was now running wind sprints from one side of the yard to the other.

"It's been a nightmare, Oona. That *Ingrid*. She really drives me crazy. She was prancing around topless in this little thong. It was unbelievable. She's so in love with herself! And now she's pressing charges against me for assault. I spent the night in jail, Oona. In *jail*! It smelled terrible! It was the worst night of my life. Do you think I could lose my job?"

"I couldn't say," Oona said, wondering if Linni's dismissal from Wendover might be to her advantage. She certainly could make it happen, if she chose. "Though I guess it *is* possible—"

"Even Tyce is mad at me," Linni went on, cutting Oona off. "The cops asked him if he wanted to take out a restraining order against me and he said yes. I just don't understand it, Oona. What was he thinking? Maybe I ... I don't know. Have you talked to him? You said you would."

"I haven't had the chance."

"But he's your next-door neighbor."

"I know. I just haven't seen him."

"Can't you knock on his door?"

"I'm not so sure that's a good idea ... I wouldn't want him to think that I was, you know, *stalking* him."

"You're right," Linni said. "He wouldn't like that."

"Hey—I have an idea," Oona said. "Why don't you give me his phone number?"

There was a long silence. "You want his phone number?" Linni finally said, with a tinge of suspicion. "Why?"

"So I can talk to him. For *you*."

"But can't you do it in person?"

"What's the difference?"

"I don't know," Linni said, though she did know. She was thinking that that's how people start flirting: they get a phone number and they start texting.

"Well, if you don't want me to help you, that's fine," Oona said. "I'm very busy anyway."

"OK," Linni said. "But just call him. Don't text him."

"Of course. Whatever you want."

"And don't tell him that I'm hurting, or that I miss him, or that I had an awful time in jail. Just say … Just say what you said the other day, that he's making a big mistake. And that he'll regret it if I meet somebody else."

"I'll do that," Oona said. "Now what's the number?"

Linni texted it to her, and Oona said she had to run.

* * *

After she hung up with Linni, Oona began composing her text. Twenty minutes and several drafts later, she settled on, "Tyce, this is Oona. Last night was great. We should meet again." It was direct and to the point, she reflected. Perfect. Then, just as she was about to hit "send," she changed her mind. She decided the message was too … tepid. Too stiff. Too *professorial*. She rewrote it, "Tyce, this is Oona. Last night was amazing! Would love to do it again." But as she read it over, she shook her head. The word "love"—*no*. It might scare him off, if only subconsciously. She was showing too much eagerness, she felt. It looked desperate. Better to play it cool. She typed, "Tyce, this is Oona. It was nice to spend time with you last night." Oh God, she thought—"*It was nice to spend time with you*"? She cringed. What the hell was wrong with her, she wondered? She had written and published three very well received books—*The Tyranny of Patriotism: A Feminist Perspective* (2009), *Technocracy and Liberation Politics: The Promise of the Twenty-First Century* (2013), and *Revolt of the Global Bourgeoisie: The Death of the Nation-State and the Rise of the International NGO* (2018)—and now she could not compose a simple text message? It was embarrassing. It was absurd. Fed up with this, and thinking she was somehow debasing herself, that this wishy-washy indecision was beneath her dignity, she typed, "Tyce, this is Oona. Last night was great. See you soon!" and hit "send" before she could overanalyze it.

Yet just as soon as the thing was sent, she felt a stab of panic. Had she just made a mistake?

* * *

For Oona, the rest of that day didn't go so well. After thirty minutes in the sun, with no response from Tyce, she had realized she was frying. Her pasty arms, legs, and chest had turned a hot pink. She went inside and saw in the bathroom mirror that her nose was already bright red.

"Mom, you look like a clown," Rosa said unhelpfully.

Oona's phone buzzed three times that afternoon with incoming text messages. Each time this happened she felt a burst of elation, thinking it was *him*. And each time her elation was dashed. The first text was from Linni asking Oona if she had called Tyce yet. The second was from her car insurance company reminding her of an upcoming bill. And the third was a spam text offering her the chance to "meet older singles."

"What happened to your nose?" Cole said after he got home from a shopping binge at his favorite used record shop in Cambridge. "You should get some ice on that. It's a good way to get cancer."

By suppertime there was still no word from Tyce, and Oona found herself in a tense, agitated state. She was gloomy, short-tempered, depressed, paranoid. She was panicking, that's what it was, she realized—panicking! Not only was Tyce not going to respond to her stupid text—"See you soon!" she had written, which now mortified her—but he was probably also going to tell Linni. And who knows what that crackpot would do. No, Oona did not like this at all. She had given away too much leverage, too much power. She had ceded control—to a man! She never should have sent that damn text message!

As she sat at the table—they were eating in the kitchen tonight —Oona looked at her husband, and her daughter, and her son, and she asked herself, Is this really so bad? Was it really so suffocating? For she had been thinking that her life *was* bad, and *was* suffocating, more and more over the last few years. She had become aware of a certain emptiness inside herself, a vague existential malaise, and she had felt sure that it was due to *them*. Yet what if her reckless hookup with Tyce were to lead to the ruin of it all? To the ruin of all *this*? The thought of it scared her. Yes, she had made a terrible mistake. She had had a memorable night with Tyce, a night she would never forget, but it would not happen again. That is, if he even *wanted* it to happen again, which now seemed very unlikely.

After supper her panicky feelings only grew worse with the arrival of another text from Linni. It read, "Oona, why didn't you answer my text??? Did you talk to Tyce—yes or no?? PLEASE ANSWER ME!" Clearly, Linni was bonkers, and it gave Oona an ominous feeling. What if the girl were to focus her craziness on *her*? What sort of madness would follow? What sort of mayhem and havoc?

Immediately she wrote back, "Sorry Linni. I did call him, but he didn't pick up. I left a message. If he calls back I'll call you. Everything will be fine."

A response came seconds later. "OK Oona, thank you. Call me as soon as he calls you. My phone will be on all night. I'll text you back in an hour to check in."

Great, Oona thought. She typed "Sounds good" and turned off her phone, now convinced that her night with Tyce Creamer was the biggest mistake of her life. Her sense of fear, or guilt, or regret—or maybe it was all of the above—was overwhelming. Whatever it was, she did not like it. She wanted the feeling gone. In response, she made an effort to be kind to her children. The two of them, plus Cole, were on the sofa in the TV room watching the latest episode of their new favorite series, something to do with alien time-traveling vampires. The program did not interest Oona. Television did not interest Oona. She preferred to read books.

"Is there anything I can get you kids?" she said with kind solicitude as she stood in the doorway to the room. "Do you want something to drink? Or maybe some popcorn?"

This generous offer, which was entirely unprecedented, was met with puzzled faces.

"No," Lucas said, giving her a longish questioning stare before turning back to the TV.

"No," Rosa said, also giving her a longish questioning stare before turning back to the TV.

Cole, however, felt differently. "Yeah, I'll have some popcorn," he said. "You don't mind?"

* * *

Later, after everyone had drifted off to their bedrooms, Oona thought it was time to make things right with Cole. He was already in bed, sitting up and checking social media on his phone.

"You know, I don't feel so good," he said as she entered the room and shut the door. "I felt a little dizzy today, on the drive home and also at supper. A little feverish too. I hope it's not—"

Oona, with her bright-red sunburnt nose, put a hand on his forehead. "Do you have a temperature?"

Cole was stunned. Oona had not touched him in months, many months, at least not willingly. "Uh … I don't know," he said with her hand still on him.

"Feels fine to me," she said, giving him a provocative smile.

Cole's eyebrows shot up. He became very alert.

In a slow, lingering motion she slid her hand from his forehead down to his cheek, tenderly caressing his face. As she did this, there was something on her lips and especially in her eyes that Cole had never seen before: a lascivious gleam, a frank promise of all manner of carnal delights. He was astounded. Her caressing hand made its way down to his chest, and then, as he remained watching her in a frozen, entranced state, she arched her back in a sensuous way and slowly took off her T-shirt. Cole's mouth fell open. The blood surged all through his body, jolting him ecstatically to life.

In bra and jeans Oona now sat on the edge of the bed, facing him. Cole dropped his phone and lunged forward to kiss her. Their mouths came together and Cole at once began groping her and making strange noises. The noises made Oona think of some frantic starving animal. An animal that was desperately snarfing down a bit of food it had miraculously found. It repulsed Oona. With a look on her face like she had just bitten into a lemon, she pulled away from him and his slobbering lips. The strange noises stopped, and Cole looked at her with dazed, confused eyes.

Thinking quick, Oona said, "Take off your shirt." She would go through with this, she decided, but she did not want to kiss him.

Cole immediately did as requested, his mind back in the moment. *It's on,* he was thinking. *It's on!* Finally, finally—they were going to have sex. He would soon be inside his wife! With his shirt off he greedily grabbed at her breasts with one hand, while with the other he hurriedly tried to get out of his boxers.

Oona helped him. She wanted to get this over with quick. Maybe, *hopefully*, a handjob would do. As she pulled down his shorts, however, something unfortunate happened.

At the sight of Cole's nude body, Oona was stricken by something like fright. Time had not been good to Cole. His chest was flabby and protuberant in an unmistakably mammarial way, and his swollen belly made him look six months pregnant. Yet while his torso had a grotesquely fecund appearance, his arms and legs were skinny and emaciated, as though all the muscle had wasted away. In grad school, where they had met, Cole had been a runner, lithe and toned, and Oona had enjoyed screwing him. She had enjoyed touching him. She had enjoyed looking at him. Now he looked like some sort of hybrid monstrosity, and it revolted her. She did not want to touch him. She did not want him to touch *her*. All at once her eyes shut and her gut clenched, and it felt like she was going to barf.

Cole, in a frenzy of lust, his entire being inflamed and ready to mate, was confounded. Something had gone wrong with his wife, he saw. Something had gone catastrophically wrong.

"Oona?" he said helplessly.

Without malice she had pushed his grasping hand off her breast and put an arm's-length between them. She could not meet his eye.

"I'm sorry," she said. "I don't feel well."

"What is it? Is it your nose?"

"No. My stomach."

She rose from the bed, went into the bathroom, locked the door, and ran the faucet at full blast. She wanted some noise. She wanted a buffer. A barrier. She did not want to see him or hear him or be in his presence in any way.

She sat on the toilet and put her hands to her face. At the sink the water gushed into the basin, but Oona remained dry. There were no tears—just a feeling like she was suffocating. A feeling like she was dying.

SIX

On Monday morning Cole tested positive for SPAARZ. Although he was double jabbed and boosted, this was the third time over the last eighteen months that he had contracted the virus. The night before he had not slept well thanks to his bizarre aborted sex episode with Oona. Long after she had fallen asleep beside him, Cole had struggled to understand what the hell had just happened. One minute she was turned on and ready to go, and the next she was gagging and running for the toilet. He couldn't figure it out. He vaguely felt that he had been rejected and even humiliated in some way, but he wasn't quite sure how. After all, *she* had been the one to initiate the whole damn thing. *She* was the one who had leered at him and pulled down his shorts. Either way, whatever she had been thinking, it was concerning. Something wasn't right. Something, in fact, was *wrong*. Troubled by these thoughts, Cole had lain awake till two a.m., and when he woke for work at seven, he felt like shit. His throat was sore, his head ached, and he had little energy.

Oona got him one of their SPAARZ Home Test Kits—Cole always made sure to keep plenty of them in stock—and he indeed tested positive. Oona immediately put on her mask, her face shield, and a pair of latex gloves.

"You know what this means," she said to him.

Cole nodded plaintively. The first time he contracted SPAARZ, he had quarantined in their bedroom and Oona had slept on the sofa in the living room. But the second time he got it, Oona suggested that he quarantine in the basement. It only seemed fair, she had reasoned. Why should *she* be inconvenienced?

* * *

Dressed in full SPAARZ lockdown gear, Oona walked into the kitchen. Rosa was eating cereal and Lucas was cooking bacon.

"Oh no," the girl said.

Lucas just laughed, and derisively shook his head.

"Your father tested positive," Oona said.

"I don't feel good either," Rosa said.

"After you eat, I want you both to take the test," Oona said.

"I'm not," Lucas said.

"Yes you are," Oona said.

"No I'm not," the boy said.

"*Lucas.*"

"Mom, he already has it. And you slept next to him all night, so if you're going to get it, you already did. Rosa can do what she wants, but I feel fine and I'm not going to do it. I haven't even caught it this whole time!" he added with feeling.

"That's because you haven't taken a test this whole time!" Oona replied with even more feeling.

"That's right! And what does that tell you?" the boy fired back.

"I'll take the test," Rosa said, hoping they would stop bickering. "But I don't feel good."

"What's wrong?" Oona said.

"I feel really weak."

"Worse than the past few days, or better?"

"Worse."

* * *

Though he felt crappy, Cole wasn't exactly upset that he was sick. It meant at least a week off from work, per Wendover College policy—a week in which he could kick back, read, listen to music, watch movies, and spend some quality time on social media. As for his quarantine accommodations, these weren't so bad either. The previous owners of the house had converted the basement into a rec room, complete with a pub-style bar and an attached half bathroom. Cole had long since commandeered the room for his own use. He kept his books, his vast record collection, and his expensive hi-fi stereo system here, as well as the two guitars that he never played. The room also had a TV, a comfy couch for him to sleep on, and a small refrigerator behind the bar. For food, Oona and the kids would prepare his meals, which they would leave on a tray at the top of the basement stairs for him to come and retrieve. In short, his SPAARZ diagnosis meant that Cole was looking at a minimum of one week's paid vacation. Not too shabby.

The first thing he did once he had settled in—he'd brought down his phone, laptop, clothes, and blankets and pillow—was to take a selfie. Donning his Pq23 respirator face mask and his N16z plastic face shield, he struck a somber yet brave attitude, clicked several shots, then posted the best one to Chirper and FaceFace. For the caption he wrote, "Even though I'm double jabbed and boosted, I just tested positive for the third time. This virus is no joke. I'm not feeling too good right now, but I'm so grateful for the vaccines, otherwise it would be much worse! #vaccinessavelives #staysafe."

Within seconds both accounts were buzzing with activity, with people he knew and many more people he did not know, liking the post and sending him well wishes.

"Be strong, friend!" wrote one stranger.

"Hang in there Cole! We can beat this!" wrote someone he had gone to middle school with.

"Thank God for Gerbyll!" wrote another stranger. "I recently tested positive for the third time too, but thanks to the vaccine, I didn't have to go to the hospital. Get well soon, and stay safe!"

And Cole smiled to himself, thinking, Yes, this is going to be a good week.

* * *

Later that morning Oona and Rosa went to Hancock-Beauville Medical Center. Because Rosa seemed to be feeling worse, and was complaining about it nonstop, and because Cole was now locked away in the basement and unavailable for parental duties, Oona had felt obligated to bring the girl in to Dr. Bumble.

"Didn't I see you last week?" the doctor said to the girl.

Rosa nodded stiffly, watching him with mistrustful eyes. She wasn't so sure that she liked this man.

"Weren't you the one with the pussy willow stuck up your nose?" he said.

"No."

Dr. Bumble laughed merrily, and to Oona, who sat in a chair beside the examination table, he said, "This girl came in with a pussy willow stuck up her nose. She pushed it way in and then it broke and her mother couldn't get it out." He laughed again, shaking his head. "Kids," he said.

"I came because of my arm," Rosa said sternly.

"Yes, that's right. The bee sting?"

"No. The vaccine."

"It wasn't the vaccine," Oona said.

"Oh, I remember," Dr. Bumble said. "Those ugly red ... *things*. Well, it looks better now. All cleared up! And what brings you in today? The nurse said you feel tired?"

"Yes. I feel tired a lot, and sometimes it's hard to breathe. I don't feel good. I feel weak."

"She's been sleeping a lot," Oona said.

"And you both tested negative?" the doctor asked.

"Yes," Oona said. She and Rosa had in fact been tested twice today, once at home and then again when they entered the clinic.

Dr. Bumble looked into Rosa's eyes, then her ears, and then he listened to her chest with a stethoscope.

"Hmmm," he murmured with a tensed brow.

"What?" Rosa said.

Oona's phone buzzed with a new text message. It was Linni. "Did you talk to Tyce yet?" she wrote. Oona sighed wearily. Why, she wondered, did she ever befriend that woman?

"I'm going to make a call," Dr. Bumble said.

"About what?" Oona said.

"It's probably nothing," the doctor said. "I just want to run a few tests."

"Tests?" Rosa said.

"For what?" Oona said.

"I just want to have her heart looked at."

"Her heart? And when would that be?" Oona said. She was concerned about her daughter, but she was also thinking that she had to get to her office. It was already eleven-thirty and she needed to start working on her overdue chapters.

"Today. It should be done today," Dr. Bumble said.

* * *

Cole's morning lost some of its shine when he made the call to the office.

"You've got SPAARZ—*again*?" Digby said.

"Yes. I just tested positive."

"But Cole, this is the *third* time. And you've already had more SPAARZ sick days than all of the department staff combined." This was true. The first time Cole came down with SPAARZ he was out of work for close to a month. The second time, it was three weeks. The total SPAARZ sick time for the rest of the Office of Student Affairs, including Digby himself, was six weeks.

"I know," Cole said. "But what can I do? It's very frustrating. I hate being sick."

"Now I know you're boosted, are you protecting yourself?"

"Yes, I always wear my mask *and* my face shield. I may have caught it at the Farmers Market on Saturday, or maybe in Cambridge. I went down yesterday. The problem is, *other people* aren't wearing their masks, and they're putting the rest of us in danger. It's ignorance, is what it is. Ignorance and selfishness."

"Cole, this really is unfortunate," Digby said. "And what about today's meeting? Is that canceled?"

"With Parkman? No, that's still on. LaKeesha can handle it. I'll prep her. It's nothing."

"And what about Thursday's meeting with Dean Munchausen?"

"It's no problem. I'll join in on video."

"Well, we hadn't *planned* on a video meeting. But since you're sick, I suppose we have no choice. And what about the report? How is that coming?"

"It's just about there, Dig. LaKeesha's been helping out. As best she can, of course. But yeah, we're just about there. All that's left now are the figures from Parkman, which we'll get today. Everything's fine, Dig. No need to worry. We're right on schedule."

"Well ... OK. I'll talk to the Dean. We'll switch the meeting to video. Same day and time—Thursday morning, ten a.m."

"That's right," Cole said. "See you then."

* * *

The rest of Oona's afternoon was spent at Hancock-Beauville Medical Center. Rosa had blood drawn and then an electrocardiogram. After that it was decided she should have a cardiac MRI. The first attempt at the MRI failed because, inside the cramped, coffin-like space, Rosa had had an attack of claustrophobia and had started crying and then screaming. She was given a sedative and also an eye mask to block her vision, which they said would reduce the claustrophobic sensation, and the next attempt was a success.

An hour and a half later, Oona and Rosa met with Dr. Bumble in an exam room.

"So, it looks like Rosa has a mild case of myocarditis," he said.

"What is that? Is it serious?" Oona said, just as her phone buzzed with an incoming text. She glanced at her phone. The text was from ... *Tyce*. Tyce! Oona's heart fluttered. "Excuse me," she said to Dr. Bumble, cutting him off just as he had begun to speak. "This may be important."

She held the screen of her phone away from Rosa's and Dr. Bumble's view and opened and read the text. "Yes, the other night was fun," he wrote. "See you soon." Oona was astonished! She read it again: "the other night was fun" ... "see you soon." She could not believe it. Tyce had enjoyed their sex too! *See you soon.* She was elated. She was ecstatic. She was aroused. *She and Tyce Creamer were going to be lovers!* She was tingly all over.

"Mrs. Perrot?"

Oona looked up at Dr. Bumble, barely aware of her surroundings.

"Mrs. Perrot?" he repeated, now looking concerned.

"It's *Dr. Pudding*," she corrected him.

"Dr. *Pudding?*"

"Yes."

A subtle yet unmistakable glimmer of amusement came into the man's eye. "Well, I do apologize—*Dr. Pudding*. But may we continue? I do have other patients waiting."

"Yes. Of course," Oona said uneasily.

The doctor explained what myocarditis was, how it involved damage to the heart, and how in Rosa's case the damage was "fairly minor." Oona caught very little of this, however. She could not stop thinking about Tyce Creamer.

"Dr. Pudding?" said Dr. Bumble.

"Oh ... Yes?"

"Do you have any questions?"

Oona hesitated. She felt it would be too embarrassing to ask him to repeat everything he had just said, so she said nothing.

Rosa was not so inhibited. "Am I going to die?" she said.

Dr. Bumble chuckled. "Oooh nooo," he said with breezy assurance and warm consoling eyes. "No no. Nope. It's a *mild* case. Of course you'll need to rest for … some time. And avoid strenuous activity. But we'll put you on medication, and we'll, uh, *monitor the situation*, and at some point, well, at some point you should be … *good as new.*"

* * *

"What do you mean you didn't ask what caused it?" Cole said, talking over speaker phone. Oona and Rosa had just left the clinic and were now driving into town for groceries.

"Cole, I was too flustered," Oona said sharply. "This situation is very distressing."

"You were reading a text message," Rosa said quietly, but Cole caught it.

"What text message?" he said suspiciously.

Oona gave Rosa a stern side-glance. "It was Linni … She's been pestering me about Tyce. She's really driving me crazy."

"You know, I'm starting to think that clown is the one who infected me," Cole said. "Either him or his floozy girlfriend, but most likely it was him because he was doing all the talking. *Mr. Charisma.*"

"Cole, what are you talking about?" Oona said with vexation.

"At the Farmers Market," he said. "We talked to Cream-boy and his bimbo girlfriend, and neither one of them was wearing a mask. They probably gave me SPAARZ."

"She's not his girlfriend," Oona said. "And hardly anybody at the Farmers Market was wearing a mask. Just you and about three other people, so don't blame him. Look, I've got to go. I'm picking up a prescription for Rosa and then we're going to the Co-op."

"Hey, would you get me some wine?"
"What do you want?"
"My Malbec. The Stepfield Valley."
"OK."
"Get a case."
"A case?"
"Yes. I could be down here for a week or two."

* * *

That evening, Cole opened his second bottle of the Stepfield Valley Vineyards Malbec. Though he was buzzing from the first bottle—it had gone down pretty quick—he was not in a good mood. He was ruffled. He was agitated. He was ill-tempered. Earlier in the day, after Oona and Rosa had returned home from the clinic, Cole had gotten a text message from Lucas. "This is your fault," the boy had written. "What's my fault?" Cole wrote back. But Lucas did not reply. Later, after he had gotten two-thirds through the first bottle, Cole repeated the question, this time with emphasis: "WHAT'S MY FAULT?" Still, there had been no answer.

All the while, as he had been drinking and fuming over the boy's text, Cole had been playing records. Cole loved to drink and play records. It was one of his favorite things to do in life, right up there with FaceFace and Chirper. Cole owned more than six hundred LPs and about two hundred 45s and 78s. More than half of these he had inherited from his father, who had been a professor of American history at Oxenberg College, near Chicago. His father had loved jazz and blues and had collected first pressings of Po-Boy McCoo, Hambone Tilliss, Silky Trainor, and Blind Huddie Watkins, among other legends. Many of the records were in near mint condition, and together they were worth a small fortune. Cole's contribution to the collection included rare examples of 1970s punk, 1980s British New Wave, and his favorite, 1990s indie rock.

Yet given his current foul mood, Cole was having trouble enjoying the music. The Roadkill Squirrels' debut album, *Prom Queen from Hell*, was spinning on the turntable. It was a longtime favorite, but right now Cole just wasn't into it. He got up and lowered the volume by half. Back on the couch, fully reclined, he put his laptop on his lap, typed "causes of myocarditis in kids" into his favorite search engine, and got exactly zero hits. This seemed odd. Very odd. He tried a second search engine, and got hundreds of hits. According to a number of recently published articles in dependable, East Coast legacy-media newspapers, including the *New York Sloth*, the condition wasn't as rare in children as had been previously thought. The latest Science pointed to viruses, such as SPAARZ for example, as a leading cause. Other causes included climate change and a meat-heavy diet. To Cole, this all made sense. Perfect sense.

Now relieved of any qualms, he sipped his wine and let out a contented sigh. As for Lucas and his not-so-subtle insinuations, the boy could go to hell.

* * *

Around eleven-thirty that night, Oona cracked open her bedroom door. She was pumped up with adrenaline and inflamed with lust. Peeking into the darkened hallway, she saw all was clear. She slipped out of the room, shut the door, and started down the stairs. Just then, Lucas's bedroom door opened and the boy came out in his boxers. Oona gasped and pressed her back against the stairwell wall as her son passed by, oblivious to her presence. Lucas went into the bathroom and shut the door. Oona sighed with relief, then quietly crept down to the first floor.

* * *

Out on the patio, Cole was seated under the stars, drunk and grumbling about Tyce Creamer. He hadn't been able to sleep and thought it might be pleasant to sit outside. It was a warm night with a full moon—a beautiful night—but the sight of Creamer's house, with several of the windows lighted up, had ruined the mood. More and more Cole was loathing his neighbor. Even more than before. *I'd love to hear your thoughts*, Oona had said to the muscle-bound cretin—the *Don't Be a Bitch* best-selling author; the *Bro2Bro with Tyce Creamer* MyToobs star; the *Chirper celebrity* with one-hundred-and-fifty-thousand followers. Oh yes, Cole loathed the guy with all his heart, with all his being, with each and every one of his Cole Perrot atoms. Now sneering and snarling, he reentered the darkened kitchen and promptly bumped into a chair, making a harsh scraping noise. Oona, who had just then come into the kitchen, was startled once again. In the darkness she went very still, hiding herself beside the refrigerator. Cole passed by her unawares and went down to the basement.

* * *

After he flushed the toilet, Lucas flicked off the light and looked out the window onto Tyce's backyard. He wanted to see if there was any action. Beginning last summer, Lucas had regularly seen Tyce out in his pool or his hot tub, late night, with some woman or even two or three women, swimming or hanging out or having sex of some sort. (Tyce had proved fairly inventive in that regard, Lucas had observed.) Yet tonight, despite the warmth and the bright moon, all was calm. There were no sexual gymnastics, no curious couplings, or throuplings, or fourplings. Lucas turned to go back to his room, and just as he did he missed the shadowy figure emerging into the space between the two houses, crossing the grass in the direction of Tyce's pool.

* * *

Around ten p.m., Linni Mudge drove by Tyce's house and began circling the block. There was an empty bottle of hard lemonade in the cup holder and another on the floor by her feet that rolled every time she turned a corner. Over the car speakers came the melancholic stylings of Linni's favorite female singer-songwriter, Edie Vayne, crooning wrenchingly about love and loss. Despite the restraining order, Linni was determined to see if Tyce was keeping any company, be it with Ingrid the Skinny Bitch or any other skinny bitch.

After her tenth or eleventh loop around the block, Linni decided she had had enough. The driving was getting boring. She pulled her car to the side of the street, one house down from Oona's and two down from Tyce's. From here, she could mount a stakeout. She saw some of Tyce's lights were still on, and she wondered what he was doing. Was he alone? Was he working? Was he thinking of her? Was he *missing* her?

Time passed, and eventually the stakeout got boring too, all this waiting and watching and seeing absolutely nothing. She decided to make one last drive-by.

Had Linni started the car two or three seconds sooner, she would have passed by just as Oona was entering the gate-door to Tyce's pool. Instead, she passed by just as the door clicked shut.

* * *

"I hope you were careful," he said.

"I was," she assured him, her face radiant with happiness and excitement. "It was no problem. Everyone's asleep."

SEVEN

The next morning Cole woke with a crushing headache and a parched mouth. He was hungover and dehydrated. He was hungry too. He sent Oona a text asking if she or one of the kids could make him breakfast and bring him some aspirin and a big glass of orange juice. Fifteen minutes passed. No response. He texted her again. Still no response. So he texted Rosa.

"How are you feeling?" he wrote.

"I'm tired," she replied. "And I think this new medicine gives me a stomach ache. Because I had a stomach ache yesterday and I have a stomach ache today."

"It might not be the pills," Cole typed back. "But speaking of pills, can you get me some aspirin? And a big glass of orange juice? And can you make me some scrambled tofu and toast?"

"OK."

"Great. And make sure the tofu is a little runny and not over-cooked."

"OK."

"And bring the juice and aspirin now, before you start cooking."

* * *

Oona woke around ten, and even though she was in her own bed, in her own home, she felt joyful. Absolutely, positively joyful. She was pulsating with joy. She was teeming with it. The joy had spread all through her body and was oozing from her pores. Cole was quarantined in the basement, for at least another week, and she lay blissfully alone under the covers, her flesh still awash in pheromones or oxytocin or whatever the chemical was that is released when a woman has been good and properly sexed. She had forgotten the exact science of it, the precise biological process, but how *wonderful* it felt! How amazing, how extraordinary, how *sublime*! For the first time in her life she truly understood why people like to have sex.

She turned on her phone, hoping that maybe he had called or texted. There were two texts from Linni and two from Cole, but nothing from Tyce. Should she maybe text *him*? He might be free now, and who knows, maybe they could meet up again this morning or that afternoon. Maybe they could go to a hotel. But no, Oona thought, reconsidering. She needed to make him start coming to *her*. Make him work for it a bit. Otherwise he might start taking her for granted.

Remaining in bed, she went through her messages.

Linni's first text had arrived at 7:26 that morning: "Oona, are you up? Has Tyce called you? Call me when you can." Her second text, from 9:07 that morning, read, "Oona, call me when you get this. It's important."

What a psycho, Oona thought. Her desire was to delete the messages, and even to delete Linni from her phone and block her number, but she was all too mindful of the girl's capacity for impulsive, wrecking-ball behavior. So she typed back, "I'll call you later. I just woke up."

A response came within seconds, "Are you free for lunch? Are you coming to campus?"

Anger bubbled up in Oona. She typed, "No. Cole has SPAARZ, so I'll be working from home all week. I don't want to endanger you or anyone else."

"Oh, I'm so sorry to hear that!" Linni replied. "Be careful, and stay safe! And let me know if there's anything I can do for you. But yes, call me later, or as soon as Tyce calls you."

"I'll do that," Oona typed back, hoping that would be the last of Linni Mudge for a few hours.

Next came Cole's two texts, both asking her to get him food and aspirin. It was true that she had forbade him to leave the basement until he tested negative. But for some reason these requests really irked her.

"Cole, why don't you sun your balls sometime?" she typed. "I think it might help."

* * *

"Sun my balls?" Cole said to himself, peering at his phone. "What the hell does that mean?" He wondered if it was a joke. Or an *insult*? Or maybe it was some new SPAARZ remedy she had seen on CNBM? Regardless, he would deal with it later, for right now Cole was eating his scrambled tofu and he hated it when it got cold. He put another forkful into his mouth and resumed watching a video on MyToobs about Nietzsche's time in Turin.

* * *

From the bathroom window Lucas saw Tyce out by his pool, exercising with kettlebells. The boy beelined it downstairs and went into the backyard. He jogged over to the soccer ball that lay in the grass and kicked it over Tyce's fence, shouting "Heads up!" He heard the ball splash into the pool and called out, "Sorry about that!"

Moments later the ball sailed back into the yard and the top half of Tyce's face appeared above the fence. "Big man, how are you?" he said in his usual friendly manner.

"I'm OK. Just working out. Sorry to bother you."

"It's no problem. I'm working out too."

Lucas nodded. "It's a good day for it," he said.

"Yep. It's too nice for the gym," Tyce said.

"Yeah, and plus, you're getting sun," the boy said. "It's good for your circadian rhythms, you know? And vitamin D."

"That's true," Tyce agreed.

There was a silence, then Lucas said, "Hey, uh, do you have a minute?"

A flicker of uncertainty passed across Tyce's face. Did the kid suspect something, he wondered? Had he seen his mother sneaking over to his house last night?

"I just want to ask you a question," Lucas said. "I'll be quick."

"OK. Sure," Tyce said. "Why don't you come over."

* * *

They sat poolside at an umbrella-shaded table. Tyce had just brought the boy a bottled water from the pool-house refrigerator and was now waiting for him to begin.

Lucas said, "So I watched your live stream last night ..." Every Monday night Tyce had a live show on his MyToobs channel where people sent in emails or typed questions in the chat on any Bro2Bro topic—from fitness and diet, to women and life advice —and Tyce answered them all. "It was really good."

"Thanks."

"And I really liked what you said to the guy who hated his job."

"Which one?"

"The guy who works at Uncle Stewie's Fried Chicken."

"Right. He said his job is boring and he just wants to smoke dope and play video games all day."

"Yeah. You said he should look for a more challenging job, and that until he gets it, he should ask his current boss for more responsibilities, and that way he'll be too busy to be bored."

"That's right. There's too much to do and learn in life for a twenty year old to be wasting away like that. At that age you should be busting your ass, setting and pursuing goals and taking chances. You should be starting to build something. Not hanging out and getting high and then complaining that you're bored and your life sucks. Life isn't that difficult. The harder and the smarter you work, the better your life."

"I agree," Lucas said. "And I really liked that, what you said to him. See, I want to build something too. I want to be a success."

"Good, Lucas. I like to hear it."

"And what I'm thinking," the boy went on, "is that I want to work for you. I want to have my own business someday, like you. And I think, for right now, it would be a good move for me to work for you and see how you do it."

"What do you mean, like a summer job? Mowing the lawn or something?"

"No. A real job. Helping you with your business."

"But aren't you leaving for college soon?"

"No. The college I got into is making all the kids get the jab, and I refuse. Screw that."

"Oh. I didn't know."

"Did you get it?"

"*Me*, the jab?" Tyce said. "The experimental, DNA-altering drug pushed by companies that have been given complete legal and financial immunity should something go wrong? Hell no. I wouldn't take a glass of water from those people if I could help it."

Lucas was smiling. "I knew you didn't," he said.

"And what are your parents saying, about you not going to college?" Tyce said.

"My dad's pissed. In his usual narcissistic way, he thinks I'm doing it just to annoy him. And my mother thinks I'm 'going through a phase,' and that I'll cave at the last minute when I see my friends going off to their schools. But they're both wrong. And plus, at this point college is pretty much useless. From what I've seen and heard, they're just indoctrination camps. Basically you pay them a lot of money to get brainwashed into hating yourself and hating America and reading from the preapproved script. Screw that. I got enough of it in high school. My parents just want me to be like everybody else. Which is exactly what they do. It's sickening."

"Sounds like there's some tension there," Tyce said.

"My dad's an asshole," Lucas said. "He thinks he's this big radical, and that he's smarter than everybody else because he studied Nietzsche in graduate school. But he's the biggest conformist I ever met. When SPAARZ first hit, he wanted us all to wear masks and gloves in the house. Even in the shower! He's such a pussy."

"You know," Tyce said evenly, "you shouldn't call your dad names. Even if they're true."

Lucas fell silent. He had thought his brash talk would impress Tyce, that it would show how independent-minded he was. But instead he had gotten a rebuke.

"The reason," Tyce explained, "is that a strong man doesn't disparage other people. And he certainly doesn't disparage his own family. It's weak. It's what beta men do. Beta men like to mock and slander other people, especially behind their back. They yell and scream. They lose their tempers. They call people names. They attack people's characters online and send angry emails and text messages because they're too cowardly to speak face to face. Don't be that guy, Lucas."

"You basically just described my father," the boy said.

"Has he always been like that?"

"Yeah, pretty much. But since SPAARZ it's gotten worse. He's always pissed off about something. Also, I know he hates his job. And I don't think he and my mother get along that well either. Sometimes I think my mother doesn't even like him."

Tyce looked away, and scratched his ear.

"I think he's pretty unhappy, to be honest," Lucas said. "But he never does anything about it. He just complains about everything. In his mind, everybody else is stupid. But he was the one saying unvaccinated people should be put in concentration camps, and that they should lose their jobs and have to wear special armbands. And he still thinks that way even though we now know the vaccines don't even work. He just can't admit he was wrong. He's in complete denial."

"It's human nature, Lucas. People will forgive you if you make a mistake. But they'll never forgive you if you tell them *they* made a mistake. That's just how it is."

"I guess," Lucas said.

"Remind me, what does your dad do for work? He's at Wendover, right?"

"Yeah. He calls it 'Bendover.' He works in some stupid office. 'Student Services' or something like that. Though I think all he does is go on FaceFace and Chirper all day, because he's always posting stuff."

"He sounds kind of frustrated," Tyce said.

"Probably. He has a master's and he was working on his PhD, but something happened and he didn't get it."

"And now his wife is a famous scholar."

"She's not *that* famous."

"But she has more status than he does. She's a tenured professor and the author of several respected books."

"That's true. The only thing he ever published were posts on FaceFace and Chirper."

"It's kind of sad, no?"

"I suppose."

"Maybe you could cut him some slack."

Lucas just shrugged.

"And so what could you do for me? If I were to hire you?" Tyce said, shifting the conversation. "What value can you bring to my business in exchange for my money? Do you have any skills that can make my life easier?"

"Yes," Lucas said confidently. "I'm really good at video editing, both visuals and sound. And while the content of your videos is good, the presentation and the graphics pretty much suck. Your videos look like they're from 2015. You need to step up your game."

Tyce chortled. "Is that right," he said, amused.

Lucas nodded.

"Do you have samples of your work?"

"Yep. Lots."

"Well, let me think about it," Tyce said. "And I'll give you my phone number, so the next time you want to talk to me, you won't have to kick a soccer ball into my pool. OK?"

Lucas laughed nervously. "OK."

* * *

Oona had just pulled into the BuffBodz parking lot, and was looking for a space, when her phone buzzed with a new text message. The grating yet very welcome sound of it sent an electric charge through her body, a potent jolt of hope. Though she had decided that morning not to text Tyce, she had changed her mind around noon, and had written to ask if he would be at the gym today. He never wrote back. Undeterred, Oona had decided to come anyway, thinking he still might show up. Typically, Tyce arrived at the gym most afternoons around four. It was now 4:10. This new text message, she felt, was likely his belated response. Ideally he would say something like, "I'm here now—where are you? Please tell me you're coming!" Or maybe, "Sorry I didn't respond sooner, I'm swamped with work. But I *have* to see you —screw work, I'm leaving now!"

Oona parked the car and snatched up her phone. The text was from Cole. "*Dammit!*" she cried. With a furious frown she read his message: "What do you mean I should sun my balls? Are you hitting on me?" This was Cole's idea of humor. At one time, Oona had thought he was quite funny. How long ago that had been, she reflected. She deleted the text.

Inside BuffBodz, there was no Tyce. Oona looked everywhere —the weight room, the cardio room, the pool, the sauna, the juice bar. No luck. But Oona did see Ingrid.

Though she had been blessed with many natural gifts—the legs, the face, the ass, the perky tits—the Blonde Bitch didn't look quite so blessed today. Covering her nose and much of her cheeks was a large white bandage. Linni, evidently, had left her mark. Yet despite this prominent facial blemish, Ingrid comported herself as she always did, with supreme queenly self-assurance. To her mind, she was still by far the hottest female in the gym. To her mind, it wasn't even close.

Oona, however, had different ideas. Yes, Ingrid was much hotter than she, but Oona was now sleeping with Tyce, which meant Oona had taken Ingrid's man. In some primal, Darwinian way, didn't this mean that Oona herself was now the queen bitch? If Tyce was the dominant male stud at BuffBodz, which he was, and if Oona could now claim him as her lover, which she could, did that not put *her*, Dr. Oona Pudding, at the top of the female status heap? To Oona's mind, it did. And how gratifying it felt! How exhilarating and how ego-stroking! Never before, from junior high to this past weekend, had Oona won a highly desirable man from a highly desirable woman. From puberty on, she had been excluded from the pretty-girl cliques, those exclusive, members-only clubs for the girls who dated the handsome, popular boys and married the handsome, successful men. From their circles, Oona had always been shunned and rejected. Attention and respect had come, to a certain degree, with her professional success. But recognition of that success was limited to a smallish number of people, mainly other academics. A small swath indeed. This new, *sexual* success, however, was of an entirely different magnitude. Not only did it feel like a triumph against the entirety of her gender, but it felt as well like an exquisite act of *revenge*—sweet, ruthless, in-your-face revenge on all the pretty girls who had ever lorded it over her.

Now, with a haughty air, puffed up with pride and maybe even a touch of grandiosity, Oona sauntered straight over to the upright chest-press machine on which the Blonde Bitch was now performing a set of eighty-pound presses. Oona planted herself in front of Ingrid, less than ten feet away, and struck a bold, confrontational pose. Like some cocky brazen man, she put her hands on her hips and stared at the Blonde Bitch with gloating, insolent eyes, as if to say, "Guess who I'm screwing, bee-atch?" Oh yes, Oona wanted to make Ingrid uncomfortable. She wanted to make her squirm. At the Farmers Market, Ingrid had asked Oona if she was a "waitress." We'll see who's the waitress now, Oona thought.

But things did not go quite to plan. As Ingrid worked the machine, raising and lowering the weights, she did not notice Oona's looming presence or catch her aggressive boastful glare. Ingrid was too preoccupied, too inwardly absorbed, to focus on anyone but herself. She had a date planned for that evening with Tyce Creamer, an early one, and she was running late. Tyce had apologized for Linni breaking her nose and had offered to pay for any reconstructive surgery if that should prove necessary. For Ingrid, that was all she needed to hear.

As soon as she completed her tenth rep on the machine, she stood and hurried to the locker room to get her things. She did not want to keep Tyce waiting. He did not like that. Thus she quickly swept past Oona without recognizing or even looking at her. And because she was wearing earphones, she did not hear the word "Slut," which Oona muttered as the girl rushed by.

* * *

Cole began drinking earlier than usual that day. He had uncorked a bottle of the Stepfield Valley Malbec around three, feeling sorely agitated. A number of different worries, anxieties, and resentments had simultaneously beset him and upped his desire

for booze. To go with the wine he had put on the Glamoramas'
mellow third album, *Onomatopoeia*, and was now staring at the
screen of his laptop. After spending an hour or two on Face-
Face and Chirper, he experienced a disquieting sensation. The
inner voice that had been subtly harassing him over the past few
days grew louder and more insistent. He tried to disregard the
voice but it would not leave him alone. It was taunting him,
goading him, disturbing him. Finally, he gave in. He opened
up MyToobs in his browser and went to the Bro2Bro with Tyce
Creamer channel. The redneck cretin's latest video was entitled,
"What It Means When Your Babe's Not Banging You."

Cole sneered, shaking his head. "What an idiot he is," he
muttered. "What a fool."

Nevertheless, Cole opened the video. The voice in his head
demanded it. There was a brief ad for a "male enhancement" sup-
plement, and another for a glitzy Las Vegas hotel/casino. Then
onto the screen of Cole's laptop came the manicured face and
Tarzan torso of Tyce Creamer. Hanging from the neck of his
painted-on black T-shirt were his designer sunglasses—evidently
this was his "signature look"—and behind him through a wide
plate-glass wall was his playboy pool sparkling in bright summer
light.

"Bros, it's time for some tough love," Tyce said as he looked
straight into the camera and into Cole's eyes. "I got an email from
my boy Barry K. out in Tulsa, Oklahoma—no wait, *Terry* K. out
in Tulsa, Oklahoma—and he asks if I have any thoughts on why
his wife hasn't boned him in six months. Oh, man—yeah, *Terry*,
I have some thoughts on that! First off, at the very least I hope
you and the missus signed a prenup, otherwise you, my friend,
are about to enter a big ol' world of pain and humiliation, not to
mention financial distress.

"Now, I don't know how many times I've said this, on this
channel *and* in my books, but if your babe's not banging you, then
she's banging someone else. I say this over and over, yet guys still

come to me, giving me the sad-sack puppy-dog eyes and telling me that I'm wrong and that *their* girl is the exception to the rule. 'Yo Tyce, me and my girl aren't having sex, but I know she would *never* cheat on me. *Ever.* I know she *really* loves me,' they say. 'She's my *best friend.* I trust her more than *anybody on the planet.* But I just don't know what's wrong. She says she doesn't want to talk about it. She says she just needs some time. And so I told her, "It's totally fine, babe. *I'm here for you.* Whatever you need, just let me know." '

"I'm telling you, bros, I hear this pathetic castrated beta shit at least once a week. Every simp out there truly thinks his case is the exception. He thinks his woman is different. He thinks his relationship is different. He thinks his 'sensitivity' is a sign of love and respect for his woman, a sign of how *evolved* and how *caring* he is as a 'new man.' 'I'm not a caveman, Tyce!' he screeches. 'I'm not part of the oppressive patriarchy! I *support* women! I'm a *feminist soyboy!*'

"Well, let me tell you something, Terry—I'm afraid you've been played, my friend. That little girl is taking you for a ride. And before you know it, you're going to have your heart stomped and your pocket picked clean, because ten to one says she's stepping out on you. Ten to one says she's getting drilled by someone at work, at the gym, or maybe the mailman. Trust me, she's doing someone behind your back, and she's loving every second of it knowing how much it's going to rip you apart when you find out. Because here's the thing, Terry: the cheating part, the actual in-and-out with Postman Dick, that's just the last step in the breakup plan. If she's doing it with her boss or the pool boy, it's only because she decided long ago that you were history.

"It's like I always say: women only have sex with men they respect, and when they lose that respect, it's bye-bye baby! The game is over, and you, my brother, have lost. The cheating part is just her way to make the break official. It means she's crossed the

Relationship Rubicon, from the land of 'I-want-to-grow-old-with-you' to the land of 'eat-shit-and-die-sucker-and-give-me-your-cash.' And what's more, Terry, is that when all of this goes down, when she suddenly informs you some night when you get home from work that she's decided to stay with her mother or with her best friend because she 'just needs some time to think,' you can be assured that she already has a lawyer and copies of all your financial papers. Then, a week or two later, she'll call and tell you what she's known for the past six months. She's leaving you, and, what's more, it's all *your* fault. That's right, on top of everything else, she's going to blame the whole thing on you: her cheating, her lying, her demand for a divorce. Mark my words.

"So my advice to you, brother, is be prepared. The hammer is about to fall, and it's going to come down hard. So take your head out of your ass and take off that skirt you've been wearing, and man up for war. Do what you can to protect yourself and your assets, and do it fast. And if you still think I'm wrong, ask yourself this: Does your wife like it when you touch her? Does she complain of headaches or other problems at bedtime? Does she avoid spending time with you and has she stopped laughing at your jokes? ... Mmm-hm. Yep. And you wonder why she's not banging you?

"Now Terry, this is the point in the conversation where the sensitive eunuch starts to panic. His capacity for denial is stretched to the very limit. He says, 'But my woman just isn't that sexual, Tyce. That's all it is.' Ha—*bullshit*! Another thing I tell guys is this: if your girlfriend or your wife hasn't screwed you in months, and you think it's just because she has low libido, check her underwear drawer or some other hiding place, and you might find a little surprise. Trust me, if your girl's not interested in having sex, it only means she's not interested in having sex with *you* ...

"OK, bros, that's it for today. Terry from Tulsa, be strong and stop being a chump. Lots of dudes have been through this, including myself back in the day. We made it through and so will you, and next time you'll be a little wiser. And if you need us, the Bro2Bro community is here to support you. Also, you might want to check out my video on how to find the right divorce attorney for your budget, and another one about how to get through the divorce process—emotionally, physically, and financially. I'll leave links in the description below.

"OK, I'll see you next time, and remember guys: give it your all, because this is the only life you get. Peace!"

The screen went black and the MyToobs algorithm readied another video from Bro2Bro with Tyce Creamer: "Best Exercises for Perfect Abs." Five, four, three—

Cole exed out of the site. Staring at the screen, he felt a little numb, a little shaken. But very quickly he regained himself, thinking, What an asshole Creamer is. What a *clown*. A phony hustler. Someone should report him.

* * *

Tyce never showed at the gym, nor did he ever return Oona's text. On the drive home in her sweaty workout gear, Oona struggled with feelings of confusion and anger, worry and despair. She resolved never to text Tyce again. That is, she would not text him again until he texted her first. More and more she felt that she was losing herself, that she was losing control and even losing her dignity. She even felt like she was maybe becoming a little obsessed.

As she drove down Lilac Lane, Oona slowed the car as she neared Tyce's place. She was hoping she might see him. She was hoping he might suddenly emerge from his front door, to check his mailbox or maybe go for a run. She was even hoping, because you never knew, that he had been waiting by the window for her to come home, and would now rush out into the street waving his arms for her to stop … But he did not appear.

Oona pulled into her driveway, eased into the garage, brought the car to a stop, and clicked the dashboard button for the garage door. The door made a racket as it slowly descended on its tracks, blocking out more and more of the sunlight and finally leaving Oona in the dark. Hating herself, she reached for her phone and typed out a text: "Missed you at the gym. Will I see you tonight?"

For the rest of that day she kept her phone by her side, awaiting his response. It never came.

EIGHT

"Dad, do you feel better?" said Rosa.

Blurry-eyed and booze-battered, Cole had just emerged from the basement and come into the kitchen. He was not wearing a mask. It was nearly noon and Rosa was making a peanut butter and jelly sandwich. Cole had just woken up. His mouth was dry, his brain hurt, and he was looking for some relief.

"Where's your mother?" he mumbled as he shuffled past Rosa to the refrigerator.

"Oh, man! *P.U.!*" the girl cried, wrinkling her nose. "Dad, you *stink*! Did you take a shower this week?"

He grabbed a carton of orange juice from the frig and drank half of it down. "Where's your mother?" he repeated.

"She's at school. She said she had to write something. Her new book I think."

"Where's Lucas?"

"He's at Tyce's. He's trying to get a job with him."

This barely registered with Cole, and the little bit that did register, did not interest him. His attention was focused on something else. Something more pressing. Something more worrisome. For much of the previous evening he had been besieged by disturbing thoughts, frightening thoughts, potentially catastrophic thoughts—until, that is, the alcohol had worked its magic. All total, he had put away two-and-a-half bottles of the Stepfield Valley Malbec. You could say he had a taste for it. Regardless, the wine had only temporarily expunged his problems, for as soon as he had woken up this morning, the worrisome thoughts had resumed their relentless attack. He took another chug of the orange juice, then trudged toward the stairs to the second floor.

"Dad, can I go over to Carrie Kim's house?" Rosa called out.

Cole didn't answer.

"*Daddy?*"

* * *

Cole shut the door to his bedroom and went straight for Oona's bureau. He rummaged through all the drawers, looking under and behind stacks of T-shirts and jerseys and socks and bras and panties. He found nothing. There was no disturbing discovery. Next he went into her closet, searching shelves and plastic bins packed with folded sweaters and sweatshirts, winter hats and gloves. Nothing. The last hiding place he could think of was the drawer in her nightstand, and there too he found nothing.

Cole let out a deep sigh, feeling a great release of tension. Screw Creamer, he thought. Screw him, the jackass. With that problem solved, Cole could now attend to another. His bladder was swollen and ready to burst. He stepped into his and Oona's bathroom and stood before the toilet. Yet before he got down to business, he once again heard from the inner voice—the inner voice that just wouldn't shut up. Why couldn't it bother someone else, he wondered? The voice was demanding that he look to the left, and Cole relented. He saw the bathroom-closet door, and for no explicable reason he felt something like dread. He went into the closet and began scouring the shelves ... And there it was. The feared thing. Back against the wall, under a stack of folded towels: an enormous rubber phallus.

For a minute or more Cole just stared at it, gobsmacked, wondering if this was really happening. *Was* this really happening? Yes, it *was* really happening. This was no drunken hallucination.

Cole did not have the DTs. Oona had truly done this. Behind his back she had purchased this thing and brought it into their home. Brought it into their lives.

Though the sight of it sickened and even horrified him, Cole also felt compelled to take a closer look. He had to see what he was up against. With some trepidation he took ahold of the thing. It felt weighty in his hand and was somewhat flexible. When he shook it from one end, the rest of it bobbed up and down. Then too there was the size. This part was hard to miss. The surrogate penis was longer than Cole's forearm and thicker than his wrist. Needless to say, it did not remind him of himself.

After he had placed the thing back under the folded towels, Cole went into the bedroom and lay on his and Oona's bed. Quite frankly, he did not feel too good. He felt dazed and bewildered and very stressed. But most of all, he felt like part of him had just been chopped off.

* * *

"I love storms. The more violent, the better," said Tyce Creamer as he surveyed the mass of black clouds that were darkening the Beauville sky. He sat poolside with a barber's bib draped over his muscle-packed torso, while a gorgeous young woman, with long raven hair and a knowing smile, held a straight razor to his neck. Seated nearby, Lucas listened distractedly to Tyce's words. In the boy's opinion, the woman shaving Tyce—her name was Amalia—was just as disconcertingly beautiful, if not more so, than Ingrid.

"Earthquakes, tornadoes, lightning, thunder—I love it all, Lucas," Tyce declaimed with grave intonation and not one whit of discernible irony. "It's the power of nature on full display, and it's sublime. One minute you have a city you think will last forever, and the next minute a hurricane takes out the whole damn thing. All of that building and striving, all of those hopes and dreams, instantly reduced to rubble. Nature is ferocious and unpredictable. But people today think nature is puppy dogs and kittens and shit they see on MyToobs. Pretty sunsets and burbling streams on a computer screen, with a bunch of morons writing comments, 'Oh that's so pretty!' This is what we've become, Lucas. Because of fear, and because there's big money in fear, men have done everything they can to tame and avoid nature, to make life 'safe.' To make life predictable and risk free. In exchange for their freedom and self-determination, men today ask to be taken care of. They beg for it. In fact, half the people in this country today think freedom is *bad*, they think freedom is *dangerous*. So they willingly give it over to other people—the government, the corporations, and the so-called 'expert class.' "

Lucas nodded with only partial understanding. He was trying to follow Tyce, but he was more interested in watching Amalia at work.

"Yet deep down, Lucas," Tyce went on, "today's man knows that something isn't right, and that it hasn't been right for some time. But rather than investigate this, rather than do a deep dive and search for the truth of how the world really works, he prefers to go along with the crowd and maybe tell himself a few lies so he doesn't have to face any uncomfortable truths, so he doesn't have to take a stand and fight, so he doesn't have to give up his porn and his Sunday football and his 1000-inch TV and his pointless job. Better to conform and swallow the lies than to jeopardize his easy life.

"But in doing this, in exchanging his freedom and his dignity for a bit of comfort and 'safety' and the approval of his fellow sheep, today's man has only made himself weak. He's given away all his power, and he's done it willingly, even convincing himself that in doing so he's done something noble, something *virtuous*. And day by day, as he becomes more and more convinced of his phony virtue, he becomes weaker and weaker. And this, my friend, is the worst thing that can happen to society. When men become weak, the whole thing turns to shit, and that's when nature reasserts itself. That's when the hurricane hits. That's when the tsunami rolls in and flattens everything in sight. Because nature is not sentimental. Nature does not reward virtue signaling or rainbow parades. Nature only rewards strength, which is why weak men and weak countries are inevitably conquered by strong men and strong countries … *Lucas?* Are you listening?"

"Yeah," Lucas said, startled. His attention had drifted from Tyce and his long-winded speech to the young woman's legs. She wore Cleopatra sandals and a very short blouse-dress that revealed lots of skin. Her legs were spellbindingly magnificent, and Lucas had become momentarily entranced.

Bemused at this, Tyce said, "I'm giving you life advice and you're more interested in Amalia's legs. Son, you're putting the cart before the horse," he laughed.

Amalia glanced at Lucas with a pleasant though mostly uninterested smile, and promptly resumed her work.

"You know, my man," Tyce went on, "to get a woman like Amalia here you're really going to have to up your game, not to mention your bank account."

Lucas flushed with embarrassment, while Amalia chuckled and gave Tyce a light slap on the shoulder.

"I've seen this twice now," Tyce said to the boy, as Amalia went back to shaping Tyce's beard. "When it's just you and me, you don't shut up. You speak well and you're insightful and you have belief in yourself and in what you say. You have enthusiasm and confidence. But when a sexually attractive woman is present, you clam up like some cowering beta. You did it with Ingrid at the Farmers Market, and you're doing it now."

Lucas, chagrined that Amalia was hearing this, chagrined that she might now think him a "cowering beta," clammed up—and thus unwittingly proved Tyce's point.

"So I'm going to tell you something, Lucas," Tyce said. "And it's something I wish I'd known when I was your age, and it's this:

You can control almost any situation, including with women, simply by how you act. Not by how you *think*, but by how you *act*. It's all about how you present yourself. With Ingrid, at the Farmers Market, I watched to see how you would handle her. And what did you do when I introduced you? You mumbled, you looked down, you looked away. Your body language said, 'I'm a pussy. Don't mind me.' And that's exactly what Ingrid did. She *didn't* mind you. She mentally wrote you off as unimportant, and it all happened within two to three seconds. You presented as a weak man, and her high-status female instincts responded in a natural way.

"Now, here's the point. Everything that happened with Ingrid could have gone the other way. In those couple of seconds you had to shape her reaction to you, you could have planted what I call 'seeds of interest'—you may have seen my video on this ..."

Lucas nodded. He *had* seen the video—"Planting Seeds of Interest."

"Well, OK," Tyce said. "There you go. Maybe you didn't pay close enough attention. But with Ingrid, you could have given her a reason to take notice of you, a reason to be interested and curious, to make her think, 'Here's someone I should pay attention to' ... Hey Amalia," Tyce said, looking up at his well-paid personal groomer.

The girl had finished trimming and sculpting Tyce's beard and was now wiping off stray bits of shaving cream from his neck. She stopped what she was doing and Tyce said, "Look at my good friend Lucas here. What do you see?"

Lucas fidgeted in his seat as Amalia, with a benign, almost big-sisterly smile, gave him a quick once-over.

"He's cute," she said in her Andalusian accent. "Though he's maybe a little shy."

"See?" Tyce said to Lucas. "We have to get rid of that. When a woman says a guy is 'shy,' what she really means is, she thinks he's a wimp."

Amalia laughed, though she tried to stifle it. Lucas was mortified, his cheeks turning red.

"I don't think that," she said, taking pity on the boy.

"Yes you do," Tyce said with a wry grin.

Amalia smiled but said nothing as she now got back to work, removing the barber's bib from her client.

To Lucas Tyce said, "Don't worry about it. We've all been there, Lucas. When I was your age I was skinny, I had zits, and I didn't know how to talk to girls. A lot of us go through this, and I'm only speaking this freely with you because I know you can take it and because I know you're an intelligent, ambitious kid. All you need is a little game, and this is where I can help. It's just about learning a few basic life truths and building confidence and a handful of skills. It takes time and work, but anyone can do it. In the end, it's all up here," he added, tapping a finger to the side of his head. "Lucas, you can get whatever you want in life, if you're smart and if you want it bad enough and if you can conquer your fears. It really is all in your head. Do you understand?"

"Yes," Lucas said earnestly. "That's why I want to work for you."

Just then there was a rolling rumble of thunder, a cosmic clamor as old as the planet itself. The air had taken on a noticeable chill, and now one after the other quarter-size wet spots began to dapple the ground.

"It's going to pour," Amalia said, hastily gathering up her things.

"How about a swim?" Tyce said, grinning at her.

"Now?" she said, beaming as the heavy drops began to pelt them.

"I've got plenty of towels," he said as he pulled off his T-shirt. "Put your stuff inside."

Amalia reached for her phone and her bag with all her grooming supplies and darted into the house.

"Big man, we'll continue this later," Tyce said, giving Lucas the signal that it was time for him to scram.

But Lucas didn't move. Becoming soaked from the strengthening rain, he watched with opened-mouth amazement as Amalia ran out of the house in black bra and black thong and laughingly jumped into the pool.

A streak of lightning flashed in the west and there came another celestial rumbling, followed by a tremendous explosion of thunder. The ground itself seemed to shake. From the pool Amalia screeched with terrified girlish glee. Tyce, still in the shorts he had been wearing, was laughing as he dove into the pool.

Astonished at all that was happening, Lucas watched the scene with full concentration. He had never witnessed anything like this before and he did not want to miss any detail. Then, seeing Tyce take Amalia into his arms, the boy turned and ran for home.

* * *

Lucas entered the house through the back, his clothes drenched and dripping on the kitchen floor. He pulled out a chair from the table, and as he was taking off his muddy sneakers, his father entered the room from the opposite side. Cole was returning from the second floor, where he had just made his cruel discovery of the rubber sex toy, and was heading down to the basement for some liquid solace. Neither father nor son seemed particularly pleased to see the other.

"Where've you been?" Cole said, dimly remembering something unpleasant to do with his neighbor.

"At Tyce's."

Cole wearily shook his head. He did not have the strength to do battle with the boy. Not now.

"I'm going to be working for him … I think," Lucas said. The job, unfortunately, had not been finalized, or even properly discussed. That had been the goal of this morning's meeting. But then came the rain and the lightning and gorgeous Amalia in her black bra and thong.

A ferocious clap of thunder shook the house. The rain was falling in heavy sheets.

"Why? Why would you *willingly* work for that guy? Or even associate with him?" Cole said in disbelief.

"I don't know," Lucas said archly. "Because he's successful? Because he knows what he's doing?"

Cole scoffed. "And this is, what? For the rest of the summer? Till September?"

"Dad, I'm *not* going to Olmsted. I already told you. I'm not taking the shot. I don't need it, and I don't want it. They can screw off."

Sighing at this, Cole said, "Where did I go wrong with you?"

"How much time do you have?" Lucas said.

Fire came into Cole's eyes. "You know something, Lucas? At this point, I couldn't care less what you do. Do whatever you want. You want to give up your education and work for that misogynist buffoon, be my guest. You want to run off and join the circus, go right ahead. You want to join the Foreign Legion, I'll drive you to the bus station. I really don't care. I don't care at all." Uninterested in the boy's response, Cole shuffled down to the basement.

* * *

That night for supper it was just Oona and Rosa at the kitchen table. Cole was in quarantine down in the basement and Lucas had already grilled and consumed his lamb steak, lamb liver, and lamb testicles. The boy had made a special trip to a local butcher for these tasty delicacies. The testicles in particular were supposed to be "insanely healthy," or so Lucas had read on the internet. Rosa, when told what the two whitish, lemon-sized things were on Lucas's plate, had screamed in horror. And she had screamed even louder when he ate them. At the moment, however, things were noticeably more sedate. Apart from the sound of Oona and Rosa chewing their meatless chicken tenders, steamed asparagus, and brown rice, there was silence in the kitchen, a distinct absence of human voices. Instead of talking to her daughter, Oona kept glancing at her phone, which lay face up beside her plate.

"Mom, is something wrong?" Rosa finally said.

"No," Oona said, not looking at the girl.

"Are you expecting a call?"

"No."

"Then why do you keep looking at your phone?"

Oona snapped. "I'm *not* looking at my phone, Rosa!" she said with a fierce look.

Rosa's head shot back as if she had been slapped. "You're such a *grouch*!" she said. "I'm never talking to you again!"

Then, as if conjured by the brute force of her obsessive longing, Oona's phone buzzed with a new text. Her face shone with elation. It was *him*, she felt. At last, it was *him*!

It was Linni.

Oona shrieked with frustration, her hands clenching into vein-popping fists.

Rosa flinched back again. "*Mom!*" the girl said in a fright.

"She drives me crazy!" Oona cried out, looking up at the ceiling.

"Who?" Rosa asked warily.

Oona tapped open the text. It read, "Oona, can you meet tonight? Can I come to your house?" Oona debated whether to respond. Part of her wanted to delete the damn thing, but another part wanted to write, "Linni—Go screw yourself! And no, don't come to my house you crazy psychopath!"

"*Mom, who?*" Rosa repeated impatiently.

"*Who what?*" Oona yelled, now glaring at the girl.

"Don't yell!" Rosa yelled back. "Who's driving you crazy?"

Oona shook her head as if to say, "It's none of your business," but then said, aloud, "Linni."

"The lady who got arrested?"

Oona didn't answer. She was focused on her phone. She typed, "Sorry Linni, but Cole has SPAARZ. I thought I told you that already. I'll talk to you in a few days. Please stop texting me." She hit send and immediately turned off her phone, knowing that Linni's reply was just seconds away.

* * *

Down in the basement, the Idiot Gurus' all-acoustic album, *Sinking Lifeboat*, was spinning on the turntable. On the coffee table was Cole's mostly uneaten supper, now cold. Meandering unnoticed atop the remaining meatless chicken tenders was a single black ant. Rather than food, Cole was concentrating more on the wine. He was currently sipping his way through the day's second bottle of Stepfield Valley Malbec.

Though the booze was more or less helping with the pain, Cole still could not believe that Oona had been cheating on him—cheating on him with a giant sex toy. It hurt. It really hurt. The betrayal. The humiliation. The shattering of trust. His wife had left him for … a vibrating piece of rubber?

Yet amid his wine-sodden cogitations, something odd happened. Rather than focusing his anger on Oona, rather than attributing his hurt and his suffering to his unfaithful wife, Cole found himself dwelling more and more on Tyce Creamer. For wasn't Creamer the *real* cause of his problems, Cole wondered? Wasn't *Creamer* the true culprit here? For it was *Creamer* who had started the flirting with Oona, flexing his veiny biceps and flashing his sugar-white fangs. *Creamer* was the one who kept kissing Oona in Cole's presence, charming and encouraging her and leading her on in who knows how many ways. Yes, it was all on *Creamer*—Cream-face Creamer. Shit-face Creamer. And now Lucas, Cole's own flesh and blood, was going to *work* for *Creamer*? *Bro2Bro with Tyce Creamer*? How was this possible? And what was next? Was *Creamer* going to make a play for Rosa? Would he abduct the girl on some cross-country sex romp, Humbert Humbert style? Cole wouldn't be surprised. He wouldn't be surprised at all.

In a less civilized age, Cole would have considered some sort of combative response. A violent retaliation. A sword fight like Caravaggio in seventeenth-century Rome. A duel at ten paces like Pushkin or Lermontov. A fistfight like de Kooning or Pollock at the Cedar Tavern. But such options were no longer open to men like Cole, thought Cole. Instead, he did as men like him do today. He reached for his laptop.

To the Chirper "Anti-Hate and Disinformation Policing Team," he wrote:

Dear Friends,

As a dedicated, long-time user of Chirper—I've been on the platform, you'll note, since 2009, one of your original "founding" members—I'm writing to inform you of a divisive, toxic, and, dare I say, *dangerous presence* in our midst. @TheReal-TyceCreamer, as I am sure you already know, is a contentious, inflammatory proponent of misogynistic right-wing propaganda. His published content includes the highly offensive book series, "Don't Be a Bitch," which promotes a hateful, cisnormative, white-supremacist agenda that threatens the very foundations of our democracy ...

The letter went on for another thousand words and concluded with Cole's heartfelt plea that Chirper "save our country from the specter of a fascist takeover" by canceling Tyce Creamer. After he read through the draft and corrected the odd typo, Cole found that he was quite pleased with his efforts. Indeed, the letter was, he had to admit, one of his finer expressions of public outrage.

A shining gem of moral indignation. Thus satisfied, he sent the e-missive into the ether and uncorked his third bottle of the day. He then proceeded to write similar letters to FaceFace, Amazin!, and MyToobs.

* * *

While Cole was drunkenly typing out the last of his "Cancel Creamer" emails to the censorship commissars, Oona was in the marriage bed watching Tyce Creamer videos on MyToobs. Rather than his videos on diet or dating or life success—which in truth Oona found a little, well, *insipid*—she preferred his exercise videos. In these Tyce wore a tank top and snug-fitting shorts as he demonstrated the various moves.

"Can you feel that in your butt?" Tyce said to the camera as he executed a series of semi-pornographic hip thrusts. "This will really develop the glutes … Yeah, yeah, yeah," he went on, his crotch thrusting back and forth. "It should be starting to burn."

Oh, yes, Oona thought. It's starting to burn. It's *really* starting to burn—

Her phone buzzed. Oona shot upright. It was a new text message … from *Tyce*. She gasped. The message read, "Sure, you can come over. Just be careful."

Oona was euphoric. She was tingly with joy. Then, just as quickly, she *wasn't* tingly with joy. Instead she was confused. The issue was this: she hadn't written Tyce a text today. He was responding to the text she had written to him yesterday. And so, was this response *also* from yesterday? She had had this problem before, where a text from Cole or Linni arrived only a day or two after it had been sent. A rare event to be sure, but still it had happened. And if that was the case now, it would mean that he had been expecting her last night rather than this night.

She wrote back, "Do you mean tonight? Wednesday?"

"Are you joking?" came the reply.

She felt a pinch of panic. Was he getting upset? Did he think she was stupid? "No," she quickly typed. "It's just that I didn't write you today."

"Oh. Yeah, I was busy," he replied.

Oona pondered this, and her brow tensed. "I was busy"? That's his response? No "sorry for not writing sooner"? And, "busy" with *whom*? Into her mind flashed an unwelcome image of Ingrid and her Olympic legs and gold-medal ass. Had she and Tyce been practicing hip thrusts together last evening? Had Ingrid felt "the burn"? But this was nonsense, Oona thought. She was just wasting time. "I'll be there soon," she typed back. She jumped out of bed, went to her bureau, and retrieved one of her new bra-and-panties sets.

Just yesterday, before she had gone to BuffBodz, Oona had paid a visit to a local lingerie shop in search of some non-mom underthings. The place was called Tanya's Treasure Chest. It was located on Main Street in Beauville and had an extremely offensive window display. For the ten years Oona had lived in Beauville, Tanya's Treasure Chest had featured the same mannequin in its window: a tall, skinny, blank-faced female with watermelon-sized breasts. Once a year, it seemed, the mannequin was done up in a different getup of supposedly sexy items—black garter belts, crotchless bottoms, pink feather boas. To Oona the place had always been a vulgar affront to women and a moral blight on the community. Needless to say, it had never occurred to her even once to go inside. Never, that is, until she started sleeping with Tyce Creamer. True, she had felt embarrassed as she entered the shop, and of course she was petrified that someone she knew might see her—particularly someone from Wendover. But these uneasy feelings had quickly passed, as the place was nearly empty and she found herself surrounded by so many interesting things ...

* * *

As Oona zipped into the shower, Linni Mudge turned her car onto Lilac Lane. She had already knocked back two bottles of the hard lemonade and had a third going in the cup holder. Tonight, she felt, was the night. Something was going to happen. She was sure of it. Since Tyce had taken out the restraining order against her, she had had no contact with him. Not a call or a text or an email. But this unfortunate situation was just temporary, Linni knew. It would end very soon. They were in love, after all. She and Tyce were soulmates. They were *meant* to be. At any moment she was expecting his call or his text or his email, and when it came, she would be close by.

She drove past his house, circled the block several times, and then parked in her preferred stakeout spot, one house down from Oona's place on the opposite side of the street. From here she could discreetly observe Tyce's house—the house that Linni fully expected to live in one day. She and Tyce, she had decided, would have three children. They would raise a family. Two boys and a girl: Tyce Jr., Ricky Robert, and Sarah June. That was how it would be.

She switched off the ignition and the lights, sat low in the driver's seat, and began her patient watch.

* * *

Freshly showered, shaved, plucked, powdered, deodorized, and perfumed, Oona got into her new lacy red bra and teeny red bottoms and went to admire herself in the full-length mirror. "Oh God," she groaned, seeing her reflection. Though she had tried the items on yesterday and had thought she looked pretty hot, she now felt differently. She now thought she looked fat. Her belly, her ass, her thighs—they all looked enormous. It was mortifying. It was also infuriating. How could she look hot one day and not hot the next? It was absurd. Maybe it was all in her head, she thought.

She finished getting dressed, and before she had even zipped up the fly on her jeans, she was back to being excited. She could not wait to see him. She went to her bedroom door and peeked into the hall. Rosa was spending the night at a friend's and Lucas was in his room. His door was closed but there was a strip of light underneath it. The boy was either reading or on his computer. It was almost eleven, and Oona knew she should probably wait another hour. She knew it would be wise. But she was ready now, and she did not want to wait an hour, or even a minute if she could help it. Her heart was thumping and her flesh was primed. She was ready to see him. She was ready to *be* with him. She was ready to be *on* him. Oh yes, Oona was ready *now*.

* * *

Linni also was ready now. She had long since finished the third hard lemonade and she now needed to pee. She considered going behind a bush—there was a good-sized rhododendron in the yard beside her car. But thinking of the restraining order, and the possibility of spending another night in that smelly jail cell should someone see her and call the cops, she decided against it. She should probably just head home. She had to work tomorrow and it was already late.

But then an idea came. It was as though a voice had whispered in her ear: "Why not take a peek at his pool? Just a quick look-see before you go." Linni considered this. Given how hot and muggy the day had turned out, following that morning's wild thunderstorm, Tyce might be taking a dip to cool off. And if he had any company—the Skinny Bitch Ingrid, for example—she would be in the pool too. If so, Linni felt it was something she should know.

Quiet as could be, she exited the car and shut the door with a near-silent click. The moon was bright so she kept to the shadows. She moved cat-like past Oona's house, cut across the grassy patch between the two homes, and went straight for the gate-door to Tyce's pool.

* * *

Back in the house, Oona snuck out of her room, slipped down the stairs to the first floor, and promptly froze. From above her came the sound of footfall. It was Lucas. He had come out of his bedroom and gone into the bathroom. Oona heard the door shut and she didn't move. She was thinking of the window in that bathroom, which looked out onto Tyce's pool. She knew she had to wait. It was the safe thing to do.

* * *

After he flushed, Lucas flipped off the light and went to the window to see if Tyce was up to any late-night action. From the moonlight and also the glow coming from the back of the house, the boy saw the pool area was empty. There were no girls and no Tyce. Yet just as he was about to return to his room—he was fifty pages into Tyce's second book, *Don't Be a Bitch: From Simp to Pimp*, and was eager to get back to it—Lucas caught a flash of movement.

Down in the yard, a dim figure was stealthily approaching Tyce's back fence. It was like something from a movie, a cat burglar or a trained assassin. Hunched over, the figure cautiously crept up to the gate-door, entered the property, and moved along the side of the house toward the pool. At the back of the house, the figure stepped into the light.

It was a woman, Lucas saw. The woman who was arrested on Saturday night: his mother's friend Linni.

Lucas hurried back to his room.

* * *

The toilet flushed and soon after came the sound of her son returning to his room. Oona breathed easily and felt a renewed rush of excitement. Her rendezvous was back on. She was just about there. In seconds she would be with Tyce, in his arms, in his face, devouring him. Mindful that Cole was beneath her, safely packed away in the basement, she tiptoed across the kitchen, quietly opened the sliding glass door, and buoyantly beamed as she stepped out into the night.

* * *

As soon as he found his phone, Lucas rushed back to the bathroom. He did not turn on the light. From the window he easily spotted Linni. She had hidden herself behind Tyce's king-size gas grill and was surreptitiously looking into the back of the house.

Lucas tapped out a text: "Tyce, that crazy girl Linni is out near your pool, spying on you." But just before he hit send, the boy saw the emergence of a second shadowy figure. This one came from near his house.

Surprised at this, he lowered the phone. He watched in wonder as this second figure also moved across the grass toward Tyce's place. The figure went to the gate-door in the fence, entered the pool area, and started toward the back of the house.

* * *

From behind the enormous gas grill Linni watched Tyce. He was seated with his back to her, at his work desk, and appeared to be alone. There was no sign of Ingrid or any other woman. Observing him hard at work—he was probably editing one of his videos or maybe writing a new book—Linni felt a pang of love. What a husband he would make. What a provider for her and her children. It was just meant to be, she felt. Of this Linni had no doubts. Soon they would be reunited and, if all went well, maybe by Christmas they would be engaged—

A slight metallic grating sound came from the fence, wresting Linni out of her romantic reverie. It was the sound of the gate-door opening. To conceal herself from this intruder, Linni shifted her position behind the grill. Hunkered down low, she wanted to know who it was but she dared not even try to peek. There was too much light. She would easily be seen. So she made herself small and waited, listening as soft footsteps approached and passed by. She then heard the glass door into the house slide open and slide shut.

Slowly, carefully, Linni rose up and looked over the top of the grill. In Tyce's kitchen now stood a woman. She had her back to Linni, but it looked like ... It looked like ... Was it *Oona*? No. Maybe. Impossible! Could it be?

Tyce had risen from his work desk and was now grinning familiarly and even knowingly at the woman. He was pleased to see her. He was *happy* to see her. He was also not surprised to see her. To Linni it was clear that this was no unexpected visit. The mystery woman hadn't knocked. She had just sauntered into the house as though she had done this before. Perhaps *many* times before.

Still trying to identify this person, Linni suddenly gasped. The mystery woman had thrown herself at Tyce and the two of them embraced in a kiss. Not a "nice-to-see-you" kiss, but a passionate kiss. A fiery kiss. A "things-are-about-to-get-broken" kiss. Their bodies were writhing and grinding, their hands grasping and clutching.

Linni's mouth fell open. Tears burned in her eyes.

She watched as Tyce reached a hand down and squeezed one of the woman's bum cheeks. Then she watched as he reached his other hand down and squeezed the woman's other bum cheek. At this, Linni nearly collapsed. Her heart was torn in two. She had always loved it when Tyce did this to her—the double bum-cheek squeeze. And to see him do it to another, to see him *share* this special move with another, oh how it hurt!

Still with her back to Linni, the mystery woman abruptly paused the passion. She pulled back from Tyce and took off her T-shirt. As she did this she turned her head to the side—and revealed her profile. The mystery woman was no longer a mystery.

"You *bitch!*" Linni cried out, louder than she may have intended, though not loud enough for the lovers to hear. "You evil bitch!" This was betrayal times two. This was heartache times two. The love of her life and one of her close friends had double-crossed her, and in doing so they had ripped her apart. To Linni, it felt like death. It felt like the annihilation of her very soul. The tears spilled and her emotions surged. She was overcome by both sorrow and rage. Her first thought was of vengeance, and her impulse was to charge into the house and go straight for Oona. Scratch out her eyes. Rip the hair from her scalp. Stomp on that big nose.

The slut, the betrayer, the two-timing deceiver, had thrown her T-shirt off to the side to display her fat tits in a red lacy bra, and was again writhing in Tyce's arms. He lifted her off the floor like a doll and carried her to the couch and set her down. He took off his shirt and she took off her bra, and Linni was audibly sobbing.

Instead of charging into the house, she decided on a second course. She took out her phone and started filming.

* * *

When Lucas recognized his mother, as she stepped into the light at the back of the house, he assumed she had gone over to rescue Linni. He guessed that Linni had texted her and told her what she was doing, and that his mother was attempting to retrieve her friend. His mother was trying to save Linni from harm.

But then Lucas watched perplexedly as Linni, who had ducked down behind the grill, remained in that position as his mother disappeared around the corner of the house. What was Linni doing? Why was she hiding from his mother? And where had his mother gone?

The boy then saw Linni rise up and peer over the grill, looking into what he knew was Tyce's kitchen/living room area. Had his mother gone into the house? Why? As he tried to sort this out, he saw Linni suddenly convulse. There was agony on her face, a look of deep suffering. Slowly it began to occur to Lucas what might be happening. But no. That couldn't be. It couldn't. His mother would never.

Then Linni began to film with her phone, filming something that was happening in the house. She was sobbing inconsolably, almost hysterically. Only one thing could be hurting her this much, Lucas knew, and all at once he felt the air rush from his lungs. He was shocked, he was disoriented. The floor seemed to wobble beneath his feet.

That his mother would do something like this had never occurred to him. That his mother would *even consider* doing something like this had never occurred to him. The vileness of the act, the sheer devious brutality of it, seemed incomprehensible to him.

Linni filmed for several minutes then rushed off. She no longer felt the need for caution. She pushed through the gate-door, left it ajar, and ran openly for the street, all the while making pitiful weeping noises that Lucas heard through the shut bathroom window.

Standing in the dark, the boy became aware of his own growing hurt. The initial shock was fading and in its place was a feeling of devastation. Lucas was crushed. Like Linni, he too felt wounded and betrayed. Something he had never put a name on, something he had always taken for granted, something that had given him a sense of stability and trust, had just been savagely destroyed.

In this painful destabilized state, the boy wavered. For some time he wondered what he should do. Should he tell his father? Should he go down to the basement and tell him right now? For the first time in a long time Lucas felt something other than disdain for his dad, something other than derision and dislike. Something like sympathy. Something like pity. But how would his father handle this news? Lucas's sense was that he would not handle it well, that he in fact would not handle it well at all. But was it better *not* to know? Lucas wasn't sure. And what about himself? Should *he* do something? Should he go over there and confront them? Should he attack Tyce? Tyce the *shithead*, Tyce the *bastard*, Tyce the *scumbag backstabber*? Should Lucas try to mess him up? Bring a knife? Bring a bat? He didn't know. He felt like he didn't know anything.

At last Lucas made his decision. He went down to the kitchen, out to the patio, and sat under the stars in one of the chairs, facing Tyce's place. He would wait for his mother and he would have it out with her right there.

* * *

Around three a.m., Oona emerged from the opened gate-door and started silently but joyfully toward her house. Her head, her heart, her body, her everything, was awash in exultant good feeling, *ecstatic* good feeling. She had never felt this way before. Though she had not said anything to Tyce, Oona could admit it to herself: for the first time in her life, she was in love. She was truly, deeply, comprehensively in love. She was suffused and brimming and drunk with love. Love for Tyce Creamer.

But then, by the waning moonlight, Oona saw something. There was a person sitting in her yard, in one of her patio chairs. A man. He appeared to be sleeping. His head was tipped to the side and his mouth was open. It was Lucas, she now saw. It was her son.

Oona wondered what this meant. But of course, it was obvious. He was seated outside in the middle of the night, facing Tyce's house—as though he was waiting for something. As though he was waiting for some*one*. He knew. Lucas knew. Oona's mind raced. What should she do? Should she wake him? Should she tell him not to say anything? No. If she were to wake him, he surely would get angry and things would get ugly. Things would get loud.

She briefly desired to touch the boy. She wanted to caress his head, his hair, very lightly, and whisper to his sleeping self that she was sorry. But she didn't do it. She knew it would not be safe. Instead, she quietly slipped into the house, crept up to her room, and shut the door.

NINE

The phone rang and rang and slowly it woke him. Cole cringed
wretchedly. His head felt like someone had kicked and punched
it all through the night, again and again and again. Wincing and
groaning, he sat up on the couch and looked for his phone. It
was easy to find. All the lights in the room were on.

At some point the previous evening, after he had gotten deep
into his third bottle of Malbec, Cole had vomited. He stumbled
to the toilet, barfed several times into the porcelain bowl, and
slept right there on the cold bathroom floor, thinking there likely
would be another round. There was. After that, he crawled back
to the couch and soon passed out, with the lights still on and
everything else: the stereo, his laptop, his phone.

The latter was on the coffee table, as was a plate of food now
crawling with black ants. There appeared to be a whole battalion
of them, fifty, sixty black ants chaotically plundering Cole's half-
eaten supper from the night before. Cole ignored the ants and
reached for the phone. It was Digby.

"Hello?" Cole said in a piteous voice.

"Cole?"

"Yes."

"Cole, where are you?"

"Hi Dig. I'm at home."

"I don't mean *where* are you," Digby said with extreme vexation. "I mean, why are you not *in* the meeting?"

Shit. The *meeting*. Cole had forgotten the meeting. "Uh ... I'm not feeling well."

"Cole, I sent you *emails*. LaKeesha called you. Several times! *Dean Munchausen* and the rest of us are waiting. The meeting has started! You *must* attend, Cole. Is that clear? For *weeks* I've assured the Dean that we would have things ready for today. *Weeks!*"

"OK. OK. Just let me ... wash up."

"There is no *time* to wash up, Cole! It is ten past ten. Dean Munchausen has been *waiting* since ten. He is *waiting!*"

"OK. I have my laptop here."

"You'll find a link in your email," Digby said. "I'm hanging up."

Digby hung up. Cole looked for his face mask, found it, put it on, then sat back on the couch with his laptop. He clicked into the meeting and saw the unsmiling faces of Digby, LaKeesha, and Dean Munchausen. None of them seemed happy to see Cole.

He held up a hand, made a genial wave. "Hi everyone."

No one waved back. No one said hi back.

"Sorry I'm late. I have SPAARZ."

"We know, Cole. I told the Dean," Digby said.

"Are we not wearing masks?" Cole said, now noticing that no one else was protected. All through the lockdowns, when Wendover had canceled in-person classes for three straight semesters and most of the administration and staff, including the Office of Student Affairs, had worked from home, college policy had strictly enforced a mask mandate for all online meetings.

"No, Cole. President Hogg sent out an email earlier this week. Evidently you did not read it," Digby said.

Dean Munchausen was squinting intently and his face grew larger on Cole's screen. "What's that you're wearing?" the Dean said, trying to get a better look.

"Me?" Cole said.

"Yes. What is that? What does it say? '*Jizcums*'?"

Cole looked down. He was still in yesterday's clothes. His T-shirt read, "The Jizcums: Cooler Than You'll Ever Be / 1998 World Tour." Even worse, the thing was stained with crusty patches of dried vomit. "Oh. Yes … it's a band," he said meekly.

Dean Munchausen frowned. He himself was wearing a coat and tie. Digby was wearing a coat and tie. LaKeesha was wearing a coat and blouse.

"Have you had a chance to look over the report?" Cole said quickly and with as much fake enthusiasm as he could muster.

The Dean paused. His critical expression made it clear he was still thinking about the T-shirt, or perhaps the crusty patches of vomit. But at last he said, "Yes."

"And what are your thoughts?" Cole said.

"Well … I'm pleased," the Dean said, his tense features now softening. "I read through it last night. Considering you've been sick, it's excellent work."

"Thank you," Cole said.

LaKeesha cleared her throat.

"And LaKeesha helped," Cole added.

" '*Helped*'?" she said with raised eyebrows.

There was silence. Then to the Dean Cole said, "Yes. We … collaborated. It was a team effort."

The Dean nodded, but LaKeesha did not. Her expression— narrowed eyes, pinched lips—did not look very collegial, Cole noted.

Now Digby cleared *his* throat. In a remindful voice he said, "The Dean was wondering about *disability access*."

"Yes. That's right," the Dean said, as if just remembering. "Why are *all* the bathrooms being made handicap accessible? Toilets, stalls, sinks, showers, doors? Given how limited our, uh, disabled enrollment is—no more than three to four percent of any incoming class—it seems rather excessive."

Digby looked on expectantly, awaiting Cole's response. The Dean waited too. LaKeesha, by contrast, was quietly smirking. Her eyes shone with a subtle, amused look.

Cole was stumped. He knew nothing about handicap bathrooms. He said, " 'Excessive' ?"

"Yes. *Excessive*," the Dean repeated with irritation. "Why do we have to make every single dorm bathroom handicap accessible? Can't we, I don't know, put all the handicapped students in one dorm?"

"I think you mean '*disabled* students,' " Digby interjected in a helpful, respectful tone.

"What?" the Dean said.

" 'Disabled students.' Not 'handicapped,' " Digby said.

"Oh. Right," the Dean muttered, understanding that he had used incorrect nomenclature. " 'Disabled students.' Yes. Well, couldn't we put them all in the same dorm?"

Cole hesitated. The question seemed ... problematic. On several levels. He struggled to find the right response. "I, uh ... I suppose we, uh ..."

"*What?*" the Dean said, turning an ear to the screen as though he was having audio difficulties. "Speak louder, Cole!"

"Yeah, I'm not ... I'm not sure that's possible," Cole said.

"What's not possible?"

"To put all the disabled students in one dorm."

"Why?"

"Well ... I think it has to do with the law."

"You '*think*'?" the Dean spat in amazement. "Cole, we're talking several million dollars here! What do you mean you '*think*'?"

There was a tense pause, though LaKeesha was trying not to grin. They all were waiting on Cole. Then, with actorly finesse, he said, "*Oh*, that's right. LaKeesha worked on that part. Sorry, I spaced it. Yes—LaKeesha?"

Now looking very satisfied, pleased at this opportunity to display her professional competence, LaKeesha took over. She launched into an explanation of state and federal educational building codes and reviewed recent trends in related policies among "other upper-tier institutions."

Ten minutes into this speech, Cole's phone chimed with an incoming email. As discreetly as possible, he took a quick peek. The email was from Linni Mudge, from her Wendover account to Cole's Wendover account. They had never exchanged emails before. The subject heading read, "I think you'll enjoy this."

Cole was intrigued. Linni might be batshit bonkers but she was indisputably hot, a real head-turner. Especially for Beauville. Cole furtively tapped the email. There was no text, just a video attachment. Cole glanced back at his laptop screen. LaKeesha was still babbling away. He nodded into the camera with exaggerated interest, to let them all know he was following. Then, with his hand off camera, he muted his phone—to prevent the others from hearing any audio—and clicked on the video.

The phone screen lit up with a frenzy of movement. He saw what appeared to be a close-up of naked human bodies. Bare shoulders and a head going up and down. A ripped male torso in a reclining position. Linni had sent him a porno? *Well*, Cole thought—*that* was unexpected. His interest was definitely piqued.

To get a better look he enlarged the magnification on the screen. Everything got bigger, and then came shots of both faces. Like some grievously wounded animal, Cole began shrieking: "Aaarrrgghhhhkkk! … Aaaaarrrrggghhkkk! … Oh God! Oh God! *Nooooo!*"

From the laptop screen, Cole's colleagues stared in wonder.

"*Cole?* What is it?" Digby said. "*Cole?*"

"Oh God," Cole gasped. He had dropped the phone and was now covering his face with both hands. "Oh God!"

"Cole what happened?"

"I have to go," he said, and he exed out of the meeting.

* * *

Lucas was in his bedroom, waiting to confront his mother. Around three-thirty that morning he had awoken out on the patio with a mosquito buzzing in his ear. He saw no lights on in Tyce's place, so he went inside his own house and up to his mother's bedroom to see if she had come home. Her door was shut. He opened it and saw she was asleep in bed, alone. He went to his room but was unable to sleep. Finally he dozed off around six and woke close to ten. He went into the hall, heard the shower running in his parent's bathroom, and returned to his room.

When at last he heard his mother's bedroom door open, he shot into the hall. She was already starting down the stairs.

"Mom … *Mom!*"

She stopped. She had been hoping to slip out of the house unnoticed. Especially by Lucas.

"I know what you did last night," he said, looking down at her from the top of the stairs. "I saw you go into Tyce's house."

"*Lucas* this is complicated. Don't start. It's not as simple as you think."

"Yes it *is* simple. You cheated on Dad, and it's disgusting. *You're* disgusting!"

"Lucas, stop! Don't you judge me! You don't understand."

"Yes I *do* understand. You snuck over to Tyce's house and you screwed him. How complicated is that?"

"Lucas, *enough!*"

"How long have you been doing it?"

"This is none of your business! I don't want to talk about it! Not now."

"Are you going to tell Dad?"

"I don't know what I'm going to do … Yes. Yes, I'm going to tell him."

"I hate you! You're such a sleaze. You're a *liar*. You're a cheater!"

"Lucas, you don't understand. And some day you'll regret that. You'll regret everything you just said."

"*I'll* regret it? What about you?"

"Oh fuck off!" she snapped, then she hurried down the rest of the stairs. As she reached the bottom step, there came an agonized bellow from the basement. It was Cole. This was the moment he had recognized Oona and Tyce in the video.

Oona turned and glared up at Lucas, who was still watching her from the top of the stairs. "Did you tell him?" she shouted.

"No. But I think someone else did," the boy said, thinking of Linni filming with her phone.

Oona wanted to know what that meant, but more than this she wanted to leave the house. The place felt oppressive to her. It felt menacing and claustrophobic. She had to get away. Without a word she went to the garage, started her car, pressed the button to retract the door, backed out of the driveway, and sped off.

Lucas went into his room, seized by violent urges. He wanted to break something. He wanted to punch someone. On his nightstand was Tyce's book, *Don't Be a Bitch: From Simp to Pimp —How to Become a Dominant, High-Value Male.* Lucas grabbed it, and then he grabbed the other one from his bookshelf, *Don't Be a Bitch: Transform Your Body and Transform Your Life in Thirty Days!*, and he took them both out to the backyard. The two books then sailed through the air, over the fence, and into Tyce's pool.

"Hey, what the hell? Who's that?" called a voice. It was Tyce. He had been doing his kettlebell routine by the water.

"It's me, you asshole!" Lucas shouted. The boy knew he could go through the gate-door and confront Tyce face-to-face, but he thought better of it.

Tyce came to the fence and looked over. In a calm yet concerned voice he said, "Big man—what's going on?"

Lucas exploded, "I know what you did last night, you piece of shit. You backstabber! How could you do that? How could you screw my mother, you scumbag! Are you kidding me? I'm going to mess you up, do you understand? I swear I'm going to mess you up." As he said this, the boy had moved closer to the fence. But not too close. He stood about ten feet away.

"Lucas, you need to tone this down," Tyce said, with the top half of his face showing over the fence. "It's not what you think. Your mother and I were just talking. That's all it was."

"In the middle of the night?"

"Yes."

"Then why was Linni crying, you shithead!"

"Linni?"

"Yeah. She was standing by your pool the whole time, filming you guys with her phone and crying."

Tyce winced and looked away.

Lucas's soccer ball lay in the grass a few paces from him. He retrieved it and fired it at Tyce's head. Tyce ducked and the ball flew past him and landed in the pool, along with the two books.

"I'm gonna mess you up!" Lucas hollered as he went back into the house. "I'm gonna mess you up, you bastard!"

* * *

As her car sped down Lilac Lane, Oona realized she didn't know where she was going. She pulled to the side of the street to think. Moments later she reached for her phone and sent Tyce a text, "I think Cole knows about us." She waited. There was no reply. She was trembling with emotion: frustration, worry, excitement, hope. She decided to call him direct. It rang several times and went to voicemail. "Tyce darling, call me," she said. "Call me soon."

She remained where she was, seated in her parked car, impatiently awaiting his response. "Oh great," she grumbled, now seeing Maeve Cutty. Maeve was walking her golden retriever, Precious. They were on the sidewalk, coming in Oona's direction. When Maeve noticed Oona, she made a pleasant but curious face as if to say, "Why are you sitting alone in your car a block away from your house?"

In no mood to explain, Oona gave her neighbor a perfunctory wave and an unfriendly look. Maeve's pleasant expression vanished. She returned the wave, and she and Precious continued on.

Oona's phone rang and she shuddered with joy. She picked it up, looked at the screen, then angrily yelled, "Damn him!" It was Cole. She muted the ringtone and a minute later the phone buzzed with a new voicemail. Oona ignored it. Cole's whiny belligerent voice was the last thing she wanted to hear. Then her phone chimed with a new email. This too was from Cole. Oona sighed with exasperation. For some reason he had forwarded her an email from Linni.

" 'I think you'll enjoy this'?" Oona said quizzically to herself as she read the subject heading. She opened the email and saw it had a video attachment. Now curious, she clicked on it.

"Eeew," she said, seeing it was a porno. What the hell was Linni thinking, Oona thought? Sending a porno—to *Cole*? It seemed very strange. But as she looked closer and got a good glimpse of the two porno performers, Oona shrieked. "Oh no! Oh no! OH NOOO!"

* * *

After she had sufficiently recovered from the shock of seeing herself performing a sex act on a video that was being passed around on the internet, Oona got out of her car and walked toward Tyce's house. Hoping not to be seen by any of her family, she covertly cut across Tyce's front lawn and went straight to his front door. She rang the buzzer. Then she rang it again.

Behind her on quiet Lilac Lane a car came to a stop. Oona nervously turned around and saw Melissa Kim. She had pulled over on the opposite side of the street, across from Oona's house. Melissa lowered her window as Rosa got out of the backseat with her backpack.

"Hey, how are you?" Melissa called out with a smile and a jovial wave.

"Hey Mom!" Rosa said, now crossing the street in Oona's direction.

Tyce opened his door. He was in snug-fitting shorts and a black T-shirt. He was not smiling.

Oona cringed. She gave him a brief, apologetic look, then turned back to Melissa and said, "I'm good … How are things?"

"Oh, you know, busy. The kids had fun. Lots of giggling last night. It's always nice to see Rosa."

"Hi Mrs. Perrot!" Carrie Kim cried out, leaning across her mother and waving from the passenger seat.

"It's 'Dr. Pudding,' " Melissa corrected her.

"Oh sorry! Hi *Dr. Pudding!*"

The Kims had moved up to Beauville from New Jersey a year ago during the height of the pandemic, and were still getting to know people.

"Hi Carrie," Oona said halfheartedly.

"We should have you over soon, you and Cole," Melissa said from across the street.

"Sounds great," Oona said, forcing a smile. "Just call me. And thanks for having Rosa over."

Melissa and Carrie waved goodbye and drove off. Holding her backpack, Rosa had come up Tyce's walkway to the front door.

"Hi Tyce!" she said brightly.

"How are you Rosa?" he said grimly.

"Good … What are you guys doing?" Rosa said, now with curiosity.

Tyce looked at Oona with a just-detectable air of annoyance. He would let her answer the question.

Oona hesitated. "Oh, I … have to talk to him about something."

"What?" the girl said.

"About … that *tree*," Oona said quickly, finding that it was becoming easier and easier for her to lie. "You know, that one that leans into our backyard."

"Oh yeah," Rosa said, and to Tyce she added, "My dad said it could fall and hit our property, and that he could sue you."

Tyce looked sternly at Oona.

"Rosa honey, I'll meet you inside," she said.

"I can wait," the girl said, smiling at Tyce. Then she said, "Tyce, last night, me and my friend Carrie, that girl that was just here, we watched some of your videos on MyToobs. We *really* liked them."

"Oh yeah? Well that's cool. Thank you, Rosa."

The girl blushed, her face glowing.

"*Rosa*, I'll see you inside," Oona said firmly.

This did not please the girl. She gave her mother an offended look and stayed put.

"Rosa—*move!*"

The child vacillated. She considered her options, and understood they were few. Deciding it best to concede defeat—at least for now—she raised her chin, assumed an expression of righteous indignation, and stormed off with her backpack.

Once they were alone, Oona said, "I'm so glad to see you. It's such a disaster." She started forward, wanting to enter the house and get out of public view. Tyce, however, did not seem to be in a hospitable mood. He remained in the door, blocking her way.

"Can I come in?" she said with a puzzled look.

He made a slight eye roll, but did not move.

"Darling, it's important," she said. "Did you see the video? Cole knows."

Tyce winced. "Oona—*please*. Don't call me 'darling.' Really."

"Oh … I'm sorry," she said, stung by this.

"It's fine," he said, though his expression made it clear that it wasn't fine. "And no, I haven't seen the video. Not yet."

"Then you know about it?"

"Yes."

"It was Linni," Oona said spitefully. "That sneaky bitch. She sent it to Cole, and he sent it to me. Do you want to see it?"

"No, I *don't*," Tyce said with extreme annoyance. Then, grudgingly, he said, "Maybe I should. I need to know what I'm dealing with."

"We can't do it here," Oona said, warily glancing over at her house. "Let's go inside."

At last, he relented. He stood aside and Oona entered the house.

The front room had a cathedral ceiling and lots of light, but it was mostly unfurnished and rarely used. Oona expected they would go into the back room by the pool or possibly up to his bedroom, but Tyce remained planted by the door.

"What's wrong?" she said.

"Let me see the video," he said.

She gave him her phone and he watched no more than twenty seconds of the clip. He shook his head, grimacing, but said nothing. He returned the phone with a peeved look.

"Are you mad?" she said.

"Of course I'm mad."

"What are we going to do?"

" '*We*'?"

"Yes. Tyce, let's sit down. Let's go somewhere more comfortable."

"Oona, I talked to Lucas," Tyce said bluntly.

Oona frowned. "What did he say? Is he the one who told you about the video?"

"Yeah. He saw Linni filming us. He's really upset. I feel pretty shitty."

"I do too. It's going to be rough on them. All of them."

"What is?" Tyce said with a questioning look.

"What do you think?" Oona said, as though it was obvious.

"I don't know—what do *you* think?" Tyce said, as though it *wasn't* obvious.

"Well ... *us*," Oona said.

" '*Us*'?"

"Yes."

Watching her with a tensed brow, Tyce said nothing.

"You know I can't go back," Oona said, as though this too was obvious.

"What do you mean? Why not?"

This baffled her. "*What?*"

"Why can't you go back?" he said, losing patience.

"Because I *can't*. Not *now*. It's over. And plus, I don't want to ... I want to be with you."

Tyce laughed. It came out abruptly, with mirth in his eyes. But he quickly restrained himself and made a serious face. "Oona, that's not a good idea."

"Why not?" she said, astonished by this and wounded by his laugh. "I don't understand."

He paused, and she stepped forward to touch his face but he flinched back. She stopped short and withdrew her hand. "I want to be with you," she repeated, now looking even more hurt.

"What do you mean, 'be with me'?" he said, both surprised and perturbed.

"Just be with you," she said. "We can spend more time together now. We don't have to hide."

"Oona, that's not something I'm interested in."

"What are you talking about? *Why?*" she said with distress.

" '*Why*'?"

"Yes, why?" she wanted to know.

"Well, for one reason, Lucas. I feel bad."

"*Lucas?*" she said, flabbergasted.

"Yeah, he's a good kid. I like him."

Oona gaped at Tyce. "You like ... *Lucas?* What about *me?*"

"Of course I like you. But Oona, let's be real. You're married. You have kids. It's not something I want to be involved with."

The words stunned her, walloped her, and she stared in mute bewilderment. Then, rethinking her tactics, she said, "I'm not saying we have to get *married*. Or even ... live together. I just want to spend more time with you. Get to know you better."

"No. I'm sorry," he said, shaking his head. "I'm not looking for anything right now. With you or anyone else. I'm actually thinking of moving to Texas."

Oona was staggered. "Texas?"

"Yeah. Or maybe Florida. I'm hearing Austin is played out."

Oona was finding it hard to breathe. She wanted to sit down. "But ... I thought ..."

"I'm bored with New Hampshire," he said. "I've outgrown it. I'm starting to think my career is only just beginning. I think I could be much bigger."

Looking at his face, looking into his eyes, Oona saw no sympathy there. She saw no tenderness or concern for her, no sensitivity or compassion for her situation. It was as though he had no comprehension of all she had jeopardized ... for *him*. In fact, there seemed to be no feeling there at all.

"I should go," she murmured. She gave him a final, plaintive look, a last-chance silent plea, as if hoping he might object. As if hoping he might change his mind and say, "No, hold on. *Stay.* I didn't mean it. We'll work this out."

But he did not change his mind, and he did not ask her to stay. He just watched her, silently, his expression firm and unmoving.

Shocked by this, shocked by it all, Oona fell into a daze. Without another word she walked past him to the door and walked out of the house. Outside the sun was bright and the street was quiet.

There was no traffic. No cars, no people. Then, from above, came the harsh cawing of a crow. It startled Oona. It gave her a fright. She stopped still and looked up into the one nearby tree, a tall leafy maple. She scanned its branches but saw no bird. The crow cawed again, abrasively and even mockingly, but still Oona could not see it. She rushed down to the sidewalk. Her house was to the right, but she turned left and hurried off in the direction of her car.

* * *

That evening, Cole was thoroughly tanked. He had been drinking all day, robustly and with determined persistence. His glass —he was now using a beer mug rather than a wine glass, as it seemed a more efficient delivery device—had not left his side even once, not even on trips to the bathroom. It was now past eight p.m. and he was nearly finished with bottle number three of the Stepfield Valley Malbec. Given all that was happening, his unquenchable thirst was maybe not a surprise.

He had begun the day thinking his wife was having an affair with an oversized rubber sex toy, only to find out that she was in fact having an affair with a real-life person, and that that real-life person was in fact his real-life enemy. He had also begun the day secure in his position at work and his expectation that he would soon be made Head of the Wendover College Office of Student Affairs. Now, he wasn't so sure on either account. That afternoon Cole had sent Digby an email apologizing for his agonized outburst and unceremonious departure from that morning's meeting. He claimed he had just gotten news that his favorite uncle had died in a "sudden automobile accident," and that grief had gotten the better of him. Digby, always a prompt and punctilious e-correspondent, had not replied. It was a bad sign. As for Oona, she too had not replied. Cole had called and texted and emailed her multiple times but with no results.

He had then texted his kids to see if they knew anything. Lucas responded with a terse "No," but Rosa wrote that she had last seen her mother at Tyce's house.

"Tyce's house? When?" Cole had immediately typed back.

"This morning. When I got home from Carrie Kim's house."

"What was she doing?"

"She was talking about the tree in the backyard. The one that might fall on our property. Are you getting a divorce?"

Seeing that last word, "divorce," Cole panicked. "Why would you ask that?" he quickly wrote. "Did somebody say something?"

"No. I just have a bad feeling," the girl replied. She was thinking about how Tyce was always kissing her mother, and how her mother was always grumpy and looking at her phone, and how her mother was now going over to Tyce's house.

"No, Rosa, there will be no divorce," Cole wrote back.

For him, this was the most disturbing thought of all, even worse than Oona cheating on him with Tyce Creamer. A divorce was not something Cole wanted. It was not something he could *afford*.

Then, around nine p.m., his phone rang. It was Oona.

Bizarrely, given his numerous earlier attempts to contact her, when he had sent one angry, desperate, and increasingly incoherent message after another, Cole considered not answering. He felt it might punish her in some way. Teach her a lesson. But after the first two rings he quickly picked up.

"Hi," he said evenly, neither friendly nor unfriendly.

"Hello Cole," Oona said coldly.

"Hi," he pointlessly repeated.

"I got your messages," she said frostily and with impatience, as if she wanted to get this over with as quickly as possible.

"Yes … Where are you?"

"At a hotel."

"A *hotel*? Why? *Where*?"

"It doesn't matter where."

"But why?"

"I need to think."

"You need to 'think'? *Now?* Couldn't you have maybe done that *before* you decided to leave?"

"Cole, I'm warning you. If you get sarcastic, I'll hang up."

There was a long silence.

Then, with raw wounded honesty, Cole said, "How could you do this, Oona? How could you do it? How could you screw Tyce Cream-boy? Mr. Redneck Steroids? How could you? Do you understand what this has done to me? My *own wife* screwing shit-face Cream-face Cream-shit?"

"Wow, you're drunk. What a surprise," Oona said drily. "You always were cool under pressure."

"*Don't change the subject!*" he screeched. "This isn't about me, it's about *you!*"

Oona said nothing.

"I can't stop seeing that video," Cole said, his eyes filling with tears. "And I only watched it once! ... Or twice ... It keeps playing in my head, over and over. I can't unsee it! I hate you, Oona. I fricking hate you."

"That was *Linni,*" Oona said, trying hard but not quite managing to sound outraged. "I did *not* make that video, Cole. Linni is trying to ruin my life! She's crazy!"

"That's true, Oona," Cole said. "You didn't make that video. You just starred in it."

"One more insult, Cole, and I'm hanging up."

After another silence he said, "I've never hurt like this before, Oona. I didn't know it was possible. I trusted you. I've always trusted you. I never thought you could do something like this."

"You've known I wasn't happy," she said firmly.

"I did?" Cole said, flummoxed.

"For years I've been unhappy."

He was astounded. "*What?* For *years?* And why am I just hearing about this now?"

"Oh come on," she chastised him. "Hasn't it been obvious?"

"Oona, what the hell are you talking about? You never said *anything*! Ever! And now you're telling me you've been unhappy for *years*?"

She did not reply.

"Oona, how was I supposed to know you weren't happy if you never said anything? How was I supposed to know?"

"It's because you're so selfish."

"*Me?*" he said, stunned by her audacity. "*I'm* selfish?"

"Oh God, are you kidding me? You're the most selfish person I know."

"*What the hell is this?*" he shouted. "Why do you keep blaming me? Am *I* the one in that video? Because for some reason, I thought it was *you*! 'Dr. Oona Pudding, Blowjob Queen'!"

"Cole, I swear—"

"And by the way," he bellowed, now losing it, "when was the last time you gave *me* a blowjob? Twenty years ago?"

"That's it, I'm hanging up!"

"Go ahead you slut!" he shouted. "Hang up you whore! *Hang up!*"

And she did.

TEN

Late the next morning Cole vacated the basement. He could no longer afford the luxury of pretending to be gravely ill. His position was precarious, both at home and at the office, and he knew he had to act. It was a matter of self-preservation. After cooking himself breakfast, he went up to his bedroom, shaved, showered, donned what he called his "wage-slave uniform"—khakis and a button-down oxford shirt—and drove to the college.

He found Digby in his office. Unlike Cole, Digby was not wearing a mask or face shield. His dour visage and jiggly jowls were on full display.

"Hi Dig," Cole said timidly from the opened doorway.

Digby looked up from his computer. His expression tensed uncordially. "Ah … *Cole*," he said meaningfully and without surprise, as if he had been expecting him. He then took several long moments to look Cole up and down, as if perhaps to make sure he was properly attired and not wearing, say, a Jizcums concert T-shirt with crusty vomit stains. "I take it you're no longer sick?" he finally said.

The sarcasm was faint but unmistakable. Helpless to fight back, Cole merely said, "No. I tested negative this morning." This was untrue. Cole hadn't thought to test himself, but no matter.

"I see. Very good," Digby said. "If you'd like, and if you feel comfortable, you can take off your mask and shield. As I mentioned yesterday, President Hogg has removed the mask mandate for all college staff. The booster mandate, of course, remains in effect."

Still standing in the doorway, so as to maintain a safe social distance, Cole hesitated. Removing his mask and shield seemed, well, *unsafe*. But he did it nonetheless. Given his predicament, conforming to the new normal seemed the smart move.

"And how is your family doing?" Digby asked with solemn concern.

"They're OK," Cole said uneasily, sensing yet another smidgen of sarcasm.

"Grieving?" Digby said.

" 'Grieving'?" Cole said.

"For your uncle. The one who died in the 'sudden automobile accident'?"

Cole nodded, now remembering. "Yes. We're all pretty devastated. The funeral is next week ..." Cole paused, giving Digby a moment to offer his condolences. But Digby said nothing. Instead he made a cryptic nano-smile, betraying just the slightest hint of mirth. Cole thought it best to push on. "About yesterday. The meeting," he said. "I'm *extremely* sorry, Dig. Emotion got the better of me. This ... this *tragedy* was a great shock. I hope you and the Dean can understand how unexpected it was, and how hurtful. He was like a father to me. But I'll get through this. I just want you to know that I'm grateful for your support. Grateful to you *and* the Dean."

Digby's cryptic nano-smile became a tad less cryptic and a tad less nano. There seemed to be, or so Cole thought, a brutal gleam in the old man's eyes, a sadistic sparkle. "That's good to hear, Cole," he said. "Now, why don't you shut the door and have a seat."

The words gave Cole a chill. But he did as he was told. He shut the door, took a seat, and submissively waited for Digby to begin. Digby, however, was in no hurry to begin. He seemed, in fact, to be savoring something. Meekly observing his boss, Cole noted a certain blithesome liveliness about Digby. In addition to the gleaming, sparkling eyes, the old man's normally pale doughy face had taken on a ruddy, vigorous cast, and his long, bony, and usually inert frame now seemed to tremble and pulsate with a barely restrained bliss.

"You know, Cole," Digby said at last, "when I took you into this office six years ago, I knew I was taking a chance. The hiring of faculty spouses for staff positions can sometimes prove, shall we say, *problematic*. Occasionally there can be a sense of ... entitlement. But in your case, my feeling was that you would work out. Indeed, I fully *expected* that you would work out. Were there warning signs? Yes. When Dr. Pudding first arrived on campus, you were given a job in the Admissions Office. You were also given, what, one adjunct course per semester?"

"Yes. In the philosophy department. To teach in the Extension School."

"But that didn't last."

"I'm really not a teacher," Cole said, feeling a pinch defensive. "I don't enjoy it. I prefer research."

"Yes. *Research*. Though you didn't finish your dissertation."

"There were good reasons for that."

"Right. Your thesis adviser *died*. A 'freak golfing accident,' I heard. And you weren't able to find another to take you on. Your position, evidently, was 'too radical'—as you yourself told me. You were writing on, what was it, Nietzsche and totalitarianism?"

" 'Nietzsche's Last Man and the Totalitarian Impulse.' "

"Yes, that's it. An intriguing topic. A topical topic, perhaps. But you never completed it."

"I got married. Oona got teaching jobs. I followed her from one school to the next."

"I understand. These things happen," Digby said in a not unkind tone. "But after a couple of years in Admissions, you were passed over for promotion, and you applied to work in this office.

At your interview you told me you were 'looking for a new challenge.' To me, it seemed genuine, and your boss at the time, Cass Sissom, gave you a good recommendation. And so I thought to myself, Well, he's nearly forty years old, things didn't work out in graduate school, things didn't quite work out in the Admissions Office, he has two kids, a successful wife, surely he's ready to *buckle down* and commit to something. Surely he's tired of drifting and, well, *failing*. So I hired you, and I was convinced it was the right move. I was even convinced that I had done a *good deed*. And Cole, I want to tell you—I have regretted that decision from the very first week you stepped into this office."

Digby paused. His rheumy, red-rimmed eyes were shining exultantly. The inner bliss that he had been struggling to restrain now broke forth in a triumphant glowing grin. This was, Cole could see, a great moment for Digby. Perhaps one of the greatest moments of his life.

"And so, Cole, it is now my absolute pleasure," the old man went on, "to tell you what a lazy, arrogant, resentful, unscrupulous, and yes, *supremely* self-entitled man you are. You show not one iota of respect for me, your colleagues, this office, or this college. You look down your nose at everyone and every*thing*. Your sense of superiority is breathtaking. You spend more of your work day on social media than you do on the projects I've assigned you. As for the Multisex Bathrooms report, I know for a fact that your input was essentially nil. Nada. *Zilch*. It was LaKeesha and LaKeesha alone who produced and oversaw that project. And I also know, and *have known*, how you've been delegating work—*your* work—to the entire junior staff and even to Victoria Fish, for years!" Victoria Fish was the department's sole secretary, an elderly woman who, like Digby, was in her eighth decade. "You have abused your authority, *and* my trust, for too long. I know the lockdown and working from home may have encouraged lax practices in all of us. But *you*, Cole, *you* were lax *before* the lockdown!

"And yet despite your continued lack of respect and commitment to the Office of Student Affairs, you had the temerity, the brazenness, the *chutzpah*, to apply for my job! Did you really think, Cole, that I would let someone like *you* take over the office that I have run and nurtured and *cherished* for over thirty years? Did you *really* think that?"

An expectant look came into Digby's heated eyes. He was awaiting an answer.

Cole blinked and said, in a not-quite-convinced tone, "Yes."

"Well, then," Digby continued with savage glee, "it might interest you to know that the hiring committee has made its decision. The new Head of the Office of Student Affairs is going to be ... LaKeesha Lovette. That's right, Cole. The Dean was *very* impressed with LaKeesha—her work on the report, her professionalism, her grit and determination in overcoming her underprivileged background. All of which means, Cole, that your new boss is going to be one of the junior staff. One of the very people whose lives you've made difficult over the past few years. I wonder how *that's* going to turn out, hmm?"

Cole lowered his eyes. Everything was falling apart. His marriage. His "career." His life. It was all collapsing, imploding all around him. He was quiet for some time.

Digby remained quiet too, watching Cole with darkly jubilant eyes. It really *was* one of the greatest moments of his life.

At last Cole looked up, and in a soft, defeated voice he said, "Is it because she's black?"

"*What?*" Digby gasped, the jubilance instantly vanishing from his face.

"Is it because she's black?"

Digby was incredulous. "Because she's ... *black?*"

"Yes. That's why we hired her," Cole said, still in a mute, downcast tone. "Because she's black."

"Cole, *really!*"

"And *you're* the one who said we had to do it," Cole said, now looking Digby straight in the eye. "You said the President's Office said 'no whites.' No whites, no Asians, no Latinos. I still have the email."

Digby's expression grew cautious and deliberative. With some alarm he was considering his legal position. Were he and the college in a potential *bind*?

"I can prove it," Cole said, growing bolder.

"Prove *what*?" Digby said defensively.

"That this is racism, Digby ... It's *racism!*"

Digby was astounded. "Cole, this is beneath even *you!*" he spluttered, his jowls jiggling with indignation.

"No, Dig, it's not! It's *discrimination*, is what it is! Blatant discrimination! *Textbook* discrimination!" Cole said fervently. He was becoming more and more inflamed, feeling that old radical fire rising up, feeling that heady zealous burn of rancor and moral offense. "You're taking that job away from me because of my race, and most likely because of my gender—because I am a *white man!* That's right, Digby—because I am a *white man! None of which is my fault!* Well let me tell you something Dig, I will not permit it! I will *not* permit it!" he shouted.

"Cole this is outrageous!"

"No, Digby, *hatred* is outrageous! *Hatred* is outrageous, do you hear me? It is the great scourge of this country, and I for one will not be victimized by your hatred or the hatred of this college. Not anymore! I am done bending over, Digby! Do you hear me? I am *done*! *I will NOT Bendover*, never again!" Cole wildly declared. He had become as if possessed, nearly levitating off his chair. The veins were bulging on his forehead, spittle was flying from his lips. In his eyes there flashed a fearsome and even maniacal rage as he exclaimed, "I will not be bullied, or demeaned, or *professionally assassinated*, Digby! Not by you or by Wendover or by any other race-baiting bigots! I oppose hatred and intolerance in all its ugly forms, and I will stand up for myself and I will fight you *and* the college whatever the cost! Do you hear me, Digby? *Whatever the cost!*"

"OK, I've heard enough," Digby said, reaching for his phone. "I'm calling security."

* * *

Lucas was lying on his bed, midafternoon, when Tyce called. For the past few days the boy had been isolating, hiding out in his room with the door closed and not wanting to see or talk to anyone. He was depressed. He was angry. He was confused. And while it surprised and maybe even fractionally gladdened him to see Tyce's name appear on his pealing phone, Lucas did not pick up. He did, however, immediately listen to the voicemail.

"Lucas, it's Tyce. I want to talk to you. I want to apologize for what happened with, uh, your mother. It was wrong. I made a mistake, a *bad* mistake, and I'm sorry. But I want to tell you in person. Call me when you can."

This only exacerbated Lucas's frazzled emotional state. Hanging up the phone, he felt somehow even angrier and even more confused than before. He had really liked Tyce. He had learned a lot from him, more than from anyone he had ever known. Through Tyce's books and videos the boy had learned about the importance of fitness and healthy food, hard work and ambition, confidence and self-reliance, and about how to meet and attract and talk to girls (at least theoretically). Nobody else had ever taught him any of these things. Not his mother or his teachers and certainly not his father. And in fact, all he had been taught at home and especially at school was that males like him were racist and oppressive and basically the cause of every evil in the world. And for a time, Lucas had believed it. He had believed all of it. And so was it any surprise that throughout his short life he had been passive and depressed? Soft and reserved? But then he met Tyce and everything changed. Now for the first time Lucas was truly excited to be alive. He was excited to be a man and excited to be himself. He was hopeful and optimistic, eager to charge into life and see and experience all it had to offer.

But Tyce had betrayed him in the worst possible way. The most despicable way. Tyce had banged his mother! It was the most basic and most grievous violation of the bro code. It was too much for the boy to forgive.

He typed out a text, "Screw you Tyce, you backstabber. I believed in you. You're a scum. I hope you die." He read the message over, and he read it over again. He deleted "I hope you die," and replaced it with, "Our friendship is finished."

He sent the text and a minute later his phone rang. It was Tyce. Again Lucas did not pick up.

In the voicemail Tyce said, "Lucas, I know you're mad, and I know you're young, but you're acting like a little bitch. Real men talk things out. Face-to-face. We don't hide. We don't send angry text messages or start screaming and throwing hissy fits. That's what women do, and beta men. You're better than that. I know you are. Now I'm not going to call you again, because in my book, two calls is enough. But as I said before, I'm sorry, and I want to apologize. You can come over anytime or I can meet you somewhere. You have my number."

* * *

That afternoon Rosa texted her mother, "When are you coming home?"

An hour later came the response, "Not today. I'll see you soon."

"When?" Rosa promptly wrote back.

"Maybe tomorrow," Oona replied.

"Are you and Dad getting a divorce?"

Ten minutes later came the response, "I don't know. I'll talk to you tomorrow."

"Dad said you're not," Rosa instantly replied.

"Not what?"

"Not getting a divorce."

"Rosa, I don't know."

Fifteen minutes later Rosa typed, "Who's cooking supper tonight?" It was after five and the girl was getting hungry.

"Ask your father," came the response.

"He's not here."

"Where is he?"

"I don't know. He didn't answer my text. He went to work today."

"I'm sure he'll be back soon."

"I'm hungry."

"Have some cereal."

* * *

Cole was now on the hard stuff. He was nursing his third double whiskey on the rocks, seated at the bar of a local dive. It was called "Froggie's Tap Room," and was a real shithole. A home away from home for local rednecks and wife-beaters, Cole thought. He had known about the place for years but had never come in. Why would he? But today, following his humiliating ejection from the Office of Student Affairs—two uniformed Wendover security guards had physically removed Cole from campus—he had not wanted to go home or anywhere else that he might see people he knew. So he had thought of Froggie's.

It was a great call, as it turned out. The place was quiet, dark, and mostly empty—an ideal spot for Cole to get steadily crocked and ponder how his life had gone so wrong, how his life, in fact, had turned into a stinking pile of *merde*. For it now seemed highly probable that he might very soon be both divorced *and* unemployed. The dreaded double whammy. Oh yes, Cole could see disaster was near. It was looming up ahead. It was waiting down the road, and it might come soon and quick.

Financially—and by now that was his primary concern, the one that dwarfed all the others—Cole knew he was screwed. He had no personal savings to speak of, and nothing of any real value except for his record collection, which of course he would never sell. It was too important to him, too much a *part* of him, far more even than his books. Yet without any money, and especially without a job, he would have trouble finding a decent place to live, should Oona indeed send him packing. What then? Would he end up in some flophouse? Or maybe the YMCA? Did the YMCA even still rent out rooms? And what would he do for work? Would he become a cashier at DeSanti's supermarket? A customer-greeter at Giganta-Mart? A line cook at Pepe's Burritos? The only full-time employment Cole had ever had was in the university setting, and the thought of going back to something like *that* was too depressing even to consider. Better a glass of strychnine or a bullet to the head than to end up in another Office of Student Affairs.

The idea with Wendover, the sole reason he had stayed there and now hoped to take Digby's job, was that Cole knew it was his one and only chance at a golden ticket. As department Head he would clear a hundred-plus grand a year, not to mention increase his already very generous, European-level employment benefits. As for the work itself, though boring and tedious and utterly soul-annihilating, it would be a breeze. For if Cole had learned nothing else in his too-many years in the groves of academe, working in libraries and alumni offices in addition to admissions and student affairs offices, first at Oberlong University as a grad student, then at Fairport College where Oona had held a junior faculty post, and finally at Wendover where she was offered a tenured position, it was that the higher up the administrative ladder you go, the easier and the less stressful the work. And after all the shit he had eaten in his life as a peon in various university craphouses, Cole felt he had earned the right to a cushy sinecure. The plan was to get Digby's job, then delegate, delegate, delegate, and ride that baby all the way to his earliest possible retirement, at which point he could finally begin to live ...

Or at least, that *had* been the plan. It was Plan A for which Cole had no Plan B. With a heavy sigh he raised his hand and asked for another drink.

"Are you driving?" the bartender said, making it clear by her reproving look that four double whiskeys in less than two hours might pose a legal headache for herself and Froggie's Tap Room. She was middle-aged, a little older than Cole, and had leathery, tanning-salon skin and big hair like someone from the Eighties. Cole wanted to ask if she had ever appeared in a heavy metal video, but he decided she might not appreciate the inference. He stuck to the topic instead.

"No. I'm on foot," he lied. "I live nearby."

She gave him the booze and Cole returned to his cogitations. He wondered firstly about the fallout of a divorce. The courts, he knew, would give Oona the house. That was a given—even though Oona was the cheater. Even though Oona was the porn-star cocksucker. That's right, Oona goes down on Bro2Bro with Tyce Creamer and old faithful Cole has to move into a cardboard box down by the Merrimack River. What a country, he thought. Deep throat your neighbor and the state rewards you with sole ownership of your house.

With his inhibitions slipping fast, Cole broke into a loud chant, pumping a first in the air as he shouted, "U-S-A! U-S-A! U-S-A!"

The big-haired barkeep gave him a baffled look. But two guys sitting in a booth behind Cole cheered and clapped for what they thought was a spontaneous outburst of patriotism, while a glazed-eyed drunk at the other end of the bar held up his thumb, offering a silent yet emphatic sign of approval.

Cole's feigned devotion to the country of his birth quickly faded, however, as he now wondered how much alimony he might get out of Oona. Of course she made far more than he did. Her salary as a tenured professor was more than three times his own as a lowly administrative flunky, and there was also the money from her books, two of which had been translated into multiple foreign languages, including Urdu. Hence their nice house. Hence their nice cars. Hence their once-regular, pre-pandemic overseas vacations and the kids' private schools. But what if Oona hired some slick, misandrist lawyer? What if things turned ugly and Cole got nothing? He'd be screwed, that's what. He'd be up *merde*'s creek without a paddle. Up shit's *merde* without a paddle. Up shit's creek without a *merde*. His lack of options, his lack of resources, his lack of any sort of power at all, was infuriating to Cole, and in his mind he lashed out at his wife. He blamed and chastised and berated Oona using all sorts of names and descriptions, terms that are too coarse and offensive for books and films and social media but which were now appearing with more and more regularity in Cole's head. His impulse was to down the rest of his drink and smash the glass against the wall, but he knew Ms. Heavy Metal Hair behind the bar would not approve. So Cole sipped and smoldered, sipped and smoldered, and soon his fury moved on to another target.

That's right—*Creamer*. *Creamer* who had seduced Cole's wife. *Creamer* who had likely told Oona to leave Cole and move into a hotel. *Creamer* who was probably pushing for a divorce. And if *Creamer* was responsible for all of this, which he most certainly was, then *Creamer* was also responsible for Cole losing his shit during the meeting yesterday and for Cole going off on Digby today, for none of that would have happened if Oona had not been screwing *Creamer*. The man was evil and was obviously trying to destroy Cole's life. This was personal, Cole felt. This was *real*. It was now life or death.

Cole took out his phone and checked his email. He was still waiting to hear back from Chirper, FaceFace, Amazin!, and My-Toobs in regard to his "Cancel Creamer" requests. But there was nothing. Not a single response.

To Cole's right a guy came and sat two stools down. He was tall, overweight, and roughly Cole's age. He wore straight-leg dad jeans and high-top basketball sneakers. He had a rough, oafish look about him. A townie, of course, and probably a Froggie's regular, Cole guessed.

"Hey Heidi," the guy said as Ms. Heavy Metal Hair came over.

"Hey Walter," she said.

And just perceptibly, Cole grinned. He was pleased by his perspicacity. The guy *was* a regular. A Froggie's Tap Room regular. Cole found it very amusing.

After he ordered a beer and a burger, the man named Walter noticed Cole was watching him. Walter nodded and said, in a neutral voice, "How's it goin'?"

Cole became guarded. "Hi," he tentatively replied.

Walter turned his attention to the television behind the bar. It was tuned to CNBM but the sound was off. A blow-dried anchor was droning on to the camera while the chyron below her read, "Vaccine Hesitancy Caused by Disinformation."

"These assholes," Walter grumbled, loud enough for Cole to hear. He then glanced at Cole to see if he might agree.

Cole understood this to mean the townie was open to a little conversation, a bit of barroom palaver. But he said nothing.

Walter tried again, now speaking directly to Cole. "I can't take the news anymore," he said, his expression both affable and resigned. "It's all lies these days. Propaganda. All of it, you know?"

Cole merely smiled, noncommittally, then made a slight shrug. The lifelong radical in him could of course relate to the townie's sentiment. Cole had begun reading Marx, Nietzsche, and Lenin in junior high, followed soon after by Saul Alinsky and Howard Zinn, and from high school on he had taken it for granted that the corporate media was incontestably corrupt, the PR organ of the country's oligarchic overlords. But by around 2008, and especially since the outbreak of the pandemic, Cole's position changed. To him it now seemed, well, *reactionary* to criticize the corporate media. Especially if it was a story about the vaccines.

Undaunted by Cole's silence, Walter continued, and it appeared he was just getting started. "You know how much money these news networks get from the pharmaceutical companies? And from the government and these transnational NGOs—the same NGOs that control the UN? Millions. *Many* millions. Maybe even *billions*. And everything you hear from these jokers —about 'safe and effective' and 'two weeks to flatten the curve' and 'let's destroy the economy to save grandma'—is bullshit. Every word. They're a bunch of criminals. Hell, from what I'm hearing, this virus might even be man-made. A kind of bioweapon that they intentionally let loose."

Cole tried not to laugh. The townie's colossal imbecility, combined with his unabashed willingness to display it in such a public way, was priceless. There was nothing funnier, Cole felt, than the fool who does not realize he is a fool. Wanting to goad the guy a bit further, he said, "You don't believe in The Science?"

Walter gave Cole a suspicious look. He detected a faint whiff of mockery in his words. "I *do* believe in science," he said, becoming noticeably less affable. "Which is why I think all of these bastards are crooks. The more boosters people get, the sicker they get. I've seen it myself, with family and friends. And Gerbyll and all the rest of them know it, yet they keep pushing the stuff."

Cole kept his mouth shut. He was in foreign territory, and this working-class lardass looked potentially dangerous. There was no need to poke the bear, he felt. He sipped his drink and looked at the television.

Walter also kept his mouth shut. He had no interest in debating the vaccines with this candy-ass liberal in his khakis and button-down shirt. For whatever reason, these people just didn't get it, he felt. They had degrees and influence but no common sense.

Heidi came with his beer.

"Hey could you put on the game?" he called after her as she
darted off to tend to another patron. "I can't watch this damn
news. And turn on the volume."

"Yep. In a minute," she said, not turning back.

Walter took a good swig of his beer, watching the silent TV
screen. Now there was footage of men in black tactical gear—
helmets and bulletproof vests—storming into an office building
with raised assault rifles. The chyron read, "Swatting: A Growing
Threat Among Right-Wing Extremists."

"Those lying bastards," Walter snarled, his eyes fixed to the
screen. "It's those millennial punks!" Then, because there was no
one else seated nearby, he turned back to Cole and said, "That
same thing happened to me."

"You were *swatted*?" Cole said.

"Yeah. I nearly got killed—in my own damn house! The cops
busted through my door and charged into my living room while I
was watching the fricking Celtics. Black helmets, guns pointed,
shouting, the whole thing. Beauville PD. And I *know* those
guys!"

"What happened?"

"Some asshole called them up and said they heard shooting
and a woman screaming for help. Of course it was all bullshit. I
had some problems with these left-wing jackasses a couple years
back, a bunch of unemployed idiots who still live with their parents, and this is how they harass me ... It's a long story," he
added, and sipped from his beer.

Cole was intrigued. On the television there now came additional footage. This time a SWAT team charged into a podcast
studio and tackled a terrified subject. With extreme violence they
dropped the guy to the floor, no doubt inflicting grave bodily
harm as well as severe mental distress.

Yes, indeed—Cole was *very* intrigued. "But how do they do
that?" he said with genuine curiosity to his townie bar-mate.

"How do they not get caught? With caller ID and everything else?"

"Burner phone," Walter said with authority. "It's pretty easy. Half of these kids today have them. Mostly for drugs."

"Hmm," Cole mused as he turned back to the screen. "Very interesting."

* * *

When he finally staggered out of Froggie's Tap Room, Cole was determined to get a burner phone. He would drive over to Giganta-Mart and look into prepaid disposable options. Ideally, so as to avoid security cameras and other potential problems, he would find some stooge to make the purchase for him. He would offer them fifty bucks. Or find a wino to do it for ten.

Froggie's was two blocks off Main Street in a derelict stretch of town. There were rundown buildings with broken windows and "For Lease" signs. Lots of graffiti and trash. On the street was little traffic. Walking to his car in the growing dusk, Cole saw a group of boys skateboarding in an empty parking lot. There were three of them, all around Lucas's age. They had long hair and ratty clothes and looked like social rejects. Stoners and dropouts, Cole felt. Offspring of the welfare class.

An idea came to Cole, and had he been sober, he would have ignored it. Had he been sober, he would have *ridiculed* it. But Cole wasn't sober, and more than this, he was mad for revenge. He was determined to get back at Tyce Creamer. Cole wanted to hurt him. Cole wanted to make him pay.

"Hey, what's up?" he said, trying to sound hip and streetwise as he walked over to the nearest boy. The kid had been standing with his back to Cole, watching as one of his buddies performed an acrobatic trick—the skater jumped his board off a set of granite steps, spun it around midair, and landed on it as it hit the pavement and rolled on. At the sound of Cole's voice, the boy turned around fast. He was heavyset, shorter than Cole, and had an unsentimental face. He gave Cole a cool look-over and said nothing in return.

"Nice night," Cole went on, grinning amiably.

The boy's face wrinkled with disbelief. He had already pegged Cole as a middle-class square. It was obvious at first glance—the clothes, the soft face, the stupid smile. But now, seeing his tipsy eyes and unsteady stance, he realized the guy was hammered too. What did the fool want?

"I'm not a cop," Cole said, as though to assure the boy that he posed no threat.

"Yeah. I can tell," the kid said.

Cole noted the glib tone. He dropped the amiable air and said, "I'm looking to get a burner phone."

This amused the kid. He turned his smiling eyes to the boy who had just performed the acrobatic trick. He was tall and had a hard look. He glided over on his board and stopped near Cole, observing him critically.

"He wants to buy a burner phone," the heavyset boy said.

"Oh yeah?" the tall boy said. "*I* have a burner phone." He pulled a smart phone from his front pants pocket and held it up, smiling with exaggerated cheer.

"Don't worry, he's not a cop," the heavyset boy said with a grin.

"Oh … OK, good. Because I wasn't sure," the tall boy said, playing along. "What else you want, Skip? Smack? Crank? Fenty?"

"Roofies?" added the heavyset boy, now laughing.

The tall boy laughed too.

"Just a phone," Cole said, wondering why the tall boy had called him "Skip."

The third boy came over, sizing Cole up as he sensed something was going down.

"He wants to buy a burner," the tall boy said to the third boy.

"A what?" the third boy said, looking confused.

"A phone," the tall boy said.

"Oh."

The tall boy again raised his phone. "A thousand bucks, Skip. Cash."

"A thousand bucks?" Cole said.

"Yeah. It's what you want. It's completely untraceable. You could call the White House with this shit and they'd never find you. You could punk the president."

"Sorry. It's too much," Cole said.

"Eight hundred," the tall boy said.

"No. I'm sure I can get one at Giganta-Mart for less than a hundred."

"Yeah, but you have to activate it," the tall boy said. "That means giving your name and credit card. You do that, then what's the point?"

Cole considered this, and the three boys watched him. They were curious to see his next move. Cole looked around. They were alone. There were no pedestrians, no cars. No witnesses.

"I've got about a hundred in cash on me," he said.

"Mmm ... OK," the tall boy said. "But just because you're a nice guy."

Cole emptied his wallet and held out the cash.

The tall boy shifted the phone to his left hand and took Cole's money with his right. He didn't count it or even look at it. Instead he put it in his pocket and said, "Thanks."

Cole nodded and held out his hand.

The tall boy returned the phone to the same pocket, and stared defiantly at Cole as he did.

The heavyset boy laughed. The third boy laughed.

"Very funny," Cole said.

"What?" the tall boy said with his hard look.

"Give me the phone," Cole said.

"What phone, Skip?"

"Come on. Just give me the phone," he repeated, again holding out his hand.

"I don't know what you're talking about."

"What phone?" the third boy said.

"Yeah, what phone?" the heavyset boy said.

"Look, give me the phone. *Now*," Cole demanded.

"What, this guy asked you for a blowjob?" the heavyset boy said to the tall boy in mock disbelief. "He asked you for a *beana*? Maybe we should call the cops."

The tall boy's hard stare was now flat-out menacing, a portent of imminent violence.

"OK. Just give me my money back and I'll leave," Cole said.

"What money would that be, Skip?" the tall boy said. "The money you offered me for the blowjob?"

Cole cracked. "Kid, give me my *fricking money!*" he screeched, with both rage and fear in his voice.

The third boy laughed loudly. The tall boy and the heavyset boy laughed too. The three of them were enjoying this. Very much.

"You shouldn't swear," the heavyset boy said.

"Yeah, that's no way to ask for a blowjob," the third boy said.

Now shaking with fury, Cole shouted, "I'm telling you, give me my *fricking money*! You don't know who you're dealing with! *Give me my money!*"

The heavyset boy laughed again while the third boy skated off on his board, repositioning himself to watch the action from about twenty feet away. The heavyset boy did the same. Cole could tell they were getting ready to do something, probably dash off. He stepped closer to the tall boy and said, "Kid, I'm warning you. Give me my money."

The tall boy didn't blink. Looking Cole straight in the eye he said, "You know what, Skip? Let's just call the cops. You can tell them you tried to buy a burner phone from us, and we'll tell them that you were asking for a blowjob. We'll let them decide. What do you say to that … *Skippy?*"

Cole lost it. He sprang at the tall boy. Yet rather than throwing a punch like someone who knew how to fight, he got the kid in a headlock, as though he was back in middle school. For several seconds Cole grunted and strained, trying to wrestle the tall boy to the ground. But the kid was strong and he remained upright. Soon the kid managed to twist his lower body away from Cole, opening up some space for him to punch Cole in the nuts. It was a vicious blow, direct to the family jewels, and Cole screeched in agony.

The heavyset boy, who had come up from behind, swung his skateboard at the back of Cole's head. The crack of contact was loud, and the force of the hit nearly knocked Cole out. Struggling to maintain his balance, Cole let go of the headlock.

Now free to move at will, the tall boy launched a counterattack. With gritted teeth and spiteful eyes he delivered a ferocious punch to the side of Cole's unguarded head. Cole dropped to the ground, hitting the pavement face first. The three boys then set upon him. Again and again they punched and kicked him in the head, in the back, in the ribs.

"You like that bitch?" the heavyset boy said, landing a kick.

"Take that Skip!" the tall boy said, punching Cole in the face.

And within fifteen, twenty seconds, it was over. The boys took off on their skateboards, laughing and hooting as they went.

ELEVEN

On Saturday morning, as the birds chirped and the sun shone brightly on idyllic Lilac Lane, Oona rang Tyce Creamer's doorbell. She had parked her car around the corner, on Mortimer Terrace, well out of sight of the Perrot-Pudding home. Her plan was to confront Tyce and then slip into her own house. She needed clothes, toiletries, her laptop, and other necessities. She was hoping to do it all without seeing her family, and was expecting they would soon be off to the Farmers Market, if they hadn't already left.

She rang the bell again, this time with impatience, ramming her finger into the button once, twice, three times. When the door finally opened, Tyce was frowning.

"Hi Oona," he said wearily.

"I have to talk to you," she said. "Why didn't you return my call? Or my texts?"

"Oona, I'm busy right now."

"Answer my question!" she snapped. "I'm not leaving till we talk. I need to know something."

He sighed. "What?"

"I can't do this here," she said, glancing nervously at her house. "I can't be seen."

Tyce looked beyond Oona and unsmilingly held up a hand. "Hello," he called out.

Startled, Oona spun around, fearing the worse: Cole and the kids on the sidewalk, on their way to the Farmers Market. But it was just Maeve Cutty, out checking her mailbox. Maeve gave Oona a friendly wave and Oona ignored it. She turned back to Tyce.

"Oona, I have a guest. I can't do this now," he said.

"I'm not leaving till we speak."

From inside the house came, "Babe? Who is it?"

Oona saw Ingrid coming toward them. The Blonde Bitch was back. The large bandage she had recently worn over her nose was now a small one. Recognizing Oona, Ingrid made a sour, unpleasant face.

"You remember Oona?" Tyce said to her.

Dressed only in a black T-shirt that barely covered her bottom —one of *his* T-shirts, Oona thought—Ingrid stood next to Tyce and casually rested a hand on his back. She surveyed Oona, head to toe, and feigned perplexity. "Uh … no. I don't," she said with an ingenuous look.

"She's my neighbor," Tyce said. "You met her at the Farmers Market last week."

Ingrid reexamined Oona. "Oh, OK—you were working at that cookie stand? The organic one?"

"No. She was with her family. Shopping," Tyce said with irritation. "I need to talk to her. Give me fifteen minutes."

Ingrid shot Oona a dismissive look. Then to Tyce she said, "OK, babe," and she slapped him on the ass. "I'll be in the sauna," she added, giving him a smile that was both intimate and self-congratulatory. On bare feet she padded off to the second floor, her bum cheeks jiggling brazenly under the T-shirt as she went.

Oona's wrath was homicidal. She could have murdered the Blonde Bitch right there, bashed her face in with her bare fists, ripped out every one of those long blonde hairs. But as this was not a realistic option, she turned her seething glare on Tyce.

"Well, come on in," he said glumly.

They sat on a sectional couch in the front room of the house, Oona on one section, Tyce on the other.

"I need to know what happened," she said, getting right to it. "Why you ended it so fast ... My God, it was less than a week! I don't understand. It's not fair! You can't treat people like that!"

" 'It's not fair'?" he said incredulously. "Oona, come on— what is this, seventh grade? You're not a kid. You're a successful professional woman. You knew what you were doing."

"But I thought you liked me."

" '*Liked*' you?"

"Yes."

This baffled him.

"You *acted* like you liked me. And I believed you," she said.

"I *do* like you," he said. "But so what? What does that have to do with anything? Are you saying you had sex with me because you *like* me?" He laughed.

The question, and his reaction to it, stung her. "Yes. I do like you," she said dejectedly.

"Oona, it was just sex. That's all it was," he said bluntly. "Beyond that, I have no feelings for you. No 'romantic' feelings, if that's what you're getting at."

"I don't understand you," she said, shaking her head with a hurt look.

"Oona, did I ever *say* that I 'liked' you? Did I ever lead you on in any way? Did I ever lead you to believe that I was looking for something *from* you? *Anything?*"

"I'm not going back to him," she said earnestly, as if this might help him better understand the situation. "I'm not going back to Cole. We're done."

"*OK*," he said slowly and with an uncertain air, as though he was wondering what any of that had to do with *him*.

"We can see each other now, openly," Oona explained in a hopeful tone. "We can do things together. Go out in public. Go away for a weekend, or more."

"No, Oona. I'm not interested. I already told you."

She exploded. "Why are you such an *asshole?*" she cried.

"Now I'm an asshole?"

"I just don't get you. We had fun together!"

Though he was becoming more aggravated, Tyce reminded himself not to react to her provocations. He knew she wanted him to lose his cool and act like a beta, but that wasn't going to happen. Indeed, he had made a video on this very topic: "How to Argue with Women—and Win."

"Why don't we just try it?" she went on, shifting to a more reasonable tone. "For a week or two. We'll see what happens. What's there to lose?"

"No," he said, calmly yet firmly. "It's not going to happen."

"You're such an asshole!" she shrieked. "You really are! A complete asshole!"

"OK, that's enough. I want you to leave." He stood up.

Oona remained seated. She wasn't going anywhere. "Then why did you do it?" she asked him. "Why did you come onto me? *Why?* I don't understand."

"Oona, *you* came to my house in the middle of the night. Remember? You and your bare feet."

"*Yes*, but only because *you* had been flirting with me, and because *you* made me think that you liked me!"

"No I didn't. That's all in your head."

"Yes you did! You kept kissing me. And you practically grabbed my breast."

"Grabbed your *breast*? When?"

"Well, you *grazed* it. *Intentionally*. At the Farmers Market."

"Oona, this is crazy. I have no idea what you're talking about. I really don't."

Frustrated, Oona shut her eyes and shook her head. She couldn't believe how pigheaded he was, and how dishonest. "So you're saying what?" she said, now looking up at him. "That you would have sex with any woman who comes to your house at night?"

"*No* ... Of course not."

"Then why did you do it? You must have felt *something* for me."

He was quiet.

"Tell me," she insisted.

More silence.

"*Tell* me!"

"You really want to know?" he said, starting to lose his patience and knowing this was the one thing he did not want to do. But she was deeply pissing him off, so screw it, he felt. "Is that what you want? You *really* want to know?"

"Yes."

"OK. I was curious to see what your breasts looked like, all right? Are you happy? You're always showing them off at the gym, and I figured there was probably a good reason." He waited for her to respond, but Oona was speechless. "Also," he went on, "I can't stand Cole. He's a smug, arrogant pussy, and he rubs me the wrong way."

Oona's mouth fell open, but no words came out. She was too dumbstruck to respond. She lowered her eyes and tried to understand. Then she said, "You used me."

Tyce laughed. "*I* used *you*? Don't you think it's maybe the other way around?"

"*What?* What are you talking about?" she said in a heated voice.

"Oona, you married a gelding. You married a spineless wimp. Cole is a complete mediocrity, and you can't stand it. You can't stand *him*. It's obvious. I see it on your face whenever you're together. And so to get out of that relationship, you used *me*."

"Oh come on!" she said. "This is unbelievable!"

"Oona, I'm sorry. I know this might hurt your ego, but you're not that complicated."

"*Fuck you!*" she said indignantly, wanting to strike him, wanting to scratch out his eyes.

"Hey—*relax*. Relax. You want out from him, and I don't blame you."

"You know nothing about me!" she said with pure spite. "*Nothing!*"

Tyce didn't flinch. He had regained control of himself. He had regained control of *her*. "OK, look," he said with a judicious air. "Answer me this: do you respect Cole? Do you *really* respect him, deep down?"

Oona tensed. "Of course I do," she said, instantly losing her fire. "What a stupid question."

"Well, you *did* respect him. At one time. Otherwise you wouldn't have married him or stayed with him this long. But at some point you changed your mind, and you realized you'd made a mistake. You realized that *Cole* was a mistake ... Am I right?"

She did not reply.

"OK, I'll go on," he said. "And tell me when I'm wrong. It started gradually, you losing respect for him, and maybe you weren't even aware that it was happening. But over time he started to irritate you. His jokes were less funny. His quirks and his mannerisms—which at one time you thought were cute and endearing—now seemed grating and pathetic. Then you started feeling depressed. You started feeling *angry*. And most of all, you started to despise him, a little more every day, because in your mind, it was all *his* fault. *He* was the one who was bringing you down. And so you began spending less time with him and avoiding his presence. You began thinking up excuses to be away from the house and reasons not to go to bed at the same time as him. As for sex, you shut that off long ago, and the thought of sleeping with him today probably makes you sick. And my guess is that your castrato husband is going along with it. The more you treat him like shit, and the more you show him how truly little you respect him, the more he's probably saying, 'Honey, whatever's wrong, I want you to know that I support you and I'm sensitive to your needs. Please tell me how I can help.' And I bet whenever he says this, that some part of you wants to punch him in the face. Some part of you wants to kill him right there. Tell me I'm wrong, Oona. What has it been, a year since you guys last screwed? Two years? *Five?*"

Still she did not reply. She was in a daze and could only stare at him.

"Like I said, Oona—you used me for your own reasons. Rather than confront Cole and your problems head on, you took the easy way. You wanted a no-going-back excuse to end your marriage, and now you have it. You'll tell yourself and your family that he was a bad husband, that he was a *terrible* husband, and that he forced you to have an affair. He *forced* you to cheat, you'll say. It's all *his* fault, you'll say. And your friends and your family will of course agree with you, because that's what friends and family do. And so you'll get what you want. You'll be rid of Cole and at the same time you'll look like the victim, rather than the sneaky deceitful bitch that you really are."

Oona did not feel well. She felt dizzy and short of breath. She shook her head, disagreeing with him, hating his words, hating *him.* "No ... No. That's ridiculous," she said at last, struggling to turn on the outrage. "*You're* ridiculous. You're a ... you're a cheap vulgar seducer. That's what you are. You and your fake white teeth."

He laughed. "Whatever you say, Oona," he said, watching her with cold, amused eyes. "And now it's time for you to leave."

Slowly she rose to her feet. She was trembling with emotion —confusion, humiliation, wild raging fury. She tried to think of a parting shot, some brutal, cutting words. Something scolding and shaming, something he would always remember with embarrassment and regret. But Oona had nothing. And because the silence was lengthening, and she was starting to feel self-conscious, she sneered and went with the first thing that came to mind, "You *disgust* me."

She walked to the door and stepped out into the late-morning sun. She cut across the lawn in the direction of her car, but then she remembered that she needed clothes. So she reversed course and started for her house.

* * *

When he emerged from the basement, Cole didn't look so good. After he had gotten pummeled and stomped the previous evening by the three skateboarding juvenile delinquents, he had lain on the parking lot pavement for a good thirty, forty minutes, moaning and groaning and too hurting to move. A number of people had passed by on the street twenty yards away, in cars and on foot, but nobody stopped to help him. Maybe they thought he was a bum, passed out from booze. Eventually, as dusk turned to night, he had gotten up and crawled to his car and driven home. Not wanting to see his kids, he had slipped in the back through the kitchen and went straight down to the basement, where he felt most comfortable. Where he felt most safe.

Now, in the kitchen, Rosa shrieked. "Oh, Dad! *Gross!* What happened to your face? *Oh,* your lip!"

Cole's lower lip looked like a hockey puck. His left eye was now black, and the part of the eyeball that was normally white was blood red. As for his ribs, his guess was that two or three of them were broken, as each breath and each step he took gave him a nearly unbearable shock of pain.

"I fell down," he said.

"You fell down?" Rosa said doubtfully.

"Yes."

"Where?"

"In the basement. The floor was slippery."

The girl wasn't buying this. With a sad face she said, "Did Tyce beat you up?"

"No … *Ow,*" he said, cringing from the pain in his ribs.

"Did Mom beat you up?"

"*No*, Rosa. I *fell*."

"Because you were drunk?" she asked sheepishly.

"Rosa, please. Enough. No. I slipped on some water. I spilled it on the floor."

"OK," she said, not believing him. "Do you want some ice for your lip? It's really gross. So is your eye. *Eeew*. It must hurt!"

"No, I want coffee."

"Holy shit," Lucas said, coming into the kitchen. He looked his father up and down. "Did Tyce beat you up?"

"I already asked," Rosa said.

"No," Cole said. "I fell."

"You *fell*?" Lucas said with extreme disbelief. "That's what abused wives say."

Cole grumbled but said nothing. He hobbled over to the counter and began to make coffee.

"Have you heard from Mom?" Rosa said to Lucas.

"No. Did you?"

Cole paused what he was doing to listen to his children. He hadn't heard from Oona in days.

Rosa said, "I texted her last night to see when she's coming home and she said she didn't know, and I texted her this morning but she didn't text me back ... Did she talk to you, Dad?"

Cole shook his head.

"Are you guys getting a divorce?" the girl said forlornly.

"*No*. I already told you, this is just ... temporary. She'll be home."

"Are we going to the Farmers Market?"

"Not today ... Maybe next week," Cole said, now with a somber face.

Lucas scoffed. He knew the family would not be going to the Farmers Market next week, or most likely ever again. Certainly not the four of them together.

Observing her brother's reaction, Rosa became even more dispirited. She lowered her eyes, looking very blue.

Then, from the living room, there came the sound of the front door opening. The girl's face lit up. She knew it could only be one person. She rushed into the next room and hugged her mother at the door.

"Mom!" she cried. "Mom I missed you!"

Oona hugged Rosa back and Rosa began to weep. Though she was moved by this, Oona expressed little emotion. She felt bad about having hurt her daughter and bad about the messy way things were unfolding, but inside she was numb. She was numb and flustered from what had just happened with Tyce. She kissed Rosa's head, and when she looked up, Oona saw Cole entering the room.

Seeing his wife, Cole experienced a powerful rush of happiness and relief. Maybe *mostly* relief. Oona had come home. She had come home to the family. She had come home to *him*. They would need to discuss a few things, he knew, and there would be some difficult moments, moments of pain and even acrimony, but in the end everything would be worked out. The two of them would resolve their problems and, most importantly, he would not have to move into the YMCA.

"I'm so glad you're home, Mom," Rosa was saying as she wept and continued to hold Oona tight. "I'm so glad you're home!"

"It's good to see you," Cole said, welcoming his wife. He wanted her to know that Tyce and the porn video and everything else was forgotten. At least for the moment.

"What happened to you?" she said with revulsion, gawking at his damaged face. "Did Tyce do that?"

Cole just shook his head as if to say, "Not now."

Then Oona saw Lucas. The boy stood in the doorway to the kitchen, keeping his distance. He had been watching the scene, and especially his mother, with a cynical wariness. Oona said nothing to him.

"Mom, can we go to the Farmers Market?" Rosa said, beaming hopefully as she pulled away to look up at her mother's face.

Oona did not hesitate. In a firm, even voice she said, "I'm only here to pick up some clothes. I'm not staying."

"You're not?" Rosa said.

"*What?*" Cole cried.

Oona let go of Rosa and focused on Cole. "I need some more time. I'm just here to get some things."

From the doorway Lucas snickered bitterly. He had had a feeling that something like this was going to happen. And now he had no doubts: their family was finished. It was over. All that remained was how it would play out.

Cole blew up. "What do you mean you 'need more time'?" he hollered. "For the past *year* you've been saying that! What the hell does it even mean?"

Frightened by her father's anger, Rosa flinched back and started crying.

Seeing this, Oona turned on Cole. "You are *pathetic!*" she shouted.

"And *you're* jerking me around!" he shouted back. "And I'm sick of it! Tell me what you mean—'more time'? More time for *what*? For *what*?"

"Stop yelling!"

Rosa did not know what to do. She felt impelled to run up to her room, shut the door, and cry on her bed. But another part of her desired the comfort of her mother. She again wrapped her arms around Oona's waist and buried her face in her chest, sobbing.

Oona held the girl and glared icily at Cole, willing him to shut up. He did. She kissed Rosa's scalp as the child wept. She could feel the girl trembling and her heart palpitating, and she could feel her own heart palpitating as well. She took Rosa's head in both hands and gazed into her tear-filled eyes. "I need some time to think," she said. "I know this is confusing for you, but I have to do it."

"I don't want you to go," the child whimpered.

"I have to."

"*Nooo.*"

"Rosa honey, some day you'll understand. I'll call you tonight, and I'll see you tomorrow, OK? I'll see you tomorrow."

"*Nooo.* Don't go."

"I have to," Oona said with finality, then added, "I love you."

She broke away from her daughter and started for the stairs up to the second floor. Cole followed. Neither of them spoke until they had entered their bedroom and Cole shut the door.

"Oona, what are you doing? This is ludicrous. It's completely unnecessary," he said, restraining himself and trying to sound reasonable. "Let's just stop and talk about this. Let's talk about it *now.*"

Yet as Cole talked, Oona kept moving. She went into her walk-in closet, got a suitcase, opened it, and laid it out on the bed.

Following behind her, Cole said, "Would you stop and talk to me? Can you stop for one damn minute?"

"No. I have to do this. It has to be done."

"You have to move out of the house? In front of the kids? Making a big scene like this? You know how much damage you just did? To Rosa? That's probably ten years of therapy right there! Ten years! That's on *you,* Oona!"

"Would you shut up!" she said hotly, as she emptied half of her underwear drawer into the suitcase.

"Oona—talk to me. What do you want? What do you *want?*"

"I don't know," she said, not looking at him as she scooped out two handfuls of socks from the bureau.

"Why do I get the feeling that you *do* know?" Cole said. "Are you moving in with him?"

She shook her head at his stupidity. "*No.*"

"How serious is it? With you and muscle boy?"

"Cole," she said, now with a look of exhaustion, "I can't do this right now. Not today."

" 'I can't do this right now,' " he mocked her. " 'Not today.' Un-fricking-believable. You're so goddamn selfish, Oona. Everything is always on your terms. *Everything!*"

She didn't acknowledge this. She had just put some tops into the suitcase and now went into the closet for pants.

Cole followed, saying, "You're moving in with him, aren't you?"

She ignored the question, and it infuriated him.

"You fricking bitch!" he bellowed. "I gave up everything for you!"

This got her attention. "You gave up everything for *me?*" she said, turning to face him. "Like what? Like living in a nice house? Like driving a nice car? Like traveling to Europe every summer? Oh, wait—you *do* have those things. And why is that, Cole? Huh? Why is that? Oh, that's right—*because I paid for them!*"

"So what! So fricking what!" he shot back. "I gave up my *career* for you! I made sacrifices. *I supported you!* And this is how you repay me? By giving Tyce Cream-face a blowjob and destroying this family?"

"Your *career?*" Oona shot right back, now with a mix of derision and disgust. "Cole, you have a master's degree in philosophy. That's it. You could have finished your dissertation but you chose not to. You could have had your PhD and done something, but you didn't!"

"Is it my fault that my adviser died out on the thirteenth hole?" Cole said. "You're putting that on me?"

"You could have gone to a different school, but you chose not to," Oona said, now marching into the bathroom to gather her toiletries.

"That's because I wanted to be with you!" Cole said, trailing behind her. "Because I *loved* you! And what a mistake *that* was!"

"Oh, that's nice. Very romantic," she said flippantly. "But as I recall, it wasn't all about me, was it? You said you'd had enough of the grad-school politicking. You said you would rather shoot yourself than 'kiss any more faculty ass.' You said you were going to write books and be an independent scholar. Well where are the books, Cole? *Where are the friggin' books?*" she shrieked.

"How could I write books," he blared, "when I was doing shit jobs to support this family, when I was doing shit jobs to support *you* while you were climbing the academic ladder? Huh, Oona? Who was wiping asses and cooking supper and buying fricking juice boxes while you were writing and going off to conferences?"

She went back into the bedroom and put her toiletries bag in the suitcase, all while saying, "That was your choice, Cole. That was your choice!"

"My '*choice*'? Now it's my '*choice*'? At the time you were saying we were a 'team'! Do you remember that, Oona—*a fricking team!*"

She stared at him coldly. And then, loading her metaphorical assassin's gun, she aimed and fired. "You *chose* your path, Cole," she said, "and you knew *exactly* what you were doing. You knew you were taking the easy way, and you did it on *purpose*. Because as we both know, you're lazy, you're insecure, and you don't have the friggin' balls to get out there and make something happen! You don't have the *friggin' balls!* You *chose* your path, Cole, so don't you *dare* blame your failure on me! Don't you *dare!*"

It was, as Oona knew it would be, a direct hit. Cole was wounded and reeling. And while the damage of the shot would likely be felt for months and years to come, a near-fatal affliction whose pain would only be salved by booze and other toxic distractions, Cole's injured narcissism sprang him robustly back to life. A murderous rage suffused his entire being. His eyes shone with vicious hate and his hands balled into white-knuckled fists. In a flash he considered obliterating Oona's face, smashing it until there was nothing left.

Oona did not miss any of this. She knew she had damaged him greatly and that he was capable of violence, maybe even lethal violence. She could see the insane rage in his eyes, as she had seen it before during previous fights. Afraid and alarmed, she looked for a weapon, something to defend herself with. All that was close to hand was a wood-framed photograph of the two of them from their wedding, perched atop the bureau beside which she now stood. If needed, she would snatch it up and smash one of the frame's pointed corners into his head.

But Cole, with his fat lip, black eye, and broken ribs, made no move. He controlled his rage and soon Oona's fear passed. Sensing his retreat, seeing the madness ebb from his eyes, she knew this was the moment to resume the attack. This was the moment to finish him off.

"Cole, this just isn't working," she said, softening her tone and gazing into his eyes with something like compassion. "You've *changed*. You drink, you hate your job, you hate your life. You're miserable to be around. It's not good for the kids, and it's especially not good for me. For years I've been unhappy, Cole ... Because of *you*."

"Why didn't you tell me?" he said sadly, his spite turning to sorrow. "Why didn't you just ... trust me? You never said anything."

"You should have known," she said resolutely. "And I'm sure you did, but you just didn't want to admit it."

"Oona, I'm telling you—I didn't know. I didn't know it was this bad."

"I think you did, Cole. In fact, I'm sure you did. I think your problem, to be perfectly honest, is that you envy my success."

Cole gaped at her.

"You envy what I've done," she went on, "and you're resentful because of it. You're *filled* with resentment, Cole. And I think you always have been, all the way back to grad school."

It was yet another bullet fired from point-blank range. This time, however, Cole did not have the internal strength to withstand it. His metaphorical legs buckled and he went down with a metaphorical thud. Oona saw he was struggling for his life, that he was gasping for breath and would likely not recover. But for her, this still wasn't enough. She reloaded her gun, aimed, and fired the killshot.

"I'm sorry it came to this, Cole," she said coolly. "I really am. But you forced me to do it. You *forced* me into the arms of another man. Tyce gave me what you couldn't. Because the fact is, Cole, you're not a *real* man. You're just a pretend one. You're weak and pathetic. You made my life miserable, and I had to act. You have only yourself to blame."

Without another word she zipped up the suitcase, hoisted it off the bed, and left the room. Cole made no move to stop her.

TWELVE

When he woke on Sunday morning amid a clutter of empty wine bottles, Cole cringed from pain—rib pain, brain pain, body pain, soul pain. He hurt all over, in places he could see and in those he could not. Lying on his back on the couch, he was dressed only in boxer shorts and a single white sock. Why he was wearing just one sock, he did not know. He did not care. Across his swollen hairless belly, a large black ant was lazily crawling in the direction of his chest. Cole brought the tip of his forefinger to the underside of his thumb, and casually but forcefully flicked the ant, field-goal style. The tiny wriggling creature arced through the air, hit the floor six feet away, then scrambled off in a confusion of directions, going this way and that.

Cole needed water. He needed aspirin. He needed coffee. He needed a lot of things, he felt. Money, for instance. *Lots* of money. Also, a new life. Yes, that would be good too. But the first thing he did was to reach for his laptop. He had a vague feeling that something *bad* had happened yesterday. Or rather, he had a vague feeling that *another* bad thing had happened yesterday, in addition to all the *other* bad things that had happened yesterday. Maybe, he hoped, he had just imagined it. It was possible. What he did remember for sure was this: yesterday, after Oona had left the house with a suitcase and the last remnants of Cole's dignity and self-respect, he had come down to the basement looking for solace in music and booze. Yet no sooner had

he chugged his first glass of the Stepfield Valley Malbec and listened to the opening track of the Idiot Gurus' melancholic fourth
album, *Woe Is Me, You, and Everybody Else*, than he got an email
from one Kelsey Flambé, the general counsel of Wendover College. It was at this point that Cole's memory got a little fuzzy,
due to his having soon afterward imbibed a massive amount of
wine. His sense, however, was that the email had not brought
good news.

Now, as he winced and squinted at the laptop screen, Cole saw
that his "sense" had not been off. The news *wasn't* good. In fact,
the news was quite bad.

The email's subject heading read, "Disciplinary Hearing," and
the message began, "Dear Cole: I'm writing to inform you
… Blah-blah-blah, blah-blah-blah, blah-blah-blah." In short,
Kelsey Flambé, along with Digby, Dean Munchausen, and the
entire Wendover College community, wanted Cole gone. In
response to his recent outburst at the Office of Student Affairs—in which he was accused of employing "racist language,"
"sexist language," "emotionally abusive language," "language of a
threatening nature," "language of a hateful nature," and "physical
behavior of a threatening and/or hateful nature with the intention of causing bodily and/or emotional harm"—Cole was being
called before the college's Committee for Equity, Inclusion, and
Kindness three weeks hence. Cole was encouraged to appear
with legal representation. He was also told that, pending the
hearing, he was placed on unpaid leave and was not welcome
anywhere on campus, either in person or digitally, and that any
violation of this "request" would result in immediate termination
from Wendover and arrest by the Beauville Police Department,
who had already been notified of the charges and given Cole's
personnel file and contact information.

Even in his severely hungover state, Cole could see that he was
screwed. This time, Bendover was truly forcing him to bendover, and what was coming would not feel good. He wondered

how much a lawyer would cost. Then he wondered if it was even worth it. The commissars of the Committee for Equity, Inclusion, and Kindness, in conjunction with the Wendover legal team, had probably already written up the verdict. The hearing itself would be a mere show trial, a kangaroo court meant to inflict as much public humiliation as possible. His termination was, Cole now understood, already in the books, a fait accompli.

Cole sighed acquiescently. He did not have it in him to get upset or distressed. Not at this point. They had him, and he knew they had him, and he knew they knew they had him.

And so what was he to do, he wondered? Should he just take it? Should he passively submit, grab ahold of his ankles, and writhe and squeal under the pain? Or was there maybe not a way he could get something out of this? Was there maybe not a way he could turn these lemons into a sweet-tasting and possibly profitable lemonade? Surely he had nothing to lose. What about a wrongful termination lawsuit? Or a charge of sexual harassment against Digby? He could claim that Digby had made unwanted sexual advances toward him over many years, resulting in emotional trauma and the prevention of professional advancement. He could even post something on Chirper right now. Why wait? Why not mount an all-out preemptive PR blitz? In fact, if he were to go all in now on a social-media smear campaign, he might not only force the college to back down but he might even force them to give him Digby's job. Or better yet, he might force them into a financial settlement. A "hefty" financial settlement, as they say. A "thanks-a-lot-assholes-it's-been-real" financial settlement. A "bye-bye-fascist-America-I'm-retiring-to-gay-Paree" financial settlement. Yes indeed, Cole mused, this could be his *real* golden ticket.

As he contemplated these things, which gave him hope and vastly improved his mood, Cole heard himself called from upstairs.

It was his son, Lucas. The boy was yelling, *"Dad! Dad!"*

* * *

Lucas was breathing into his sister's mouth and pressing down on her chest, just as he had learned at the Beauville Swim and Racquet Club back when he was in junior high. Two breaths, thirty chest compressions, then repeat. Lucas had been out in the yard going through his muscle-building routine—squats, pushups, planks, and wind sprints—and had come into the house for water when he saw his sister sprawled face down on the kitchen floor. He rushed to her side, turned her onto her back, saw her eyes were closed, and thought she had fainted. It was a hot muggy day and she had been out in the yard with him earlier, kicking the soccer ball and running around. But checking her breathing and then her pulse, Lucas realized her condition was dire—that she was in fact dying, if not already dead.

That was when he had yelled to his father and began giving her the breath of life.

"Oh God—what happened?" Cole cried as he hobbled into the kitchen, straining from the pain of his fractured ribs.

Lucas was on his knees at the girl's side, pressing down on her chest with rhythmic thrusts. "Call 911!" he said.

"But ... what happened?" Cole stammered.

"Her heart stopped! Call *now*!" the boy yelled.

"Her heart?"

"*Yes!* Stop diddling!"

"Diddling" was a word Cole had used to chastise the kids when they were younger and took forever doing some basic task, like eating their food or brushing their teeth. "Stop diddling and dawdling," he would say. Now, as best he could, Cole scampered down to the basement, found his phone, and made the call.

When he returned to the kitchen Cole saw Lucas shaking and crying. The boy was still on his knees at his sister's side with tears on his cheeks. But Lucas was also radiant with happiness.

"She's breathing," he said. "She's breathing."

* * *

With sirens wailing and horns blasting, a Beauville fire truck and rescue squad soon arrived at the Perrot-Pudding residence. Rosa was conscious but very weak and still lying on the kitchen floor. Lucas, recalling more of his safety training, had thought it best not to move her. Instead, he had remained at her side, holding her hand and comforting her, telling her he was there and that she would be all right.

Cole went to the front door and led the firemen and EMTs, all wearing blue paper face masks, into the kitchen with their equipment and rolling gurney. The gurney, which had a warped wheel, squeaked gratingly as it moved. Cole thought one of the EMTs, a tall guy with a pronounced beer belly and a thick red beard, looked vaguely familiar, but he could not place him. The guy questioned Cole and Lucas about Rosa and what had happened, and then he joined his partner in tending to the girl.

Rosa was moving and alert. The EMTs checked her pulse and blood pressure and placed an oxygen mask on her face, all the while asking her questions. Then, very gently, they got her onto the gurney and strapped her in. As they were preparing to leave, Rosa looked in the direction of Cole and Lucas, who stood beside two firemen watching from ten feet away. The child was trying to speak.

The second EMT, a very short woman in latex gloves and a plastic face shield in addition to her blue paper mask, tried to calm her and told her not to talk. But Rosa only became more agitated. There was panic and fear in her eyes and she continued to emit garbled words. The female EMT lowered the oxygen mask and Rosa said, in a scared, weakened voice, "Don't leave me." She was looking at her family.

Cole stepped toward her. "Do you want me to go with you?"

Rosa shook her head. "No … Lucas."

Cole turned to his son, and as the firemen and EMTs looked on, Lucas came forward. Rosa raised her hand for him to hold, and he held it.

"Don't leave me," she said.

"I won't. I'll come with you."

The female EMT interjected. "You'll have to meet us at the hospital," she said from behind her mask and shield. "Civilians aren't allowed in the vehicle."

"I'm not leaving her," Lucas said.

"I'm sorry. It's the rules," the woman said. "It's for your safety and ours."

"Screw the rules," Lucas said. "This is my sister."

The woman looked at her partner, and the big guy looked at the two firemen. One of the firemen just shrugged. The other looked off to the side. Then the big guy said, "It's fine with me."

"OK," the woman said to Lucas. "But you have to wear a mask."

* * *

By the time Oona arrived at Beauville Hospital, Rosa had been in the Emergency Room for more than two hours and was now in surgery. Cole and Lucas were seated at a picnic table outside the hospital's cafeteria, which faced the Emergency Room parking lot. As Cole watched Oona coming toward them from her car, he wondered how he should play this. What angle should he take? Should he act the embittered, cuckolded husband and say something venomous and snide? Something like, "Glad you could make it"? Or, "I hope we're not inconveniencing you"? Or should he instead view this more as ... an *opportunity*? Specifically, might he not use this family tragedy as a means to repair their relationship? Or at least, if "repair" was perhaps asking for too much, might he not use it to prevent an imminent divorce? It was, Cole realized, an easy choice. He shot to his feet and assumed a solemn yet compassionate air, making it clear that he was prepared to provide comfort and support, a strong shoulder for Oona to lean on in this great hour of need.

Lucas, who sat across from his father, turned and saw his mother. His look became hostile.

"How is she?" Oona said to both of them in a frantic voice. "Have you heard anything? What's happening?"

Cole went around the table to be closer to his wife and possibly embrace her, should she be open to it. But Oona wasn't open to it. Her look of worried concern shifted to frosty reproof as she sensed what Cole was thinking. Cole in turn caught this and instantly stopped short. Now feeling rejected, he switched tactics.

"*Where have you been?*" he sneered with withering contempt.

"I came as soon as I could," she said. "I just got your message. My phone was turned off. What happened? Why are you outside?"

She looked at Lucas, but he turned his back to her and resumed his former position, facing the hospital. Oona looked at Cole and he gruffly explained. They were outside, he said, because of the hospital's SPAARZ policy. Only one family member at a time was allowed into the waiting room, and so Cole and Lucas had decided to wait together. As for Rosa, the ER doctor said that she had suffered a "sudden cardiac arrhythmia," and that her heart had sustained significant damage. The girl was now being fitted with an internal cardiac defibrillator.

"A defibrillator?" Oona said. "How could that be? She's only eleven years old!"

"She's *twelve*!" Lucas said, turning around in his seat to glare at his mother.

"It's a routine operation," Cole said, addressing his wife. "The doctor said she should be fine."

"*Fine?*" Lucas snapped, now glaring at his father. "Her heart is significantly damaged, Dad! The defibrillator is for life! She is not *fine!*"

It offended Cole to be scolded by his son, Mr. Teenage Smartass, but in this instance he could not refute the boy's logic.

Oona, sensing the potential implications of this medical disaster, became circumspect. Surely something—or rather, *someone* —would be held to blame. In a wary voice she said, "Do they know ... what caused it? Was it—?"

"Gee, I wonder," Lucas said caustically.

"*Lucas*, not now," Cole said. To Oona he said, "The doctor didn't know. He said it was too early to tell."

"Does he know she has myocarditis?"

"Yes."

"But I thought she was doing well? I thought the pills were helping?"

"I did too," Cole said. His phone, which he had left on the picnic table, started to ring. "That might be Dr. Bumble."

"You called him?"

"I left a message with his answering service." Cole removed his face shield and face mask and answered the phone. It indeed was Dr. Bumble.

"Doctor, thanks for calling," Cole said.

"It's no problem," the man said. "I'm out on the golf course, but that's OK. Go ahead."

"Oh," Cole said, taken aback. "I'm, uh, sorry to bother you."

"It's fine. Really. Go ahead."

"Well, I'm calling because Rosa's had an emergency," Cole said, and he relayed all the details. Afterward, the doctor expressed his concern and said Rosa was "in good hands."

"I guess what I'm wondering," Cole said, "is how could this happen? How could a healthy twelve-year-old girl have cardiac arrest?"

"Well Mr. Perrot, I'm afraid Rosa *wasn't* a healthy twelve-year-old girl. She has myocarditis."

"But I was told you said it was a 'mild case.' Was that incorrect?"

"No. No no. That was a, uh, *joint* diagnosis, made in consultation with a number of specialists. And it was made based on the girl's condition *at that time.*"

"But that was on *Monday*," Cole said in amazement. "Less than a week ago!"

"I understand, Mr. Perrot. But evidently Rosa's condition *worsened* since then. Trust me, it's not unprecedented. I've seen stranger things. Human biology can be very unpredictable."

"OK," Cole said, trying to think this through. "So you're saying that her myocarditis worsened—in less than a week—and that her myocarditis caused the arrhythmia? Is that your position?"

"It's a theory."

"A *theory?*" Cole said.

"Yes."

"And what are your, uh, *theories* on what caused the myocarditis? I've looked into it myself and—"

"There are a number of factors involved, Mr. Perrot," Dr. Bumble interrupted with growing impatience. "Genetics, viruses —including SPAARZ, of course—climate change and ... other causes. The etiology of these conditions can be very complex, and difficult for laymen to understand."

"Right," Cole said uneasily. "I have read about the climate change theory. But how, exactly, does that work? I mean, how does climate change cause a young girl to get myocarditis?"

"Well Mr. Perrot, The Science is quite compelling. But as I say, it's very complex."

"The Science," Cole murmured.

"Yes," Dr. Bumble said.

"Well … I believe in The Science, of course," Cole said earnestly. "I always have. But again, how exactly does a change in the *weather* cause myocarditis in human beings? I mean, what exactly is the, uh … mechanism?"

"The 'mechanism'?"

"Yes."

"Mr. Perrot, I'm not a meteorologist—"

"You're not a weatherman?" Cole said, baffled.

"I mean, a *climatologist*," the doctor corrected himself. "The point, Mr. Perrot, is that there is growing consensus in the scientific community around the multiple health threats posed by climate change, including myocarditis."

"Yes, I … understand," Cole said weakly. "It makes perfect sense."

By now, Oona had become thoroughly annoyed. She had been listening all along, and the more Cole spoke, the more it drove her crazy. Her husband's utter fecklessness, on full display at this critical time, was intolerable. She snatched the phone from his hand and said, "Dr. Bumble? This is Dr. Pudding."

"Ah, yes … *Dr. Pudding*."

She detected amusement in the man's voice, a touch of sardonic disrespect. Because she was already worked up, it required tremendous effort not to go off on him. As much as she would have enjoyed telling this uppity asshole off, she knew it would only make the situation worse. In a firm yet restrained voice she said, "Am I to understand, Dr. Bumble, that you're saying Rosa's heart attack was caused by *climate change*?"

"Dr. Pudding, first off, Rosa has not had a heart attack. According to your husband, she had a cardiac arrest. They are not the same. And second, I did not say that climate change *definitively* caused Rosa's myocarditis. What I told your husband was that the girl's condition could have been caused by any number of factors, including genes, viruses, and yes, climate change. Also, stress can play an important role too. Has Rosa been under any unusual stress lately?"

Oona fell silent. In her mind she saw Rosa, just the day before, begging her not to leave the house. Rosa with her arms wrapped tightly around her waist. Rosa sobbing and saying, "Mom, don't go ... *Don't go.*"

"Dr. Pudding? ... *Hello?*"

"Yes, I'm here," Oona said. "Uh, no ... Not that I know of," she added, answering the doctor's question and making sure not to use the word "stress." Cole was watching her and listening closely. Lucas, surely, was listening too. She did not want to give either one of them anything to think about—or use against her.

"What about anti-vaxxers?" Dr. Bumble went on. "Is there anyone close to Rosa who may have been giving her misinformation about the vaccines?"

Oona's eyes widened. She could not believe her good luck. For a tenth of a second she did feel a slight pang of conscience over the rightness of taking advantage of this gift, but she quickly stifled it. In a puzzled, innocent voice, and loud enough for everyone to hear, she said, " 'Anti-vaxxers'?"

Still seated at the picnic table, Lucas spun around and gave his mother an acid stare. Cole was roused as well. At the word "anti-vaxxers," he turned his accusing eyes on Lucas.

"Yes," Dr. Bumble said. "These anti-vax, anti-Science people are causing severe mental stress in vulnerable persons. This stress in turn can lead to serious health problems, including cardiac-related issues. These people are *very* dangerous."

"I see," Oona said, now speaking primarily for her husband and son. "I'm sorry to hear that, doctor. But no, Rosa *hasn't* been exposed to any anti-vaccine rhetoric, as far as I know."

Cole stared furiously at Lucas.

After Oona hung up, the boy said, "*What did that idiot say?*"

"He said Rosa's cardiac arrest could have been caused by anti-vax misinformation. I kept you out of it."

"*What?* Are you fricking kidding me?" Lucas bellowed.

"I knew it!" Cole said with triumphant scorn. "What have I been saying all along? Huh, kid? *What have I been saying?*"

"No, I'm *not* kidding," Oona calmly replied, looking at her son. "That's what he said."

"But how can an *idea*, whether it's right or wrong, cause a medical condition? That makes no sense! It's absurd!" Lucas said.

"Because ideas can cause stress, Lucas," Oona said. "And stress affects our health."

"Of course it does! Stress *kills*!" Cole declared.

"Mom, the guy is lying! He's just trying to pass the buck! He's trying to scapegoat the people who know this is all bullshit! Can't you see that? How blind can you be?"

"I'm sorry, Lucas," Oona said. "But stress *does* play a role in our health. So it is possible."

"You're damn right it's possible!" Cole said indignantly.

"OK, fine," Lucas said, now with a cold, shrewd look in his eye. "If that's how you want to do this, sure. Stress is bad for your health. I agree. And what about the stress caused by your mother sleeping with the next-door neighbor and moving into a hotel? Does that count too? Or is it only the 'anti-vax stress' that counts?"

Oona was silent.

For his part, Cole sensed another opportunity. Here was a chance, he felt, to pay back his son and possibly score a few points with his wife. He erupted on the boy, saying, "Lucas, you've been upsetting your sister for two years on this issue! *Two years!* Spewing out your internet nonsense and your conspiracy theories and everything else. You've refused to wear masks, you've refused to get the vaccine, and you've refused even to get tested. You've been completely irrational, and unbelievably selfish! You put your ego ahead of the safety of this family, and now there are consequences! Do you understand? *Consequences!* I hope you're happy, kid, I really do."

"I can't believe you guys are trying to blame *me*!" Lucas said. "*You're* the ones who made her get the vaccine—*you* did! Both of you!"

"Are you not listening, Lucas?" Cole roared. "Did you not listen to a single word your mother just said? Has all of that meat you've been eating gone into your ears? Dr. Bumble said *viruses cause myocarditis*, not vaccines!"

"Then if that's true, then how do you know she got it from *me*? The vaccines don't provide immunity and they don't prevent transmission, so maybe *you* gave it to her! What about that, you jackass!"

Under any other circumstances, Lucas calling him a jackass would have triggered Cole into a frenzied rage. But now, because he was convinced that he had finally and definitively defeated the boy in their two-year-long debate over SPAARZ, because he was convinced there was now no doubt over who had been right and who had been wrong, Cole merely smiled at his son, serenely and gloatingly. Then, because he could not resist, he said, "Do you know what the difference is between you and me, Lucas? Do you know? ... I care about people. I *care*. Unlike you, I don't put my vanity and my desire to be a rebel ahead of other people's safety. That's why I wear a mask. That's why I wear a face shield. That's why I got the vaccines. And that's why I isolate in the basement when I test positive. So no, if Rosa caught the virus from someone, it was from *you*, not me. And if you can't figure out something so basic as that, then I don't know what else to say."

Seeking to position herself as the neutral party, as the sympathetic mediator, Oona spoke up. In a measured, pacifying tone she said, "Lucas, I never said you were to blame, and I don't think you are. This is a difficult time—for all of us—and I know we're all doing the best we can. Right now, we just need to think about Rosa."

* * *

The operation was a success. The surgeon, a Dr. Pye, phoned Cole with the good news. For the duration of the procedure, Cole, Oona, and Lucas had remained outside the hospital, sitting, standing, walking around, checking their phones, and generally trying to avoid each other. Now, they wanted to see the girl. She was in recovery, in a private room in the ER, and was expected to stay for an additional one to two days. However, per the hospital's SPAARZ policy, Rosa could only have one visitor.

"I want to see her," Lucas said. "I'm going to spend the night. I'll sleep on the floor if I have to."

"You can't," Cole said. "You're not vaccinated. They won't let you."

"That's not true," Lucas said, though he had no idea if it wasn't true or not. "Plus, how would they know?"

"Are you kidding me?" Cole said. "You would lie to them? *And* put your sister at risk? *Again?*"

"*Dad*, I don't have SPAARZ! What the hell is wrong with you?"

"How do you know you don't have SPAARZ? When was the last time you were tested? Oh, that's right—*never!* You were never tested for SPAARZ because you don't care about other people!"

With tired exasperation Lucas shook his head. "I'm not having this conversation again. I'm going inside. I'll see you guys tomorrow."

"No," Oona said. "I'm going in. This is my daughter. She needs me."

"Oh, now you care?" the boy said.

With this, Oona finally broke. She could take no more. "*Shut up Lucas!* Just shut up!" she screeched. "I am sick of your superior tone! You know nothing about life. *Nothing!* I'm going in and I'm spending the night. The two of you can come back tomorrow."

* * *

Rosa was asleep when Oona entered the room. The child lay on her back with tubes and wires attached to her body. Seeing her little girl like this, her baby, the product of her flesh, still so innocent and so fragile, pierced Oona's heart. She stood at the girl's bedside, watching her, and her eyes burned and became wet. The child had been damaged. Great harm had been done, and not just to her heart, Oona realized. Something equally delicate and precious had been broken, and Oona wondered if it could ever be repaired. She wondered too if *she* could ever be repaired. With more and more force, the tears came. They spilled hotly down her cheeks and into her paper mask. Overcome by a strength of feeling she had never known before, a mix of sorrow and remorse, Oona suffered and wept.

* * *

That night, Cole was back on the hard stuff. He had finished off the last bottle of the Stepfield Valley Malbec the night before and had forgotten to pick up something on the way home from the hospital, so he had started on a bottle of gin that hadn't been touched in many months. In his despair—and Cole could now admit to himself that he *was* in despair—he turned to the only source of intimate human connection that remained to him. He turned to social media.

For his first chirp, he wrote: "My dear daughter Rosa had a cardiac arrest today. She's just 12 years old, and I'm hurting. Please pray for Rosa. #hurting #heartbroken #prayforRosa."

As for his request—"Please pray for Rosa"—Cole himself was not a believer. He considered himself too intelligent for belief. Too modern, too enlightened, too sophisticated. His mother had emigrated with her family from one of the Baltic states and had remained, all through her life, deeply devoted to the ancient faith of her people. Cole had found the religion, and the people and their Old World ways, a source of embarrassment. They were not cool. They were very *uncool.* So he jettisoned all of it at a young age, deracinated himself, and became an American. Like many before him, he reinvented himself. Popular music and philosophy, particularly the works of Nietzsche, helped him become the person he wanted to be, the person he *chose* to be. He believed, as Nietzsche wrote, that Truth does not exist, and that we must create our own truths, and that religion is merely a psychological crutch for weak people. Such had been the credo of Cole's life. But given his present circumstances, with Rosa lying in an ER bed with a damaged heart, he felt that maybe public requests for prayers were permissible for someone like him. Tragedy evokes atavistic feelings in even the most evolved of men. And if nothing else, Cole knew that a request for prayers for a twelve-year-old girl would certainly illicit some sympathy.

And on this last point, he was correct. Almost instantly the deluge of responses began. The likes and comments and re-chirps grew and grew beyond anything he had ever experienced. Within fifteen minutes, the chirp had more than three hundred likes— a new record for Cole. Within thirty minutes, it was up to eight hundred.

Cole was elated. He was euphoric. He was riding the dragon of a dopamine high.

In the comments, all from people he did not know, someone wrote, "Oh, so sorry to hear this!" The commenter then added five consecutive broken-heart emojis, and concluded with, "Sending you good wishes!"

Another wrote, "I'm not religious, but I am spiritual. May the Divine Presence be with you and your daughter. Namaste."

A third wrote, "I'm re-chirping this to my church prayer group. We'll pray for Rosa."

A fourth wrote, "Was she vaccinated?"

Cole let this last one slide. He knew that a slew of people would attack the guy, barrage him with clever and vicious put-downs. Instead, Cole re-posted the chirp to his FaceFace account. There too the love was immediate and plentiful, further spiking Cole's already exorbitant sense of gratification and good feeling. He was pumped, enthused beyond measure. He knocked back the rest of his drink—he had mixed the gin with a splash of tonic—then made himself another and put on some up-beat music, the Vile Bodies' reggae-and-disco-influenced second album, *The Revolution Will Be Commodified*.

* * *

Up on the second floor, Lucas stood in the darkened bathroom, looking out the window at Tyce Creamer's place. The lights were on in the house but there was no movement in the pool area. With phone in hand, Lucas was debating if he should call Tyce. He wanted to. But part of him was still angry at Tyce. Part of him still wanted to *kill* Tyce. But like his father, Lucas was in despair, and he too had no intimate human connection to turn to. He too had no other person to confide in and share his burdens with, someone who would listen and provide comfort and maybe even some guidance.

This past year at school Lucas had lost his two closest friends. Since ninth grade he had been best friends with Jules Brandt, and since junior year he had been going out with Laney Moreau. Through Lucas, Laney and Jules had become good friends too. Then last summer Laney began saying that monogamy was "oppressive" and "patriarchal." She even said it was "capitalistic," though she couldn't quite explain why, at least not in a logical, coherent way. Then soon afterward she began saying that polyamory was not only "progressive" but "natural." It was "sincere" and "honest." People should be free, she said, to do whatever they wanted, to explore any desire, any fantasy, and not be constrained by "old-fashioned morals," which were just "fascist" and "racist" anyway. And plus, all the cool people were doing it, she said. Polyamory was hip. It was in. After weeks of such observations, Laney ultimately said to Lucas, around Labor Day, "If you really love me, then you'll let me be my true self."

Lucas did love Laney. Or at least, he thought he did. He had never been in love before, so he had nothing to compare it to. Regardless, the girl's demand gave him pause. Something didn't seem right. Something seemed *off*. "Do you have someone in mind?" he said. At this, Laney had acted surprised, and also offended. "*No*," she said sharply. "At this point it's just ... hypothetical." "Oh," Lucas said, feeling a touch relieved. Finally, because he had come to feel that it maybe *was* oppressive and patriarchal of him to prevent Laney from being her "true self," he relented. And within a week Laney announced that she wanted to sleep with Jules. "But he's my best friend," Lucas said. "He's one of my best friends too," Laney countered, again acting offended. "He'll never do it," Lucas said. "Yes he will," Laney said, "I already talked to him."

And so it began. Laney started sleeping with Jules while still going out with Lucas. This was mid-September. Over the first few days Lucas felt hurt and depressed. By the end of the week he began to feel jealous. And just days after that he became enraged. One morning in the school parking lot, less than two weeks into Laney and Jules's affair, Lucas threw a punch at Jules. The punch hit Jules in the face but Jules recovered quick and gave Lucas a thorough beat down. Lucas didn't know how to fight or even how to defend himself in a fight. Jules bloodied his lip and bloodied his nose. The kids laughed at Lucas. They mocked him. His best friend had stolen his girl and then whooped his ass in front of half the school. After this, Lucas became a loner.

Now, standing at the window, he decided he *would* call Tyce. He needed to talk to someone, and he felt, despite everything, that he could count on Tyce. Yet, as he was scrolling through his contacts to find the number, a woman emerged from Tyce's house into the pool area. It was the blonde girl, Ingrid. She was nude and she dove into the water. Tyce himself appeared and he too dove into the water.

Lucas went back to his room.

THIRTEEN

Over breakfast with Lucas, Cole was in high spirits. His "pray for Rosa" chirp was up to twenty-three-thousand-plus "likes," twelve-hundred-plus comments (almost all positive), and nearly nine-hundred re-chirps. As an unexpected bonus, Cole's followers had rocketed from seventy-eight to more than seven thousand six hundred. The response was similar on FaceFace. Additionally, he had received a number of inquiries from the press about potential stories and podcast interviews. Some of the journalists, so-called, had written from conservative outlets to ask about Rosa's vaccine status. Those messages were promptly deleted. Other inquiries, however, came from journalists affiliated with dependable left-wing or left-leaning organizations written in response not just to the "pray for Rosa" chirp but to the follow-up chirp in which Cole had addressed questions about the cause of the girl's cardiac arrest. About this, Cole had laid the blame directly to "climate change" and "stress caused by anti-vax lies and scaremongering." To further develop this latter idea, he had composed yet another follow-up chirp, stating, "The anti-vax troglodytes have blood on their hands, and I call them out today before the world: How dare you harm our children like this! How dare you!" This chirp alone was up to nearly six-thousand-three-hundred "likes," including from a famous movie actress, a famous professional basketball player, a famous former network anchorman, a famous former astronaut, a famous teenage climate activist, and the current CEO of Smollox Pharmaceuticals, one of the two primary makers of the SPAARZ vaccines.

All in all, Cole had realized one of his most cherished dreams
—he had gone viral. He was now, at last, *somebody*. He was
even, you might say, a celebrity. Or at least, he was *on his way*.
Yes indeed, he was in *very* high spirits.

"I saw what you wrote on Chirper," Lucas said, eating his now-
regular breakfast of one pound of raw, grass-fed hamburger, six
strips of bacon, and four fried eggs. "I think it's despicable."

Cole ignored this. As his kale burger and scrambled tofu got
cold on his plate, he was mesmerically focused on his phone. The
comments to his assorted chirps, from hundreds and hundreds
of progressive, likeminded strangers, were so uplifting, so ener-
gizing, so *inspiring*, that Cole was even starting to rethink his
lifelong misanthropy. Maybe people weren't so bad after all, he
thought. Maybe people didn't *completely* suck.

Presently, Cole looked up at his son. With his still-black
eye and his still-fat lip, he said in a coolly superior tone, " 'Despicable'? Is that what you said, Lucas? *'Despicable'*? Hmm?
Well, that's very interesting. Let me ask you something—who's
projecting now? You're familiar with the concept of projection,
right? You've read Freud, in addition to 'The Complete Works
of Tyce Creamer'? I ask because I'm guessing you don't feel too
good about yourself this morning, with your sister in the hospital, and that you're maybe having second thoughts about your
many anti-Science positions. But rather than admit you were
wrong, rather than admit you were wrong about *everything*—
masks, testing, social distancing, and yes, the vaccines—you're
instead focusing your anger on me, rather than on yourself where
it belongs. But I'm not going to let you get away with it, Lucas.
I'm not. Because what you need to understand is, ideas have
consequences.

"Now, am I saying that you and your ignorant views are responsible for Rosa's cardiac arrest? No, I am not saying that. At
least, *not quite*. The fact is, we may never know for sure what
caused it. But your views certainly did not help. If nothing

else, you *did* cause your sister severe mental distress, which is something that *I* think is despicable. So my hope for you, *boy*, is that in time you'll learn something from all of this. Perhaps in time you'll even gain some humility and a sense that maybe, just maybe, you're not the smartest person in this house."

Cole took a bite of his cold kale burger, and turned his attention back to his phone.

* * *

An hour later, father and son drove to the hospital in tense silence. To break up the awkwardness, Cole put on an Idiot Gurus CD.

"I hate this shit," Lucas said.

"Tough," Cole said, and he raised the volume.

Two songs later they pulled into the hospital parking lot, where they ran into Maeve Cutty.

"Oh great," Cole muttered.

She came up to their car as they got out. "How are you?" she said with concern, looking from Lucas to Cole. Then, seeing Cole's battered face, she gasped. For several long uncomfortable moments, Maeve stared at him in silent horror. It appeared she wanted to ask him what happened, then it appeared she thought better of it. Regaining her composure, she turned to Lucas.

"We're OK," the boy said somberly, answering her question. "Thank you."

"I just talked to your mother," Maeve said to him. "I tried to see your sister, but the hospital wouldn't let me because of the policy. I knew they wouldn't, but I just had to try. I've been so upset." She glanced briefly at Cole, then looked back at Lucas. "How are you holding up?" she said, placing a hand on his upper arm. "Are you sure you're OK?"

With the feel of Mrs. Cutty's warm touch, and the tender caring look in her eyes, Lucas choked up. He did not expect this. His eyes stung and he tried to hold the emotion in, but he couldn't do it. He began to convulse with muffled sobs and he turned his head away, feeling ashamed.

Watching this, Cole was baffled. Completely. He could not understand what he was seeing.

Maeve Cutty embraced Lucas, holding him tight with both arms. "It's OK," she said softly. "It's OK to be sad. I'm sad too."

Unused to being hugged, unused to a sympathetic human touch, the boy nearly broke down. His eyes flooded with tears, yet he kept his arms stiffly at his sides. His desire was to hug Mrs. Cutty back, to fully connect with her, to fully receive the love and the consolation she was offering him, but something inside restrained Lucas. And soon that something inside grew stronger. It rebelled against this vulnerability and this outpouring of feeling, and suddenly the boy felt awkward. He felt embarrassed.

Sensing his unease, Maeve Cutty released him and stepped back, though she kept one hand on his arm. "Are you all right?" she said.

Lucas nodded and wiped his cheek with his hand.

"If there's anything I can do, Lucas, you just let me know, OK? You can come over any time. You're always welcome. Andy and I are always happy to see you."

"Thank you," he said. "I will."

After Maeve departed, Cole sent Oona a text to let her know they were here.

* * *

"I'll be right down," Oona wrote back. She had slept in a reclinable chair in Rosa's room but had spent most of the night awake, thinking about her life. With her little girl asleep at her side, still hooked up to tubes and wires, Oona had concluded that she had done almost everything wrong. At the top of the list was her failure as a mother. She had put herself first in nearly every imaginable way, and now her baby had almost died and would spend the rest of her life in a diminished state. Rosa's heart was permanently damaged, and the threat of death would always be potentially near. Whether the cause of the myocarditis and cardiac arrest had been stress or climate change or a virus or even the vaccine seemed less consequential to Oona now than the larger and more terrifying fact of her own culpability. In some way, at some level, she felt *she* was responsible for what had happened to Rosa. It was on her. That is, it was on her and *Cole*. Cole and she had done this. Cole and she had failed their daughter.

Outside in the bright sunlight she approached her husband and son.

"How is she?" Lucas said

"I'm not sure," Oona said. "I just talked to Dr. Pye. He said she's recovering, but I have a feeling he's not telling me everything."

"What do you mean?" Cole said.

"I don't know. It's just the way he's acting. He won't look me in the eye."

"I want to see her," Lucas said.

Oona gazed at the boy. There were many things she wanted to say to him. Most of them would be difficult, so she went with the easiest. "Dr. Pye said you saved Rosa's life. He said without the CPR she would have died." Oona wanted to thank Lucas for this, for saving her little girl's life, but she couldn't do it. She held back.

Lucas only said, "Can I go in?"

Cole made an exasperated face but said nothing.

Oona nodded. "Yes, though she's sleeping now."

Lucas went into the ER.

"I hope they test him," Cole said. "Did they test you?"

Oona did not answer this. She remained silent, just watching him.

For Cole, this seemed to be the moment. This seemed to be the moment they could begin to make up. "How are you?" he said.

"It's been hard," she said.

"I know," he said.

There was a pause, and when she didn't speak Cole said, "Oona, why don't you come home?"

She made no response, still watching him.

"Everything is forgiven," Cole went on. "All of it. We can work this out. Rosa needs you. We all need you."

"I am coming home, Cole," Oona finally said.

"Oh good. Good. I'm so happy to hear it," he said with instant relief and a joyous face. "We'll get through this, Oona. We'll get through it."

"No, Cole," she said evenly. "*I'm* coming home. You have to leave."

"What?"

"*I'm* coming home," she said, clearly enunciating her words. "And I want you to leave. I want a divorce, and I want the house, and I want Rosa. Lucas is eighteen, he can do what he wants. It's my house and my child. I'm giving you a week. I want you gone by next Sunday night."

Cole was astounded. "But I just *forgave* you!" he cried with injured feeling. "I forgave you! For *everything!*"

She shook her head exhaustedly.

"Are you getting together with Creamer?" Cole raged. "Is that what this is?"

"Cole, I'm not having a long discussion here. It's over, and I want you out of the house by next Sunday night. It's done. I've made up my mind."

"You *can't* do that!" he said incredulously. "You can't *force* me to leave."

"Yes I can. I know what happened at Wendover. That you were escorted out of Student Affairs by campus security and that you're having a disciplinary hearing for violent behavior and racist language. I know all about it, Cole, and I'll tell the police all about it when I say that you just threatened me and the kids. That's what I'll say if I have to, that you're violent and that you threatened to harm us, and you'll be locked up within an hour. You see this?" She raised the sleeve on her right arm to display the still-visible bruise from her nights with Tyce Creamer. "If I have to, I'll show them this and say it was you. I've already taken pictures of it. This and other bruises. Bruises you've never seen. So for the last time, you've got till next Sunday night. If you're there on Monday, I'll call the police and press charges." She reached into her pocket and removed a small piece of paper with a name and phone number written on it, which she handed to him. "This is my lawyer. From now on, you'll only communicate with me through her. If you try to contact me in any way—by phone, email, or in person—I'll call the police and press charges. And this starts today. Right now. As for Rosa, I'm going to spend the nights here until she's released. You can see her when she comes home. And if you disobey me and I see you back here, I'm calling the police and pressing charges. As you can probably tell, Cole, I'm kind of itching to call the police and press charges. So my advice to you is—don't *fuck* with me."

Oona started back for the hospital, but then abruptly stopped. She turned to face him. "Oh, and I've emptied our joint accounts. The bank and the portfolio accounts. I hope you've saved some money, because the free ride is over. Goodbye Cole."

* * *

Wearing the mandatory blue paper face mask that he was given at the check-in desk, Lucas entered Rosa's room. He felt nervous and stiff. He was expecting something depressing, something grim. But it was worse than he had feared. His little sister, six years younger than him, was lying on her back in a bed. Her eyes were shut, her face was masked, and her small body was perfectly still. Tubes and wires were connected to her chest and arm. It was terrifying to the boy, a brutal, jarring sight. He had only ever been to two funerals in his life and he was reminded of them now—Rosa looking as though she were laid out in a coffin. His emotions surged and tears prickled his eyes. His desire was to run away, to flee the room and the hospital, but he felt it would be wrong. He felt it would be weak.

For some time he remained near the door, watching her from a distance. He did not want to go near the bed. The two funerals he had gone to had been for old people that he barely knew—his grandmother from Illinois (Cole's mother) and his grandfather from Michigan (Oona's father)—and while the sight of the corpses had creeped him out, he had not felt anything deeper. Now he understood that people you love could die. People you love could be no more. Even your little sister.

Rosa opened her eyes and turned her head toward the door, as though she knew he was there. Startled at this, Lucas froze. He did not move, he did not speak. Though the girl was wearing a mask, Lucas could tell she was smiling. He could see the smile reflected in her eyes, which shone with muted happiness. He approached the bed.

"Hi Lucas," she said.

"Hi Rosa," he said.

"You look funny with a mask," she said.

He was struggling with his emotions, so he just nodded.

Seeing the tears fall from her brother's eyes, Rosa said, "Why are you crying?"

"I'm not crying," he said as he wiped the wetness from his cheeks. "I'm happy to see you."

The girl smiled again.

Though it felt awkward to him, because he had never done it before, not in this way, Lucas reached out his hand and placed it on top of hers. Rosa watched as he did this. She watched his hand settle on hers, and she understood. She then turned her hand over, so that their palms were touching. Gently but firmly Lucas squeezed her hand, and Rosa squeezed his hand back.

* * *

For the first time in his life Cole thought he might have a drinking problem. At the hospital he had been waiting in the car for Lucas when the boy sent him a text saying he would get a ride home from his mother. That was fine with Cole. He drove straight to the liquor store. The plan was to get another case of the Stepfield Valley Malbec. But once inside the bottle-stacked store, a toper's paradise filled with endless tempting selections, Cole decided he wanted gin instead. The previous night's G&Ts had really hit the spot. So he perused the different offerings, settled on a top-shelf English brand, grabbed a liter bottle, and started for the cashier. But before he got there he decided to exchange the liter for a half gallon. And then he thought, Why not get two?

As soon as he returned to his car he opened one of the oversized bottles and knocked it back. It burned his throat and shocked his flesh, but within moments it felt good. *He* felt good —that fire in the blood, that soothing lightness in the head.

Yet after he re-capped the bottle and ignited the car, Cole paused when he noticed the dashboard clock. It was just after eleven-thirty a.m. What, he wondered, was he doing? Two half gallons of gin? A desperation chug out in the parking lot before noon? What was happening here?

In some uncanny way, Cole realized this was a *moment*. A significant moment. A *life-determining* moment. He had arrived at a cosmic crossroads and was faced with a choice. He could put a stop to things right now. He could chuck the two gin bottles out the window and make a pledge to himself to turn his life around (whatever that meant). Or, he could just say screw it and give the middle finger to the world.

His decision came quick. He reached for the bottle that he had just drank from, uncapped it, and took another chug. A long, willful, "everyone-can-go-screw-themselves" chug. The impact was immediate and twice as potent as the first chug. This double dose of booze jolted him, and a look of maniacal exhilaration came over his face. Into the CD player he put the Smack Grannies last album before their breakup, the hard-driving, metal-infused *Let It Burn*. He cranked it up, then sped off across the shopping center parking lot toward the exit. At the stoplight, waiting behind another car, he was bobbing his head to the aggressive beat when he snapped to attention.

Passing through the intersection in front of him, heading east on Depot Street, were three teenage stoners on skateboards.

Cole was giddy. "Thank you Jesus!" he said sarcastically as a devilish gleam came into his eyes. He watched as the boys—the tall boy, the heavyset boy, and the third boy—continued in the direction of Froggie's Tap Room. Cole hoped, Cole *prayed*, that they were heading back to the vacant parking lot where just days before they had stolen his money and stomped him silly.

The light turned green and Cole tailed the kids for two blocks, and sure enough, the little bastards made their way back to the scene of the beating. Cole pulled to the side of the street, twenty yards from the entrance to the lot. With a cold, predatory grin, a grin of malevolent intent, he scanned the scene for potential witnesses. All was clear except for traffic. On the street a pickup truck was coming in his direction. Behind him, in the rearview, he saw two cars coming his way from the opposite direction. Though this was a quiet section of town, it was still a Monday afternoon, business hours, which meant the traffic, though light, might also be constant. But Cole was fine with it. He would take his chances. He was done playing things safe.

He took another slug of gin, secured the cap, and set the bottle on the passenger-seat floor, all while keeping his eyes fixed on the boys. They were doing jumps and acrobatic tricks on their boards, unaware that they were being stalked.

Cole scanned the street again, saw no car coming his way from the front, and just a lone motorcycle coming his way from the back. With a mad manic grin he lowered the car's four side windows and raised the music to full blast. The Grannies' blistering cover of "Me and Mikey McGee" rang out at eardrum-destroying volume. The motorcycle passed by. Cole waited a few seconds, then floored it.

The car shot forward, though perhaps not as fast as Cole would have liked—it was an electric vehicle after all, a GAIA GX, designed to save the planet. But it moved fast enough, and as he made a sharp left into the parking lot the tires screeched and the car rose up on the driver's side. All three boys turned to look. At first their faces were puzzled. Then they became alarmed. A music-blaring vehicle was barreling straight toward them.

Like some crazed, wild-eyed demon, Cole laughed with demented glee as he locked in on the tall boy. The kids scrambled for cover, each of them fleeing in a different direction. The tall boy had abandoned his skateboard and was running for an alley. Cole swerved to hit the board—there was a violent cracking sound as debris flew off to the side—and though the music was deafening, he pressed down on the horn to heighten the terror. At the last instant Cole swerved to the right and just missed the boy, then immediately spun the wheel to the left and hit the brakes. The car screeched to a halt, cutting off the kid. Fearing for his life, the tall boy bolted in the opposite direction. Cole floored it, making another crazy laugh, and beelined after his prey. Panicking, the tall boy looked over his shoulder as he ran, to see where Cole was, and as he did he stumbled and fell. Cole hit the brakes again and the GAIA GX fishtailed to a loud, tire-shredding stop just inches from the boy.

"What the hell, man? What the hell?" the kid shrieked from the pavement as Cole killed the ignition and hobbled out of the car, moving as fast as he could with three broken ribs. The kid tried to stand and scramble away, but Cole kicked him in the head. Howling in pain, the tall boy fell over on his side. Cole kicked him in the back and then he kicked him again in the head.

"How does that taste you little piece of shit?" he bellowed. "I told you not to mess with me!"

The tall boy writhed and groaned.

"Now give me my money, or I'll stomp your ass some more!" Cole said, and he quickly looked around. A car passed by on the street but the driver didn't look over. She was talking on her phone. As for the other two boys, they now stood together about thirty yards away, watching from the front of an old brick warehouse.

"*You want some of this?*" Cole shouted at them. Neither of the boys spoke or moved. Cole flipped them the bird, then he turned back to the tall boy. The kid was still sprawled on the pavement, moaning and holding his side.

"My money, douchebag," Cole said as he delivered another kick.

The kid reached into his front pants pocket and held out some cash.

Cole snatched the bills and counted them. "You're fifty bucks short, shithead."

"It's all I've got."

"I don't believe you." He kicked him again.

"*Ow!* Stop kicking me!"

"Give me your phone."

"I don't have it."

"Give me your fricking phone!"

"I don't—"

Cole kicked him. "Give it to me, punk!"

The boy handed it over.

Cole looked at it and said, "Thousand-dollar burner phone, huh?" He smashed it on the pavement, shattering the glass front.

He brought his heel down on it several times, breaking it into more and more pieces. "Time to get a new one you little shit!" he hollered and delivered another kick to the tall boy's head. The kid sprawled backward, wailing in pain.

For Cole, this was a glorious moment, a volcanic release of a lifetime's worth of pent-up rage. All of the countless slights, humiliations, resentments, and failures—the pressurized magma of his psyche, years and years of it—were now gushing forth in one magnificent eruption. It was beautiful and sublime, a moment he had waited for his whole adult life.

Yet, like every other moment that ever was, this one too passed.

From thirty yards away, he saw, the heavyset boy and the third boy were now filming him with their phones. Minutes before Cole had had little concern for consequences of any sort. Now he felt differently. He knew he could not catch both of the kids and confiscate their phones. They would run in different directions.

To the tall boy he said, "Listen dog face, if any word or any video of this gets out to the cops or onto the internet, from you or either of your two boyfriends over there, I'll find you and I'll kill you, you understand? I'll cut off your head and chop off your dick, and I'll bury you in the woods, you got that? I'll feed you to the squirrels! And I'm *not kidding!*"

Cowering on the ground and looking up fearfully at Cole, the tall boy said nothing.

"And then I'll kill your mother and your father!" Cole added, wanting to make his position perfectly clear. "You *understand?*"

"My father would beat your ass," the tall boy said, finally finding some courage. "My mother too."

"Screw your mother!" Cole said, and he gave him a final kick. "I'll kill all of you!"

He jumped into the GAIA GX and sped off, squealing his tires as he turned onto Depot Street and nearly crashed into an oncoming car.

FOURTEEN

Seated out on the patio, under the hot summer sun, Cole was drinking gin straight from the bottle while ebullient women frolicked next door. There were three or four of them, these ebullient women. With extreme delight they were laughing and shrieking, splashing in Creamer's pool, horsing around, and generally having the time of their lives.

Cole's mood, however, was less cheery. Over the past hour, as the good times rolled on the other side of the fence, he had been pondering his situation. He had to admit, it didn't look so good. In fact, he felt fairly certain that he was well and truly screwed. Not just divorced screwed and unemployed screwed, but now cops screwed and maybe even jail screwed too. Had the tall boy fallen for Cole's bluff? Had the kid bought Cole's threat to decapitate him and cut off his dick? And then kill his parents? And would the tall boy also convince the heavyset boy and the third boy not to take their video to the cops or post it on the internet? Cole wasn't so sure. In fact, he half expected the cops to pull up for him at any moment. Tonight, maybe. Or tomorrow. Or *now*.

"Hey, easy!" said the voice of Tyce Creamer, ringing out from the pool. "There's enough for all of you!"

The women pealed with laughter. "Heeheeheeheehee!"

This inflamed Cole. Sparks of spite flashed in his eyes. *There's enough for all of you.* What an asshole, he thought. He tipped back the bottle and filled his gullet with gin. For some reason, the more he drank, the less it seemed to burn going down. He wondered if that was good or bad. Either way, the booze did help to steady him. It calmed his nerves and made it easier for him to think. Returning to the issue at hand, he knew that running from the cops was out of the question. He was no Clyde Barrow or O.J. Simpson. If they came for him, he would submit peaceably and his lawyer would plead temporary insanity. Something along the lines of, "Your honor, due to extreme emotional stress caused by his wife cheating on him with his redneck neighbor, my client suffered a severe mental breakdown that led …" Or better yet, "The extreme emotional stress caused by his young daughter's cardiac arrest, coupled with his wife cheating on him with his redneck neighbor …" Yes, that would do, Cole thought. They would buy it. The jury would buy it. The press would buy it. The entire *system* would buy it—particularly once they checked his social media and discovered he was one of *them*.

"Meggie, give Amalia a kiss," came Tyce's lighthearted voice. "You know you want to."

"*Tyyyyyce!*" cried a merrily scandalized female voice. "You are *so* nasty!"

"Hahahahaha!" laughed Tyce in his manly voice.

"Heeheeheeheehee!" laughed the women in their feminine voices.

Listening to this, listening to every word, every syllable, Cole was smoldering. How he loathed Creamer. How he despised him! He was tempted to text Oona that her boyfriend had a harem of drunken trollops reveling in his pool, but he was mindful of her threat to call the cops should he attempt to contact her. He knew she meant it, and he knew she would do it. Well, screw her, Cole thought. Screw her and screw Tyce Creamer.

He took another belt from the bottle, and as the booze sloshed in his belly, Cole got an idea. It was another of those inner-voice suggestions, almost like someone was whispering in his ear: "If the cops are coming for you anyway, which they most assuredly are, then why not go out with a bang?"

Musing on this, Cole decided it wasn't a bad idea. For the fact was, having gotten his first taste of blood, so to speak, Cole found that he had rather liked it. That's right: despite twenty years of committed vegetarianism, Cole found that he liked the taste of blood. It tasted *good*. It tasted *real* good. He had immensely enjoyed inflicting real-life violence on a real-life enemy. He had enjoyed imposing his will on the tall boy and administering physical pain. Without question it had been far more pleasurable than doing it virtually, over the internet with typewritten words. And so, what harm could one more bodily assault do, really? Particularly if that assault was against the man who had seduced his wife and ruined his marriage and broken up his family? Surely no jury would hold *that* against him—right? Hell, it might even help his case. Other men might support him. Women too.

"Amalia, slap Sasha's ass," came Tyce's playful joking voice.

"No! No! ... *Aaaaahhhhh!*" a jovial female voice screeched as the sharp slap of a hand hitting a well-cushioned bottom echoed over the fence.

"Hahahahaha!" laughed Tyce.

"Heeheeheeheehee!" laughed the women.

For Cole, that settled it. One more assault would not harm anything *at all*. In fact, *this* attack, he felt, would be a sort of service to the community, a gift to town and country.

"You're drinking gin now?"

Cole turned and saw Lucas, who had just come from the house. On the patio table, in front of Cole, the half-gallon gin bottle was a quarter empty.

"Just a little nip before supper," he said.

"Right."

"Were you with your mother?"

"No, I walked back. I wanted to think. Mom told me she wants a divorce. I knew this would happen."

"It's because of this asshole," Cole said, pointing at the fence as the laughter and frolicking continued on the opposite side.

"Who knows?" Lucas said. "Maybe. Maybe not."

"Listen to you," Cole sneered. "Maybe he'll be your stepfather. You'd like that, wouldn't you?"

"You shouldn't drink, Dad."

"What is it about the guy that appeals to you? The money? The bimbos? He's a total clown. How can you not see it? I thought you were smarter than that."

"You're cherry-picking, Dad. As usual. He has a good message."

"And what's that—that it's OK to steal another man's wife? That it's OK to destroy someone else's family? This affects you too, you know."

Lucas glanced at the ground. "I know. It's bad."

" 'It's bad,' " Cole said snidely. "Yeah, I guess you could say that. '*It's bad.*' "

Lucas was silent.

"Then what is it?" Cole went on. "What's the attraction? I really don't understand. The misogyny? The steroid muscles? The white nationalism? He's obviously a fascist. What are you going to read next, *Mein Kampf*?"

"This is so ridiculous," Lucas said, resignedly shaking his head. "Do you really even believe half of the stuff you say?"

"Yes I do!" Cole burst out. "I believe what I say because it's true! The guy is dangerous. His *ideas* are dangerous. *Don't Be a Bitch*? That's not misogynistic?"

"Dad, he's *not* a misogynist! For Pete's sake, he's a chick magnet! Women love him. They fall all over him. What do you think's going on over there right now, a torture session?" the boy said, pointing at the fence as the ladies giggled and made merry.

Cole kept quiet.

"And he's not a Nazi or a fascist or any other slander you have," Lucas went on. "He's just a guy who's trying to help men be men instead of weak beta wusses. His whole message is about self-reliance and doing your best. Reaching your potential. Why is that so threatening to you?"

"Threatening to *me*?" Cole snapped with blazing eyes. "Threatening to *me*? Lucas, I don't need to read a book by some uneducated hillbilly grifter who preys on insecure boys to know how to be a man. I *am* a man, you understand? I *am* a man, and I prove it every day!"

"OK. Sure. Whatever you say," Lucas said with a bored look. "I'm going inside. You really should stop drinking, Dad. You're just going to get into trouble."

* * *

When Rosa woke from her nap Oona went to her side and took ahold of her hand.

"How do you feel, sweetie?"

"OK," she said. "Though my chest hurts."

"Does it hurt, or is it just sore?"

Rosa thought about this. "Both."

"I think that's just from the operation. I'll tell the nurse."

"Where's Lucas? And Dad?"

"They're at home. You can only have one visitor at a time, because of SPAARZ. I told them I'm going to stay here tonight and every night till you come home. You can see Lucas again tomorrow … He cares about you very much," Oona added, feeling a sudden tug of emotion.

"I know," Rosa said.

Oona smiled.

"Mom, I had a dream, I think. Something bad."

"What, sweetie?"

"I saw Dad hurting Tyce. He was hitting him with something. A stick, I think."

Oona pondered this. "It's nothing. Like you said, it was just a dream."

"I'm worried though," the girl said. "It seemed real. More real than a dream. And Daddy was really hurting him."

"Sweetie, it was just a dream."

"Can you call him?"

"No. Your father is fine. He can take care of himself. He's a big boy."

* * *

That evening Lucas went into the upstairs bathroom to look out the window. He wanted to see if the women were still at Tyce's place. Lucas wanted to call Tyce, but not while he had company. All that day, since he had returned home from the hospital, he had wanted to call, but every time he looked out the window he saw that the girls were still there. The four of them—Tyce, Amalia, and the two other girls—had swam, and lain in the sun, and grilled steaks and drank wine over the course of several hours. Now, Lucas saw the pool area was empty. Tyce and the women had cleared out. Yet holding his phone, Lucas wavered. He didn't want to interrupt Tyce if he was … *busy*. Also, he knew that Tyce would shortly be going on air for his weekly MyToobs live stream. It started at nine and it was nearly eight-thirty now. Maybe, Lucas thought, he should just wait till tomorrow. Or maybe he would send in a question to the live stream, some message to let Tyce know that he was no longer mad at him. Or at least, not mad enough to want to kill him.

* * *

Around nine-thirty p.m., Cole crept up the stairs to the second floor. Although he was shitfaced—the half-gallon gin bottle was now nearly half gone—he was still mentally alert. His head was buzzing and he was stumbling a bit, but he knew what he was up to. Keeping an eye out for Lucas, he happily saw that the boy's bedroom door was shut. Cole proceeded on. He slipped into his and Oona's room and entered the bathroom. For the past couple of hours he had been plotting his attack on Tyce Creamer. Fighting mano a mano was out of the question. With his bulging pecs and veiny biceps it was obvious that Creamer was rugged and in great shape, and Cole was neither. So, to even the odds, to make the fight *fair*, he had decided to take along a weapon. But what sort of weapon? Cole, of course, did not own a switchblade or brass knuckles or a pair of nunchucks. This meant he had to improvise. He considered a hammer. A baseball bat. A bike chain. A frying pan. But none of those had seemed ... *satisfactory*. To be clear, the idea was not to kill the guy. Rather, Cole just wanted to give Creamer a proper pummeling, a memorable thrashing. Knock out a couple teeth, bust his jaw, crack his skull. That sort of thing. Something the wife-stealer would never forget. And then the idea had come to Cole, an idea so magnificent, an idea so perfect and true, that it seemed as though preordained, something that was just meant to be.

Reaching under the pile of folded towels in the bathroom closet, Cole pulled out the sixteen-inch heavy-rubber sex toy. For Oona, it had been a pole of pleasure, but for Creamer it would be a bludgeon of pain. Gripping the thing at one end with his right hand, Cole brought the rest of it down against the open palm of his left. It made a solid, ominous smacking sound that Cole found utterly delicious. "Ooooh yes," he muttered with satisfaction. "This will do *just fine*."

Next he went into Oona's underwear drawer. It was nearly empty, but not quite. Seeing a pair of tan-colored pantyhose socks, Cole smiled. He took one of the socks and left the other. He then snuck down to the first floor, went into the living room, and looked out the window at Creamer's driveway. The two cars that had been there earlier in the day—presumably the cars of the frolicking floozies—were now gone. That made things easier. Though come to think of it, having a few terrified screaming women on hand to witness the assault potentially would have been better, Cole thought. It would have added more drama, more thrill, more *artistry* to the spectacle, and would have been doubly more humiliating for Creamer, to get smacked down in front of his hussy harem. But those were the breaks.

With as much stealth as a gin-soaked man could muster, Cole passed through the kitchen, stepped out to the patio, and scanned the surrounding houses to make sure he was unobserved. There was no one around. He put the sex toy on the patio table and pulled the pantyhose sock over his head. Though the sock reduced his vision, and also kind of stank—in fact, it stank pretty bad—Cole nonetheless was exhilarated. He was at war and going into battle. He was mounting a sneak attack on his archenemy and would soon extract some much-deserved revenge. Tingly with excitement, he broke into a distorted, crazy-man grin.

It was showtime.

* * *

Up in his bedroom, Lucas was watching the Bro2Bro with Tyce Creamer live stream on his desktop computer. As always for the live stream, Tyce was filming from the large room that looked out onto his backyard. It made for a stylish setting. Viewers saw a section of the high-ceilinged room with its swanky décor and, behind that, the pool through the plate-glass windows. And now, with the pool only partially lit against the dark of the night, the effect was frankly cinematic, like a mise-en-scène from some neo-noir film. You half expected a femme fatale to slip into the frame.

Taking up most of the frame, of course, was Tyce Creamer himself. Seated at his desk, he had already answered questions about how to reduce belly fat, the best exercises to build sexual stamina, and whether he thought crypto was a good investment.

Presently he looked away from the camera and off to the left, where he kept the monitor that displayed the incoming comments and queries. "OK," he said to his audience, "the next question comes from, uh, 'Doobie Doodareno.' 'Tyce, love the show.

My question is this: over the last year or so, I've become more and more depressed. My girlfriend wants me to go on antidepressants, like her, but I don't want to. At this point, after the whole SPAARZ thing, I have little trust in doctors or the pharmaceutical companies. Any thoughts? Thanks, and keep up the good work, Doobie Doodareno.' "

Turning back to the camera, Tyce said, "Well, Doobie, it's a good question, and to me it sounds like you're starting to wake up. So there's hope. Now, it's possible that your depression was caused by some serious physical or emotional trauma, in which case medications of some sort might be helpful or even necessary while you work things through and heal. But it's also possible that you're depressed for the same reason that most people are depressed today—because your life sucks. Why? I don't know. I don't know you. But men's lives can suck for a thousand different reasons, most of which are self-inflicted. For example, do you drink alcohol regularly? Do you smoke weed? Do you do other drugs? Do you spend your free time on the couch playing video games and watching movies and TV that make you stupid? Do you eat shit food? Are you overweight? Are you in good shape? Do you watch porn? Do you spend hours every day on social media? Do you hate your job? Are you happy with your girlfriend? Do you have a close group of guy friends? Are you spending more money than you make? Do you have goals that excite you? Do you have a plan for your life and are you working every day to achieve that plan? What do you say, Doobie? Does any of this resonate?

"Now, I can't tell you how many bros come to me and say, 'Hey Tyce, I'm really depressed. No girl will bang me. My life really sucks.' Then I go down my list and they say, 'Yeah, I smoke weed, yeah I hate my job, yeah I watch porn, but so what? What does that have to do with anything?' What does *that* have to do with anything? Are you *kidding me*? It has *everything* to do with it! You've *chosen* to live like a pathetic loser. You've *chosen* to be lazy and weak. You've *chosen* to sit on the sidelines for the only life that you'll ever have, and now you're surprised that you're depressed and no girl will bang you? Seriously? How stupid can you be? 'But, oh, Tyce,' the guy will say, 'I have a chemical imbalance.' 'Says who?' I say. 'My doctor,' he'll say, 'and I saw a story about it on CNBM. A lot of people have this. Life's not easy, man.' Of course life's not easy, you fool! Life is and always has been hard, *very* hard, especially for the ninety percent of us who weren't born with a silver spoon up our ass. And nowadays it's become even harder, and that's because over the past thirty, forty years the game has become completely rigged against us.

"What you need to understand, Doobie—and I wrote about this in my most recent book, *Don't Be a Bitch: The Sissyfication of America and How to Resist*, which you can get on Amazin! or on my website—is that the System, as I call it, meaning the various financial interests that control countries and governments, *wants* you to be depressed. The System *wants* you to feel helpless and hopeless. It *wants* you to feel beaten down and overwhelmed by life. So what you and millions of other guys are going through right now isn't an anomaly—it's intentional. It's the result of careful planning over many years at the very highest levels of society. And not only does the System want you to be depressed, it wants you to be weak, it wants you to be lazy, it wants you to be stupid, and it wants you to be unhealthy, mentally *and* physically. Why? Because the System wants your money and your dependence, and most of all, it wants your servitude. The System wants to control you, Doobie. The System wants to *own* you. The System wants to make you its castrated little bitch.

"This is why for the last fifty-plus years the System has been going after men. Think of the nonstop brainwashing and propaganda coming out of the government, the news, the schools, Hollywood, television, social media, the corporations. The messaging is continuous and omnipresent: Men are oppressive. Patriarchy is evil. Fathers are unnecessary. What's the goal here,

Doobie? Why do movies and TV shows portray fathers as clown-ish fools? Why do schools teach children that their patriarchal heritage is bad and the cause of all evil? Why are the western governments and all the corporations shoving rainbow flags down our throats, and especially down the throats of kids? It's because the System wants to weaken and feminize men—men and especially boys. The System wants to disempower men. Why, Doobie? Because strong, healthy, productive men, and in particular, strong, healthy, productive fathers, are the last line of defense against the System. The System knows that once men are finished, once fathers and families are finished, then the game is up. Then the System will have what the System has always wanted—complete control.

"Now Doobie, if you or anyone else watching this thinks I'm crazy or paranoid or that this is all just 'conspiracy theory' nonsense, then let's look at the past few years. Because of a *flu virus*, you were made to hide inside your house, separated from your family and friends. You weren't allowed to exercise at the gym or go to a house of worship. You maybe lost your job or had to close your business or stay home from school. You were made to feel afraid of your neighbors and other people. You were made to take an experimental medical product, and if you had the good sense to question the safety of this experimental medical product or even ask any questions about it at all, you instantly became the target of the System and its army of well-paid henchmen and its legions of useful idiots. People were censored and gaslighted. People were fired from jobs. People had their reputations destroyed. People were publicly slandered and ridiculed, sometimes by their friends and even their own families—just for asking questions.

"And what was the result of all this? The result is that the people behind the System, the people who *are* the System, they doubled their wealth, they made billions and billions, whereas the rest of us got significantly poorer. The result is that the System got more powerful and the people got weaker. The result is that the System has never had more control over you or over society than it has today, and trust me, they're just getting started.

"And so Doobie, given everything that has gone down these past few years, I'm not surprised that you're depressed. My advice to you, my friend, is start looking into how the world really works. That way, you'll understand why you feel the way you do, and from there you can begin to take steps to improve your life. This is true empowerment, and it has nothing to do with pills. And Doobie, look into the whole thing. Geopolitics. Money and banking. Hollywood. World history. Look into the food they want you to eat, the water they want you to drink, the drugs they want you to take, the ideas they want you to believe. You just might find that most of what you thought was true, isn't true at all ..."

* * *

With the pantyhose sock on his head and the oversized sex toy in his hand, Cole scurried over to Tyce Creamer's property. Despite his drunken state he was careful to maintain a clandestine air. Hunched over, looking all around, he kept an eye out for peeping neighbors. He saw no one. At the gate-door to Creamer's pool he listened for voices. He heard no one. Even the birds were quiet. Cole gingerly opened the gate, slipped inside, and made his way to the back of the house.

From the edge of the enormous plate-glass wall that faced the pool, he crouched low and cased the scene. The entire back of the house was lit up. Near him was a sliding glass door, now closed, that led into the kitchen side of the large open-plan room. And there, over in the living-room side of the space, Cole saw his victim-to-be: Tyce Creamer. Tyce the wife-stealer. Tyce the life-wrecker. He had his back to Cole and was seated at what appeared to be a work station with monitors and bright studio lights.

Holding his breath, Cole gripped the handle of the sliding glass door and gently applied pressure. The door cracked open. It made just the slightest sound. Cole could now hear Creamer talking, and he cautiously paused. He did not see anyone else in the room or hear a second voice. Perhaps Creamer was making one of his famous videos, which would explain the bright lights. Well, good, Cole thought. Creamer had made a video with Oona. Now he would make one with Cole. Though this time there would be no sex—just a whole lot of violence and pain.

Cole slid the door open a little wider, and still Creamer kept talking. He was going on and on in his arrogant muscle-man voice, bloviating some foolishness about doobies and geopolitics. Cole stepped into the kitchen and slowly slid the door shut. Crouched over, he snuck along the side wall of the kitchen, passing behind a large marble-topped island on which were three empty wine bottles and several empty wine glasses. In silence Cole made it deep into the kitchen, and from there he began making his way closer and closer to Tyce Creamer.

* * *

"Oh, and Doobie, I just remembered something," Tyce said to the camera, and to the thousands of people watching live in the United States and across the globe. "It's very important. Maybe the most important thing I'm going to say tonight …" Yet just then, something strange happened in the video, and viewers' attention shifted from Tyce to the puzzling distraction. On the left-hand side of the screen, and wholly unbeknownst to Tyce, there emerged a human figure. The figure appeared small on the screen, due to the camera being focused on Tyce, but viewers could still make out that it was a man. An odd-looking man. He appeared to be wearing a pantyhose sock over his face, like some B-movie bank robber, and he was also holding an odd-looking tubular object in one hand. In a furtive manner the man moved straight toward Tyce, and as he did, he grew larger and larger on the screen. Soon his T-shirt became legible. It was a Smack Grannies concert T-shirt from their 2003 North American tour, "Babylon Has Fallen."

The comments poured into the live-stream chat:

Mackalicious69: Who the hell is that?
Rooster: is that a nylon on his head?
FredZeeSpamford: wtf?
MuffinBoyBillyBob: Yo Tyce, you have a guest?
JanieQ: What's in his hand? It looks like a ...
Pookie_Zee: sumbitch, is tyce on the down low???

* * *

When Lucas recognized the T-shirt he said, in a stunned voice, "No." Not wholly trusting his eyes, he leaned closer to the computer screen, wanting to get a better look at the sock-covered face. "*No*," he repeated, now with more feeling. But of course the answer was "*Yes*." Of course the man on the screen in the Smack Grannies' concert T-shirt was his father. Who else could it be? Who else in Beauville even owned a Smack Grannies' concert T-shirt?

"*What are you doing?*" Lucas cried out. He shot up from his seat and ran to the stairs.

* * *

The only one unaware of the intruder was Tyce himself. He remained wholly focused on the camera and was now fervently explaining the single best way to "fight the System." The commenters in the chat, however, were not listening. They had other concerns.

SpankyGoes2Bollywood: Is this a gag?

265

TurboTodd12: Tyce turn around!!!!
Pookie_Zee: cant be real
LanaKarenina: this is weird, I think its AI
Phenix510: lmfao
Stevie Trofimovich: is that a dildo?

The first blow came swift and hard, the sex toy smacking Tyce flush on the right temple. He had no idea it was coming. The heavy rubber made a loud *thwak* sound as it connected, knocking Tyce off balance in his rolling chair and half out of the picture on the screen.

MuffinBoyBillyBob: Dawgs, this shit is real!!
JanieQ: Tyce look out!
LanaKarenina: yes that is a dildo
Sigma Sal: DAMN!!!!!!!
Rooster: oh man!

Discombobulated from the blow, baffled by what was happening, Tyce turned his head to see his assailant. He tried to rise from the chair but before he could the next blow hit him square on the nose. There was a grisly sound of cartilage cracking and an instant spray of blood, some of which splattered on Cole's T-shirt. Tyce fell to the floor and was now completely off screen. Cole hovered over the supine figure and continued his attack, directly in front of the camera.

FredZeeSpamford: shit this is real! somebody call the cops! where does he live?
JanieQ: Oh God! Tyce!!!!
Phenix510: This is pure genius, his best live stream by far.
SpankyGoes2Bollywood: I think this is real.
Mackalicious69: He's in Texas.
LanaKarenina: he's in tennessee. nashville I think.

ManquéUltra: This is fake, you idiots, hahahaha!

Without pause the man on the screen with the pantyhose sock over his head brought down the sex toy again and again and again.

* * *

Though his intention had been merely to hurt Tyce, to cause acute physical pain and perhaps disfigure him a bit, Cole found that he could not restrain his bloodlust. He had his enemy on the floor, vulnerable and defenseless, and he could not hold back. In fact, with each successive blow he seemed to grow more delirious, more frenzied, more crazed. As he pounded away at the face of the now unconscious man, pulverizing him a little more with each additional strike, Cole began to rave and taunt his senseless victim.

"Take that you porno wife-stealer!" he cried. *Thwak!* "You misogynist flag-waver!" *Thwak!* "You racist steroid hick!" *Thwak!* "You fascist cow killer!" *Thwak! Thwak! Thwak!*

* * *

Lucas raced across the lawn, dashed into the pool area, and now entered the house through the sliding glass door. His father stood over Tyce and was bashing his face with some type of club. There were three wine bottles on the kitchen island. Lucas grabbed one of them by the neck and went straight for his father. Raving madly, Cole neither saw nor heard Lucas coming. With tremendous force the boy knocked the bottle against the back of his father's head. Cole fell limply to the floor, face down beside Tyce.

What Lucas saw was ghastly. "Oh God," he said. "Oh God."

Tyce lay unmoving, and where there had once been a head, there was now a bloody pulpy mess. His face was hideously disfigured, nearly unrecognizable even as a human being.

For some seconds Lucas could only stare. The gruesome image had transfixed him. It was beyond his understanding. His father had done this. His angry, depressed, cowardly, conformist father had committed a horrific atrocity. It was incomprehensible. Yet at the same time, Lucas realized he was not surprised. He was not surprised at all, really. There was even a certain logic to this. Maybe even a certain inevitability.

Then, something occurred to the boy. Still holding the wine bottle by the neck, he realized he was being watched.

From amid the bright video lights, the live-stream camera was pointed straight at him. The internet could see him. The world could see him. They were watching him, and Lucas knew he needed to act. He did not have his phone, nor did he see one on the work desk. So he gazed into the camera and cried out, "Somebody call the police and ask for an ambulance! Tyce might still be alive. We're in Beauville, New Hampshire. The address is 28 Lilac Lane. Tell them a crime has been committed, and that someone is dying. Tell them to hurry. Do it *now*! There might still be time! There might still be time ..."

Lucas then went around the desk and unplugged the camera. On screens all across the globe, the video went black.

FIFTEEN

Months passed. Fall came, then winter, and now it was spring. There were flowers again and trees with green leaves.

Inside the visitors' room at the Central New Hampshire Penitentiary, Lucas was seated at a graffiti-covered table. Around him were watchful guards, prisoners in blue shirts and pants, and an assortment of civilians: wives, children, parents, girlfriends, lawyers. Many in the room were discreetly watching Lucas and exchanging hushed words. One of the visitors, an older woman with a missing front tooth, had even come up to him and said, "I just want you to know, I think you're a hero. A real hero for what you did, stopping your father." But Lucas was hearing a lot of that these days—both good words and bad.

Presently Cole entered the room accompanied by an armed guard. The people who had been watching Lucas now redirected their attention. All talking ceased. An air of anticipation filled the room. The onlookers were expecting some drama. They were hoping for a scene.

Cole sat opposite his son and promptly made a stony, critical face. The boy was wearing a red trucker hat with an American flag on it. Cole also noticed that Lucas had bulked up. He had become more muscular and there were veins showing on his forearms.

"Hi Dad," Lucas said grimly.

Cole sighed. "Hi Lucas."

They both grew silent, each struggling to control their respective animosities.

"Where's your sister?" Cole finally said.

"At home. Last time she came here she had nightmares afterward, because of that guy who was yelling, and Mom said she shouldn't come back. She said she needs to be careful about her heart."

Cole felt the anger rising. "You're fricking mother," he muttered. "I'm sure she's giving Rosa ideas. Planting little seeds in her head. What a manipulative bitch she is. I can't believe I married her!"

Now Lucas felt the anger rising. But he restrained himself and made no reply.

After a long silence Cole said, "Did you guys see the interview?" In his eyes was a proud, expectant look. The previous day, Cole had sat down in this very room for a televised interview with CNBM's Jess Murdlow who, along with hundreds of other members of the national and international press, would be on hand for tomorrow's opening statements at the Superior Courthouse in Beauville. Cole's trial for the attempted murder of Tyce Creamer would be broadcast live across the globe, as the story had become a worldwide sensation. On MyToobs alone, the video of Cole attacking Tyce with the large rubber phallus, and Lucas knocking Cole unconscious with an empty wine bottle, had been viewed more than 1.2 billion times.

"Yes, we saw it," Lucas said gruffly.

This pleased Cole. The hour-long interview, in which Jess Murdlow gushed with fawning praise over Cole's "courage" and "moral commitment," had covered a range of topics, including Cole's determination to continue his "tireless fight, even behind bars," against "misogyny," "white supremacy," "climate change," "vaccine hesitancy," and also the consumption of red meat, which was, as Cole assured Jess Murdlow, "destroying the planet." By that morning, Cole's followers on Chirper had risen from 1.9 million before the interview, to 2.3 million.

"What did you think?" Cole said to his son.

"I thought it was bullshit," Lucas said.

A subtle, boastful grin came over Cole's face. "That's not what the country thought," he said. "That's not what the *world* thought."

On this point, Cole was certainly correct. Both the country and the world could not get enough of Cole Perrot. Since his dramatic assault of Tyce Creamer, he had become a figure of international renown and a global media darling. From Bangkok to LA to Reykjavik, from London to Kyrgyzstan to Tierra del Fuego, Cole was a hot topic of conversation. In homes and barbershops and cafés and seminar rooms, on podcasts and campaign trails and websites and television talk shows, he was lionized and reviled, analyzed and debated, censured and praised. Without question, Cole had made it big.

"Good for you, Dad. Congratulations. But I didn't come here to talk about the interview. I came to tell you that I'm leaving Beauville. I have to get out of here. I'm going to travel for a few months. I want to see the country and figure out what I want to do."

For Cole, the news was unexpected but not a surprise. "When are you leaving?"

"Today. After I get out of here—"

"*Today?* But what about the trial?"

"What about it? It's going to be a circus, and I want nothing to do with it. I've already given testimony. I'm done."

This was true. As Cole already knew, neither Lucas, Rosa, nor Oona would be testifying in person. Oona had fought for this, and the judge had consented. Instead, the Perrot-Puddings had already given videotaped depositions—Lucas as a witness to the alleged crime and Rosa and Oona as reluctant character witnesses. Still, Cole had been hoping that his family might attend the trial, to show support. With a bitter look he said, "Well, that's your choice. But if you're looking for money, you came to the wrong place. If you haven't noticed, I'm currently unemployed."

"I'm not here for money," Lucas said. "I just wanted to tell you what I'm doing. I also want to tell you that I sold your record collection, and that Mom gave me your car."

Cole exploded. *"You sold my record collection?* That's *theft*, Lucas!" he shouted, banging the table with his hand. "That's theft! You had no right to do that!"

People were staring, and some of them looked quite happy. They would have something juicy to report on the outside. A guard appeared and told Cole to keep it down or he would be sent back to his cell. Cole composed himself.

"You would've had to sell your stuff anyway," Lucas said. "They're saying that after the criminal trial there's probably going to be a civil trial. Tyce has already had three reconstructive surgeries and I know there's going to be a few more. You're going to owe him millions, Dad. Better I got your records and your car than the lawyers."

"Fine," Cole said grudgingly. "But you should have asked first!" he added, pointing angrily at his son. "That was incredibly disrespectful!"

Unbothered by this, Lucas said, "I'm sure you'll make plenty of money when you get out."

Thanks to his newfound fame Cole had become the happy recipient of numerous celebrity perks, including a slew of commercial proposals. The volume of offers had been so great, in fact, that Cole had been forced to hire an agent. There had already been many of the expected film and book proposals, but there had also been endorsement offers from a sex-toy manufacturer, a video-game maker, and a well-known light beer company, among many others. And in addition to these, Cole could also look forward to money from a popular crowdfunding website, which Cole's lawyer—America's top defense attorney, Wyatt Keller—claimed would likely amount to several or more million dollars, enough to cover legal fees and make Cole a rich man to boot. The online pledge appeal would be going live at the start of the trial, tomorrow morning at ten a.m. Contemplating all of this, Cole decided the loss of his record collection wasn't so catastrophic after all. In a year or two, or however long it might take for him to regain his freedom, he would be able to buy all the records he wanted. And if the civil suit against him was successful, he would just do another online campaign to raise the needed funds.

With a disdainful smirk he said, "You're right, Lucas. I'll be fine. So feel free to take full advantage of the situation while you can, and go and enjoy your little holiday on my dime. I hope you have a great time. And don't worry about me, rotting away in this place."

Lucas's eyes narrowed. "Worry about *you*?"

"Yeah, *me*. Your father."

"My *father*," Lucas said deliberatively, as though he maybe had mixed feelings about the term.

"Yeah, your *father*," Cole repeated sharply. "You should be supporting me, Lucas, in my hour of need—not selling my fricking records and going on vacation."

Lucas was stunned. "Supporting *you* ..." he quietly said, dumbfounded.

"Yeah, that's right—*me*," Cole seethed.

"Dad, it's because of me that you're not going on trial for murder tomorrow. I think that's support enough."

"Oh, right," Cole said sarcastically. "I forgot. You're the big hero. 'The kid who saved Tyce Creamer.' The new right-wing poster boy. I've seen the articles."

"I've had nothing to do with any of that. I haven't spoken to the press even once. Unlike you."

A sly smile came over Cole's face. "You will, at some point. When the offer's right," he said with a taunting look. "It'll be the easiest money you'll ever make. And you'll be more than happy to throw dear old Dad under the bus."

This disgusted Lucas. "Dad, I'm trying really hard with you. Really hard."

Cole scoffed. "As if you've done me any favors."

For some moments Lucas was silent, trying to control himself. Then he said, with feeling, "Dad, let me ask you something. Do you not realize how much damage you've done? Not just to Tyce and his family, but to Rosa? To me and Mom? Rosa has panic attacks now. Kids make fun of her at school and she has reporters sneaking onto the playground trying to talk to her. Mom is embarrassed to go out in public. Everyone knows who she is and what she did. She's talking about moving to Europe now. And I've gotten death threats. Many death threats. Do you not get this? Do you not get that you've ruined people's lives? Or is it just that you're more interested in how many Chirper followers you have?"

"*Me?*" Cole said with a shocked look. "*I've* ruined lives? Lucas, *I'm* the one who's fighting to save this country! I'm the one who's fighting for *change*! I'm the one who's stuck in this place, getting assaulted in the shower and eating terrible food and sleeping in the same cell as a pedophile whose breath smells like dog shit! *Me!* And what support do *I* get? What support do I get from *any* of you? Huh, kid—*what support do I get!*" he hollered with mad bulging eyes as he again violently smacked his hand on the table.

"OK, that's enough," said the guard as he and one of his partners roughly seized Cole by the arms, lifted him up, and led him to the door.

"You can go screw yourself, Lucas!" Cole cried over his shoulder as he went. "You little fascist! You Nazi! And I want my

records back! Do you hear me? *I want my fricking records back!*
Every single one, or I'll sue you! *I'll sue your ass!*"

As soon as Cole was gone, everyone in the now-quiet visitors' room turned to Lucas. They were watching him, some with amused faces, others with sober concern, but Lucas did not care. A feeling of peace had come over him, a tremendous feeling of release. He knew in that moment that he was finished with something. Something big. He was finished with his father, he was finished with being a boy, and he was finished with this great idiotic clown world that currently existed all around him. He was embarking on a new life, he knew. A life apart from the tyranny of fools. What this new life would be, exactly, he wasn't quite sure. But he knew it was going to be good. He knew it would be daring and free and exciting and it would definitely not be safe. His new life would not be safe at all. Caught up in these hopeful exhilarating thoughts, Lucas stood with a serene knowing smile, ignoring the curious gazes of those around him, and confidently started for the exit and all that awaited him on the other side of the prison walls.

About the Author

Michael Lacoy is the author of *The Mystical Adventures of Stavros Papadakis* and *Making a Better World*. He lives in New Hampshire.

www.MichaelLacoy.com
Facebook.com/michael.lacoy.9
Twitter: @MichaelLacoy
Instagram: @michaellacoyy

Made in the USA
Middletown, DE
19 September 2023

38570117R00168